Nothing to Hide

Nick Simon

Deux Voiliers Publishing

Aylmer, Quebec

First Edition

Copyright © 2015 by Nick Simon

Published in Canada by Deux Voiliers Publishing, Aylmer, Quebec.

www.deuxvoilierspublishing.com

ISBN 978-1928049258

Cover Art - Paul Zacharias

Cover Design – Ian Thomas Shaw

For Friends

It's Power that needs the gallows: 'That man's a Jew, he's a Negro, he's a worker, he's a slave…he's different…that man's the Enemy!'

Elsa Morante, History: A Novel.

Report on William Potenco
by Doctor Officer Elias Degair
I

It's raining, and William Potenco—who is usually the last to leave work, even on a Friday—is sitting at his desk on the tenth floor of the J. Griffin Building. I'm watching him and I can see that he's lost in his thoughts. He's ignoring his work and looking out the window above his monitor contemplating what is likely some sad idea, as is his habit lately. The rest of the data management team, a group of part-timers and interns, have already gone home. The whole floor—all the employees of Eureka!, "the social network for academics"—have gone home. William is alone. He's staring out of the rain-spattered window, over Victory Square and the city of Vancouver, lost in a depressing thought.

The grey sky he sees is nothing special. The mist, the wall of rain awaiting him when he steps outside, is nothing new. The Vancouver skyline, or what William can see of it anyway, is no more exciting to him than a postcard, or a painting of a landscape hanging over a grandmother's couch. The way the rain taps at the window, evenly and rhythmically, the way the water runs down the pane—this is what seems to interest our sad William.

Sighing deeply, he looks back down at his monitor. *Maybe time to get out of here*, he must think. But as he begins closing the windows and programs on his computer, he pauses. Perhaps he's thinking: *One quick update before I leave—why not?* He brings up *Real*. My computer records it—he never even logged out; his Canvas is still open and I can see him do it through the camera.

Since he last checked an hour or so ago, there's really no updating to do, so after scanning old messages and compositions, he decides to compose something new. On his Sketchpad, William quickly draws a mountain with a snow-covered top and a pine tree on its side. Next to the mountain he draws a skyscraper standing, for some reason known only to William, as high as the mountain. Above the skyscraper and the mountain he draws a raincloud, from which little drops of rain fall. He colours it all in different shades of grey, presses the "animate" button to have the rain look as if it's falling, and cuts and pastes it onto his Canvas. I suppose this is meant to be a representation of Vancouver. Next, from *Real*'s online music files, William finds what he thinks is an ideal companion song to his rather dismal-looking drawing—it's The Smiths's rather drab "There Is a Light That Never Goes Out." It must not be the lyrics but rather the sad tone that makes it work for William as the drawing's companion. He drags that over too.

He's almost done, but he obviously feels there's something missing, since he's stopped and is contemplating his composition, mulling over what particular kind of punch he feels is still needed. He leans back in his chair again to have another look out the window—the rain, the mountains, the wind—and an image pops into his head.

Where did the image come from, William? Is it a happy memory from a childhood trip to a museum or a Grade 10 art class, or maybe from a postage stamp you once saw? Hard for me to know, but with a quick search through *Real*'s database he's found what he wants. It's

Emily Carr's 1931 painting, *Big Raven*. William drags the image—a great raven staring out at a rain-swept landscape—over to his composition. He leans back to have a long good look at it, likely thinking: *Sad and funny. Perfect.* He then hits "compose" to finish it up and, typical of him, hits "send" to issue his particular, grandiose form of bleakness to all of his friends. It is 5:14 p.m.

Moments later, a message arrives underneath William's composition. It's from his friend Mike, who has been "affected" by William's post:

(5:18 PM) Mike George: another raven? and raining in van again, huh?

Mike is one of William's closest friends—one of his few friends, actually. They went to university together where Mike lived in the dorm room next to William. The two have remained friends, and stayed connected on *Real* over the years since Mike moved to Ottawa. Mike's *Real-ID* photo shows a young, smiling man with a round face, brown eyes and short brown hair, wearing a white unbuttoned dress shirt over a black t-shirt. Mike's *Real-ID* number is #fifteen-three-thirty-nine. According to Mike's profile, his favourite musicians are: Dire Straits, Coldplay, The Tragically Hip, and the Red Hot Chili Peppers. His favourite directors are: Sam Raimi and Quentin Tarantino. His favourite authors are: none. His cultures are: Canadian. Mike always communicates in lower case.

William replies promptly to Mike:

(5:19 PM) William Potenco: I like ravens, and it's always raining here.

Shortly after, another message appears from William's other friend, Ryan. Ryan is neither "affected" nor "unaffected" by William's post. His message reads:

(5:23 PM) Ryan Jeffreys: haha, nice picture. Depressed much?

Ryan is William's best friend. He went to university with William and Mike, and shared a Computer Science major with William. Like Mike, Ryan left Vancouver just after graduation and moved back to his hometown, Winnipeg, to take a job at Bombardier. Recently, Ryan has started to change his *Real-ID* picture often. On this particular day, he's representing himself on *Real* as a young Tom Cruise. Ryan's favourite musicians are listed as: Coldplay, U2, The Strokes, and Jay-Z. His favourite directors are: M. Night Shyamalan, Peter Jackson, and J.J. Abrams. His favourite authors are: none. His abilities are: smart.

Ever sensitive, William reads over Ryan's response, probably thinking that Ryan is pretty jerky to respond in such an unfriendly way. His initial reaction, because of his short temper, is likely to tell Ryan to go fuck himself, but he reconsiders, perhaps thinking it wouldn't be nice to reply like that, especially online where everyone could read it, so he ignores Ryan's comment and responds:

(5:26 PM) William Potenco: Anyways. I have to get out of here. See you guys later tonight.

As he's posting, another message pops up in William's designated "Family Room." It's from his mother:

(5:29 PM) Margaret Potenco (MOM): Happy Birthday, Willy. Big kiss. From mom. And Frank too. We miss you.

II

Leaning back again in his chair, William Potenco lets out a long, deep sigh and stares out the window, through the rain and over our great city of Vancouver.

What is William thinking as he looks out over the city? It's hard to know exactly, but it's likely about his life—perhaps about what drew him to Vancouver in the first place: the fresh air, the mountains, tolerance and so forth. Obviously, a lot has changed since he arrived, though. That was years ago, and now many of those reasons—some today even call them myths—have lost their original lustre.

It matters little, since it's not the myths but the rain William cares for now. Is this because he's depressed? Not exactly—not clinically, anyway. He's happy in a way. Lonely for sure, but happy. From what I've gathered so far, he seems to take some mysterious joy in life, feels remarkably content, likes his job and his friends and so on. So, no, it's not because he's depressed that he likes the rain. He enjoys it because, like a poor bum who finally lands a windfall, he thinks it enables his happiness. The rain gives him a reason to be inside working at Eureka! his dream job, or connected on *Real* watching films and chatting with Mike and Ryan. Inside is where William feels safe and content.

I wouldn't say he's against going outdoors for some healthy recreation. The problem with William is more that nature sort of frightens him and offers nothing in return, as if the time he would need to spend on carrying out recreational activities would be a waste of his energy, and more risk than it's worth.

Take the mountains, for example. People in Vancouver love the mountains—they write poems and sing songs about them, they revere them as religious sites and pray to them, they paint pictures and sculpt them, they are driven to map, record, conquer, and dominate them. According to what we know, however, William has never once been to the mountains. The mountains form an integral part of our lives in this magnificent city, but William, he just stares at them every day, never going farther than that. He may secretly even hate the mountains. Part of the problem, aside from a youthful and misguided disregard for physical activity, is that William (and this is a truth that he has never admitted to his friends) is a rather anxious person. He is afraid of what might happen to him if he goes to the mountains. He has it in his head that if he were ever to attempt a trip to the mountains, it would end in his own tragic death. On many occasions he has written in his *RealDiary* of his fears: of the "terrifying winter avalanches," which actually do kill people every year; of falling; ("What if I slipped on some moss or a loose rock and fell off of a cliff to my death?"); of bugs that "swarm and terrorize to no end;" and of the hot sun and the terrible sunburn ("I might as well just ask a doctor to give me cancer.") The list of hazards and personal fears he's written of is almost endless. On top of the fears are the overpriced and complicated equipment he's convinced himself he would need to buy for such an undertaking. There are all the shops that he would need to go to, all the salespeople he would have to talk to to get the top-quality hiking shoes, shorts, shirts, composite walking sticks and so on that are needed for such a trip. For all of these reasons and more, William has made up his mind that it is simply impossible to make any kind of a trip to the mountains.

William also does not ride a bike, much less rollerblade or even jog. He thinks car drivers a frightening, unpredictable bunch of lunatics who might cut him off at any moment or open a car door as he's riding by, sending him sailing over his handle bars and right into a coma. Nope, that's not for him, and neither is skateboarding, hiking, camping, or even going for long walks. William Potenco doesn't play sports of any kind, and ever since the Hockey Riots, he won't even go outside when any major sporting event is happening in the city. He refers to sports fans, regardless of gender or age, as "lugs" and they scare the shit out of him. So no, none of that. William is quite comfortable, quite content, indoors, and it's the rain, and more recently of course, the Scare, that allow him to stay inside where he is convinced he's happy, safe and secure.

Indoors, at his computer, on *Real*, watching and discussing films, talking with Julia, his girlfriend, talking and working with his friends Ryan and Mike—these, and his job at Eureka!, and all the tasks associated with maintaining a healthy online presence, are what make William feel good.

It's 6:28 p.m. when William finally gets bored staring at the rain and stands to leave. He electronically punches out of the system and turns off his computer. In the elevator, the advanced camera records him as he stares at the floor. When he steps out of the elevator, he pumps a few squirts of hand sanitizer into his hands from the dispenser. As he walks toward the front doors, public health and security cameras accurately record his temperature and appearance. As he approaches, almost out of the J. Griffin Building, William looks up and smiles contemptuously.

Outside, the rain has turned into a fine mist, a cold drizzle. William zips his coat up to his chin and pulls his hood over his head to begin his familiar walk home.

The rain. William didn't know about the constant rainfall before he moved to Vancouver. He would have heard that it rained a lot, but you just don't see many postcards of Vancouver in the rain. You might see it on a postcard of the mountains or the West Coast rainforest, but not the city. But can you blame the postcard makers? Rain is bad for a city's reputation. After living in Vancouver for almost ten years, though, William knows that the rain in Vancouver is a permanent feature that goes without saying, like the cold in Yellowknife.

The other thing he's learned about Vancouver is that the seasons are barely discernible one from another. Beautiful as they are, the seasons are perceptibly different only in the temperature of the falling rain. Sometimes the rain is a relief, like in August, when for two or maybe three full weeks, the sun is hot and the photographers take pictures for postcards. At most other times, though, the skies are grey, the roads are sloppy and the rain is either cold or very cold. At these times, the mood can get downright depressing. A miserable place, some say, is

Vancouver.

But I think that's unfair. In the spring, in certain special places like the manicured Japanese and Chinese gardens, and on the university campuses, there *are* beautiful flowers: cherry blossom, English daisy, spiderwort, butterfly bush, magnolia and many more. In the summer, during those three hot weeks in August, the ocean water even gets almost warm enough for swimming. And very rarely, but sometimes, toward the end of December or in January, a layer of fluffy white snow might blanket the entire city. William loves the snow. It reminds him of home and his childhood in southern Ontario. And it's even better than the rain for keeping him indoors, for the city, without the needed equipment—snowplows and such—is unable to cope with even an inch of snow and must shut down and wait it out, while he and every other citizen remain cozily indoors.

But the rain, unknown to many of our good people, is treacherous too. Downtown Vancouver is not like its suburbs. While the buildings on William's walk home are largely constructed of brick, stone and glass, the suburbs are something else altogether. The old wooden houses in Vancouver's suburbs absorb moisture from the ground and the rain and remain in a permanent state of dampness. Some are covered in green and black mould. Some have mushrooms and ferns growing on them. Some are decomposing before our eyes, being reclaimed by the earth. The picture is far from quaint, and the health risks are serious: malaria, West Nile and other waterborne diseases, pests and vermin, have sprung from far less. I know William has never seen this, never thought about it, never even ventured to the suburbs— the farthest he's been from downtown is the university—but for us working at the Public Health Bureau, these are serious issues.

Like most people, what William knows of Vancouver, and what he knew of it before he came, is skewed, a representation built on a lot of stories, misconceptions, and the tall tales of the outside media. Take Vancouver's citizens, its human geography, for instance. The people here have a very complicated nature, but you would never know it from the lies spread about them in the rest of Canada. What can be said and what is entirely true of our citizens is that since the Scare they have become humbled and, many say, slightly stoical. But this is relatively new, and any sympathy that they might now receive from the rest of Canadians is quite novel. For, before the Scare, Vancouverites did not enjoy a good reputation in the rest of Canada. They were lied about and misperceived, with most Canadians thinking them a decadent, arrogant bunch of assholes.

Stories and tall tales. Vancouver was, and I assure you, will be again, a Canadian paradise, a place where all got along, where the progressive merits of the generation of the '90s were really on display, where tolerance was the mantra, and "politically correct" meant something. Oh yes, back in the golden age of globalization, Vancouver truly was a global village and Canada's shining achievement. Before the Scare, Vancouver was a model of progressive liberalism, and it pulled William, as it pulled many from around the world and across the country, to its shores.

But history is a cruel animal. Vancouver was young and we needed more time. It turned out that some of its citizens were far from the people we had thought they were. For some observers, it was the Hockey Riots that first challenged the harmonious reputation of our city. The images seen on television and the Internet of thousands of drunk, marauding hockey fans, randomly destroying private property, setting fire to anything they got their hands on, fornicating in the streets and laughing in carnal lust, will do that. If that weren't enough, it was the Anti-Chinese Rampage a year later that solidified for many the fallen image of Vancouver. William saw. We all saw, and it was

9

shameful.

III

Returning to William, we watch him. After smiling cynically into the cameras, stepping out into the rain and bundling up, he begins to make his way towards home. But for a pair of Syndics plastering up city-beautification posters, there is no one else on either side of the street. William crosses to look at the new posters, many of which I had a hand in writing and designing. William stops to investigate. He's looking at one of my favourite pieces, a picture of a physically fit, beautiful young man and woman jogging on the beach on a sunny day. Under the image it reads: "Vancouver is only as beautiful as its citizens. Stay fit." Very nice, very direct—a clean message with no rough edges or dirty words, it gets right to the point of the matter. I call this style of writing —one that I probably invented—"direct poetry." I like to think of my posters as a poetry for the coming hygienic age, when we will all be, like my posters, clean, crisp and devoid of filth, sickness and disease.

William, however, is clearly a non-believer. Our cameras watch as, in an unhealthy burst of emotion, he begins to laugh hysterically at my poetry. He bends over and clutches his stomach, slaps his thigh, then snaps and sends pictures to his friends with his eyePhone. He's even infected the idiotic Syndics who, instead of filming him as they should, join in the laughing. If William wasn't so sick, I would hate him for laughing so cruelly at my work and hurting my feelings. Everyone's a goddamned critic. Does he think poetry is easy to write, or these messages are stupid? He should know that exercise helps the mind and body alike. If he took my message seriously, maybe he wouldn't be where he is now—he might even be healthy and good. But it's too late for that.

Recovered from his bout of laughter, William continues walking.

He stares at the ground, occasionally looking up to see where he's going. The walls of the buildings are immaculately clean and free of graffiti. Since the Scare, the sidewalks, the roads, the entire city is in a strict state of coded hygienic cleanliness. Spitting, littering, body odour, obesity and a host of other health offences deemed harmful to the well-being of the citizen-at-large have been forbidden. In the case of smoking, we've simply circumscribed the offenders so that those who remain have become second-class citizens, looked at as social pariahs derided by the rest of us. "No smoking" signs have been replaced by the now-familiar "No smokers," and smoking, like all health-related crimes, is punishable by fines and its ban enforced with cameras, drones, and the Syndics.

These measures are a necessity; William and everyone else must follow them. They've been put in place for the citizens' own benefit and protection. When H8N8 first attacked, the authorities were slow to react because the people and the city were already unhealthy and susceptible. They were not then being monitored or cleaned. The virus's first victims were the elderly, the weak and the homeless—a few here, a few there, misdiagnosed, not enough cases to worry about or tie together. Perhaps, though, with the sophisticated monitoring cameras and drones we have now, human error could have been avoided and we would not have seen those people die. We would have been able to tie the cases together, diagnose them more quickly, and lessen the overall destruction of H8N8. All hindsight and wishful thinking, I suppose.

William's relationship with the monitoring is ambivalent. The memories he gives us of his youth, recorded in detail in his diary, point to an early fascination with the technology. We have a picture, a memory written by William, of him as a young boy with his parents in the electronics section of the Sears department store. William's father is looking at the new VCRs; his mother waits patiently, watching William play in front of a big row of television screens. William is laughing and hopping around, looking into the line of cameras above the screens and at his own image on television. He's trying to draw his mother's attention. Did she not see him? He's on TV. William is fascinated with his image on the screens. He plays with it, approaching, laughing, jumping back and forth, like Peter Pan with his shadow, in and out of the camera's lenses, on and off of the television screens. His mother has a hard time pulling him away, and he cries. He wants one. His parents tell him not today. They promise to bring him back again to the electronics section to play. He was only four or five years old, but the memory is obviously a vivid one for William.

The next time he describes a camera, it is done in passing. He and his generation are getting used to them. William, twelve years old, rides a school bus to school. On the ride, bad children torture the bus driver by calling her names and flinging garbage at her. The school board installs a box above the driver and tells the students there's a camera inside. Many don't believe it; they think they're being tricked. But it works, and the bad kids stop tormenting the poor bus driver. By the time he's an adult, video cameras are a common feature in most places—shopping malls, convenience stores, airports—and William, like everyone else, has gotten comfortable with them. After the Scare, when we installed them in every public building, major intersection, public park, entrance to every hockey rink, bus stops and so on, we received little opposition. William, like everyone else in Vancouver, hardly noticed at all.

Walking down West Pender, close now to Carrall and home, William passes another row of posters. They read: "Doctors are your friends," and show a doctor holding a toddler by the hand, walking on an immaculately clean sidewalk. Anyone of intelligence will see the importance of the message, how it conveys the new-found goodwill among science, the people and health.

When William enters Harmony Cooperative, where he lives, he passes by another pair of cameras, at which he again smiles contemptuously. The cameras, now always in pairs, record far beyond just what he is doing; one camera notes and transmits to our office his body temperature, while the other, using facial recognition technology, picks up unhealthy or alarming anomalies in appearance.

I know that William, now riding the elevator up to his room on the eighth floor, will have only one thing on his mind—get to his room as fast as possible so that he can grab his reusable plastic container, go down to Harmony's first floor cafeteria kitchen which serves food until eight o'clock every evening, take his food to go and return to his room so that he can get back on *Real*. Normally he completes this routine with astonishing speed and efficiency. There is never anyone eating in the cafeteria, which means that his trips are guilt free. (The unwritten rule in Harmony is that residents should eat together to foster socialization, but no one ever does). Furthermore, this evening, the pretty young woman who often works in the kitchen—with whom shy William is clearly infatuated—is not at work, but instead it's the elderly Chinese man, so William's anxiety is kept in check and doesn't get in the way of his determination to get back to his room as quickly as possible.

IV

Safely back in his room, William leans back in his chair to have yet another long look out the window at the rain. In the distance above the mist, he sees the tops of the mountains in the fading light. Vancouver is a lucky city—it is grafted onto such magnificent natural beauty. William turns *RealNews* to the local Vancouver feed.

On the news is my colleague, Doctor Chief Medical Health Officer of Vancouver Stacey Starr, who spoke today in front of a delegation of the press, civilians, and top Conservative Party government members in from Ottawa. "It is only a matter of time," she is saying. "In fact, our top scientists and engineers are making this happen right now. Soon we will all be equipped with technology that will store our personal health histories on our bodies, on our phones, and in our wallets. This data can be read remotely by our health and safety drones and medical-detect cameras. The data we have been collecting from each and every citizen since the Scare has not been gathered in vain. In the near future, whenever a person walks past a camera or is viewed by a drone, they will get an on-the-spot, remote medical examination to determine if they have cancer, an STD, TB, a minor headache, or almost any other health-related ailment. The cameras and drones will detect it before you yourself know about it, and you will be saved." The Conservative Party officials applaud and look pleased. *Real*'s reporter then clarifies that Doctor Chief Starr's speech was part of the day's ceremonies. The Public Health Agency of Canada has honoured Vancouver as this year's healthiest city in which to live.

"Vancouver," says the Public Health official now on-screen, "is a vision of the future for the rest of Canada. It has emerged from darkness to show the rest of us the light that lies ahead. As it was before the Scare, when Vancouver was a trailblazer, so now is it again a model for the rest of the country. We are happy to honour the city and its hard-working citizens with this award." The speech is followed by more applause and smiles from the Conservative Party officials.

William turns it off. Ryan and Mike are both online. To them he sends a message:

(7:23 PM) William Potenco: Vancouver's back on top again. Honoured as healthiest city in Canada to live.

14

(7:24 PM) Ryan Jeffreys: Good for them. winnipeg [sic] could learn a few things. This place is a dump.

(7:25 PM) Mike George: i like ottawa.

(7:27 PM) William Potenco: Ya well, I guess it's good.

(7:33 PM) William Potenco: Hey guys, I'm a bit tired tonight. I thought I would do some work but I don't think I can. Think I'll just watch a movie and then crash. But I'll get on tomorrow early and catch up. Okay?

(7:34 PM) Ryan Jeffreys: whatev.

(7:35 PM) Mike George: no problem, it's late here.

(7:37 PM) William Potenco: Okay, I'll be on if anything comes up. See you both tomorrow.

William must truly be tired. He's worked hard and long. His thoughts are unclear and clouded, and so, as like on every night, he opens his diary to clear his mind. He's been writing in it for some years. He has recorded that he enjoys "emptying his mind" at the end of the day; he has said, too, that in the diary he can write many things that he can't talk about with his friends Mike and Ryan, who, William believes, always want to turn his most personal confessions into jokes. William's diary is our most reliable source on his condition. It was certain disturbing phrases in his diary that first caught the attention of our highly sophisticated and accurate surveillance software.

After saying goodnight to his friends, he writes the following. Note the italics, the alarming indications of William's sickness that our software has detected.

Friday, April 4.

Today, during what was supposed to be an engaging task, a task that required independent thought, my mind unexpectedly floated off. I lost focus on what I was doing and I ended up in a place far from work and the office building, and far from my computer screen. I ended up in a dark place, a place too impossible for me to describe, a place not quite right and somehow *disjointed. I felt I was disjointed,* but I felt happy too, afraid but happy in this place. It was weird, I had perfect clarity of thought, but absolutely *no sense of purpose or direction.* I'm not entirely sure, it doesn't really make sense, but I think that maybe it was my subconscious telling me that I might *not be well suited* to my work, or that maybe I need some kind of change.

It's strange, though, because I'm not bored at work. I like what I do. I've mastered all the tasks and I actually like the boring ones because they don't interfere with my deep thoughts—they don't even touch them. It's the difficult tasks that make me tired. It was a difficult task I was doing today when my mind wandered. Strange. Perhaps the feeling came because of a certain lack of excitement lately about being at work. I remember when I first started, and even after three months working at Eureka!, I was excited, almost nervous, every day before work. I was full of so much anticipation. I felt as though I was part of something big. I saw Eureka! and I knew that they would go places, and I wanted to share that journey with them. Some day, I thought, *Real* will buy them—some day, I'll be working for *Real.* That really got me going and I was so happy. But now, I don't know, *I'm not as happy* about that. I guess there still is that possibility, me one day working for Sydney Rothsteen, but it hasn't happened yet, and I'm getting pretty bored waiting. It's a *sad feeling* when you wait so long for something, only to realize you maybe don't want it anymore.

I turned 30 years old today. Do you think that has something to do with it, my *unsettled thoughts?* I've always been impatient. Ever since I can remember, I've been the first to arrive to meetings, to work, to appointments of any kind. I've always thought of my punctuality as a virtue. But what if instead it's a weakness, a vice? I just need to wait, to have a little patience, that's all. Patience, that's the virtue, not punctuality. Punctuality is a sign of impatience.

Ryan always said that I needed more patience. Fucking asshole—what he said today really pissed me off. I don't know why he acts like that. He knows that it bothers me. He knows I'm not depressed.

What an idiot—he spelled it wrong too, haha, the moron. He never used to be mean like that.

I don't know. Anyway, the rain has eased and it's almost totally dark now. The sign on the Chinese import shop across the street has lit up and it's shining in through my window directly onto my pillow. I would be sleeping in its light of it weren't for my curtains. The hum of the cars passing down below and the drone of the drones flying overhead has died down finally letting the quiet of the night take over. It feels so late. I should get some rest, and tomorrow I'll be back to my normal self. Everything is fine.

It's 8:32 p.m. when William finishes writing. After saving and closing his diary, William searches through *Real*'s online film catalogue for something to watch. He decides on something he considers funny, *The Jerk,* with Steve Martin. William knows this movie well; we know that he's seen it many times. Tonight, though, it barely starts before his eyes close, the screensaver switches on, and he slumps asleep in his chair.

William and I
by Thomas Vickers
I

I'm not a writer. I'm a reader. I read books. It's what I do now. They say good readers make good writers. They also make shitty ones. But I'll do it anyway. I'll do my best and try to write it down. Record it all as it happened.

It's Wednesday morning and it's a little cool, but at least it's not raining. I hate the damned weather. I'm early, because I make it a priority to arrive early to new jobs. It's all about first impressions. At a new job, the boss sees you there early, and it shows that you're keen, that you want to get right at it, a real team player, like. The boss doesn't forget that. I know they don't forget you're there early with a big smile on. That's the key to success at a shitty job—looking like you care. It's the same with interviews, meetings, and all other appointments of any kind, even drinks with pals—you show up early and you make a good impression.

So, I'm early. It's around 8:30 a.m. and I don't start until nine. I'm dressed up too, wearing some nice blue slacks, slightly tapered. Nice dress shirt, brown with blue pinstripes, not too wrinkly. Good brown leather shoes. On top, my blue wool pea coat. My hair is combed and my glasses are on. I'd say I look pretty damned sharp—professional and intelligent.

Unfortunately, the goddamned door to the building is locked. I buzz a bunch, but no one gets off their ass to open it so I'm left here to just stare up at the nondescript grey building. The engraving above the entrance says J. Griffin, whoever the hell that is. There's also some ornaments carved into it. I'd say it was definitely built sometime before 1970. It's not quite as boring as the 70s shit, since there *is* that kind of art-deco flare. At least it's not all glass like these new Hong Kong buildings—man, those are ugly as shit. I guess I shouldn't ask so much from buildings. Anyway, this J. Griffin building in Gastown is fairly central—a good place to work.

Before the Scare, this part of town was a bit dodgy at certain times of the day. It was a fucking train wreck of drunks and the homeless, especially around the Victory Square monument. I find it ironic that Vancouver builds a war monument, calls it Victory Square, and that's where the drunks and the homeless flop around. That's not the case anymore, of course, since all the drunks and bums are either dead or driven off. But I remember what it used to be like before the Scare, when my good friend Eugene used to visit me. He liked to go and sit by the monument at Victory Square and drink with the drunks. I went a couple times, but I never really got into it. There were a lot of natives —Indians. Eugene has some kind of affinity with them, but no matter how drunk I got, I always felt kind of awkward and out of place, guilty and all that. Anyway, it was always a total circus—shopping carts full of discarded junk, clothes, blankets, beer bottles and cans, booze and wine bottles, random garbage strewn on the ground next to people passed-out every which way—a real fucking catastrophe. Like a bomb had gone off. Now, of course, the monument and park are shipshape— clean as an unused park should be.

I look back at the doors and buzz again. I put my hands up to the glass to block out the light and peer into the lobby. All I see are two cameras staring back at me, probing me with their electronic eyes. I buzz again and hide around the corner from the cameras. Finally, I hear the lock open and someone come out—an Asian guy in coveralls, probably the janitor. He holds the door open and lets me in.

"Thanks," I say.

"Yep," he says. He's a bit grumpy.

"Sorry," I say.

I know he probably hates his job—jobs suck. And when you have to work some shitty job cleaning a building, or any shitty job, you get these routines to make the time go by, make it less shitty, but then some dickhead like me comes along and disturbs your routine, makes you do something you're not getting paid for.

"I didn't mean to disturb you," I say as we ride the elevator up.

"Meh."

He gets off at the eighth floor, but I keep on riding up to the top, to the tenth floor where Eureka! is. I step off the elevator, but there's no one else there. When I had my interview, I was given a quick tour of the place, so I know where to go. I walk past the front offices and down a long corridor with doors inscribed with names or departments —Programming, Marketing, Creative—until I get to the last big room marked Data Management. The setup inside the room is pretty weird. When I was first shown the place, I was expecting to see cubicles, like the "veal fattening pens" Douglas Coupland talks about, but instead, what they have are these tables, fifteen or so, each with two laptop computers. They're arranged in three semi-circle rings around one bigger table with a proper desktop computer, where the manager sits. It's like a panopticon where management can see you at all times and it's pretty fucking gross.

Anyway, I'm standing there and I don't really know what to do, since there's no one there, so I just go and sit at the desk farthest away from the manager's in the far back corner next to the window. That seat has the best view.

The manager is the person who gave me my interview. His name is Stuart, but he told me to call him Stu. Stu has messy, curly hair and he wears shorts. He told me that he wears shorts every day and that he rides his bike every day no matter what the weather. On his left calf he has a giant black tattoo of a Haida raven. He's nice, I suppose, one of those bosses with an attitude like "I'm your pal, we're all in this together. Let's have a beer sometime." I don't really fall for that though. If he's my superior, he's probably a dickhead. Anyway, I'll find out soon enough.

I'm sitting in the corner and waiting and having a good look around. To be honest, the place is disgusting. I mean, it's well-lit and very modern, with big windows and all that. The carpet is new. It's red and the chairs are red, which is a bad colour. Red makes people get crazy violent. I did my Masters in Toronto and the student bar there had red carpet and all-red furniture and there were fights there almost every night. They couldn't figure out why until they finally remodelled the place and made everything blue, and there was no more fighting. Anyways, the chairs in this office are red but comfortable, the computers are new, the office even smells new. But it's not the new smell or the colour that makes it disgusting. What makes it so gross is the feeling of subservience I get just sitting here. First, there's the layout—like I said, a panopticon prison where the boss can observe us, but we can only stare at the back of one another's heads. I would honestly prefer cubicles to this. Second, it's the décor, which is minimal, empty-like. There are three types of picture on the walls: one is a pinned-up poster of a group of penguins huddled together on an arctic beach. In bold white letters above them is printed the word "Conformity." The caption at the bottom reads, "It's the one who's different that gets left out in the cold." I can hardly believe it. I seriously hope it's meant to be ironic. Another is a framed enlargement of *Time*'s "Person of the Year" from 2006, that iconic "You" year, with the ridiculous caption that reads, "Yes, you. You control the Information Age. Welcome to your world." What a fucking lie that turned out to be. The last thing on the wall is above a door with the name Dana Burrows on it. It's a bunch of words printed on fluorescent pink paper—one black word on each pink page spells out the lyrics to the Daft Punk song, "Harder, Better, Faster, Stronger." They read, "Work it *harder*, make it *better*, do it *faster*, makes us *stronger*." Unbelievable.

It's revolting; it immediately makes me feel like a lackey, a stooge, a surf, a slave—and it makes me sincerely want to revolt against it. It's a fucking instinct with me. I instinctively feel oppressed and censored, surrounded by this shit. I mean, okay, this might be the first time I've worked in an office like this, but I'll tell you, and I've had lots of jobs so I know. At the other places I've worked they at least try to hide that they're a dictatorship. They try to make you feel like you have a say, or make you feel that your opinion matters and that you can influence things. Like they might have a suggestion box or something (to find out who the complainers are so they can fire them). And it's not like we're unionized in these places—we can't fight back—and even then, the unions are fucked these days. But that's another story. Here at Eureka! there is no suggestion box and no union, and unless it's all just a joke, I can tell by my surroundings—actually I'm being told by my surroundings—that I'm nothing but a mindless penguin who better not venture too far from the pack or my family, this corporation, will abandon me and I'll freeze and then die. I can tell all this in five minutes.

And look, I don't want to hear that I'm complaining too much, that the wage is supposed to compensate for this type of shit. I say no to that. No. The wage doesn't compensate me. I was hired at Eureka! at nine dollars an hour to work twenty hours a week. I almost have a PhD in history, for fuck's sake! I speak Russian, for Christ's sake! Nine bucks an hour. No one can live on that in Vancouver. Yeah sure, it's not awful. It's not fucking McDonald's, and the guy who let me in, he probably makes less. But since they got rid of minimum wage to bring back investment after the Scare, they get away with murder at these places. It's a fucking crime against humanity.

And it's not like the job is easy either. You might just sit at a desk in front of a computer all day, and maybe that seems physically easy, but it's not. I've done it and it takes a toll. Headaches, hand cramps, back problems, eye problems. The worst is what I call "fuzzybrain." It's sort of an amalgamation of the sore, tired eyes and the mild but super-annoying headache. There is this static in your head behind your eyes, and it prevents you from thinking right or seeing clearly, because your depth perception is all out of whack; you can't even communicate like a normal human. Like after talking to a computer for eight hours, you've forgotten how. You can't do anything after that kind of work— you have fuzzybrain and walk around like a fucking non-communicating zombie.

The good thing is that I'm not nervous. I've worked a shit ton of different jobs. You might even say that I'm a bit of a factotum. So I've mastered the emotional experience on the first day on the job. What I feel comes from a lot of experience combined with total indifference. I mean, I don't want to get fired and I'll work hard, but you can't confuse hard work with caring about a job. The fact is, low-wage, part time jobs don't pay you enough to care. Nine bucks an hour doesn't buy my emotional attachment, loyalty to a company, or commitment to a product. It gets my labour power and nothing more.

Anyway, I've been sitting here fifteen minutes now, ruminating on this stuff. I'd really just like to draw a huge cock on one of the conformity penguins and get the fuck out of Dodge. But as I'm working up the courage to do it, I hear the elevator doors open down the hall, so I stay seated. A minute later a guy walks into the room with his head down. He's tall, around six feet I'd say; young, slim, good looking, dressed in dark blue jeans and wearing some black synthetic, outdoorsy coat. He comes in and walks right up to me before he lifts his head and finally actually sees me. He gives a little start, but not much. He looks confused more than anything. He stands with his eyes all twisted up, head moving side to side like he's searching for something to say.

Background to the Report on William Potenco
by Doctor Officer Elias Degair

It began much like SARS with poor monitoring, human error and a lack of vigilance, resulting in gross negligence and misdiagnosis. We should have learned from the mistakes made in Toronto, but no one ever wants to think about the worst-case scenario; no one ever wants to believe that it can happen to us. The real bad ones—Ebola, polio, small pox, the plague—are always imagined happening in far-off places, in both space and time, as if we're too privileged for something similar to strike us; as if here in Canada, we don't warrant a visit from one of these great masters of death.

And so, it was twenty-two people—that's how many died before British Columbia's Ministry of Health finally realized they were connected. Twenty-two people were sacrificed before our pride and arrogance, and our belief that it couldn't possibly happen here were silenced.

But that was really only the beginning. Soon after, more died and it spiralled. Vancouver's Chinese community was made into a scapegoat —they were the first ones blamed. Their exotic tastes and their documented unhygienic methods of food preparation were held responsible. As the bodies mounted, answers were demanded where none could be given. Who did this to us? Where did it come from? At the time, those of us working in public health, even lowly volunteers like myself, knew as little as anyone else, and were just as scared. When no answers came, responsibility was assigned. After around a hundred had died, anti-Chinese rhetoric flared and violent acts towards Chinese people and Chinese businesses intensified until we and all the rest of Canada and the world were forced to witness what was left of Vancouver's image as a tolerant, multi-cultural society get flushed down the toilet.

Small but very organized, angry mobs of Vancouverites marched into downtown Chinatown demanding answers and blood. They were soon joined by thousands of frustrated citizens caught up in the mood of misplaced vengeance. Anti-Chinese slogans like "dirty Chink, dirty food," and "Chinese no clean" were chanted and sprayed on walls; bricks were lobbed through Chinatown windows; Chinese signs were sprayed over and rewritten in English or torn down altogether; businesses, import/export shops, grocers and restaurants were ransacked for their goods and set on fire. Even the beautiful Dr. Sun Yat-Sen Classical Chinese Garden was destroyed—dug up, defecated and pissed on, and set on fire. The police were conspicuously slow to act, letting people die. And we watched it all on TV. In total, one white rioter (a housewife named Cindy who had two kids and a dog named Richie) and forty-four Chinese died. In the aftermath of this tragedy, most Chinese in downtown Vancouver, gripped by fear, left, thus abandoning one of the oldest Chinatowns in North America.

Afterwards, even after we had traced the infected turkey, the one responsible for H8N8 to a free-range farm outside of Calgary and a butcher at an organic market on Granville Island, Vancouverites persisted in their anti-Chinese racism (god forbid in this day) and rhetoric. Chinatown after the Rampage was like an empty fortune cookie. Even today, only a few Chinese-owned import/export shops remain.

One of them is located across the street from where William lives. He, like many others, took advantage of the plummeting cost of rent in the area, and found a place in the sharply reduced apartment complex called Harmony Cooperative.

I wished that the Federal Government had acted then. Send in the troops, I thought. If not for the Chinese, then for the virus. But it was not until over six hundred diagnoses and two hundred deaths later that the weak-kneed Federal Liberals finally stepped in and issued Special Decree 451, putting Vancouver into a state of emergency. Health officials and doctors from other parts of Canada and a military unit from the Canadian Joint Operations Command were flown in to fight what we had now correctly diagnosed as the H8N8 virus. Normal, run-of-the mill rights, such as the freedom of movement and the freedom of association, were suspended in the name of the greater good. The police and people like me working with the health authorities had permission to enter homes without warrant, diagnose and forcibly remove the sick. Traffic both in and out of the city had to pass through health and security checkpoints. Everyone was issued, and required to wear, a mask. Malls and schools closed, public transportation ceased, and even the first home games of the Vancouver Canucks hockey season were cancelled. The city shut down, people stayed inside and H8N8 ran its course.

In an emergency like this, some people shine. They seem made for situations like the Scare, as it came to be called—they can act quickly, make on-the-spot decisions, and like me, know who to say yes to, and when. Quick field promotions were made and I soon found myself in charge of a small team tasked with house-by-house on-the-spot diagnoses. I had a knack for it, a feeling in my gut. Even before even the medical equipment showed that someone was infected, I could sense it. I thrived in these circumstances and got the results we were looking for. Six months after the issuing of Special Decree 451, I was the head of an entire unit, and the Scare was proclaimed "over." City authorities declared victory in destroying the virus and pledged to the citizens of Vancouver that a tragedy such as this would never befall our glorious city again. To commemorate those who died, a statue was erected on the former site of the Dr. Sun Yat-Sen Garden; it depicts a doctor cradling a child in her arms and honours the more than two thousand citizens who succumbed to the virus. The statue and renovated gardens were renamed The Monument Greens.

William never visits The Monument Greens even though Harmony Cooperative is practically next door. Maybe he doesn't give a damn about those who died, or maybe, like most these days, he's simply scared and wants to forget. We were all of us, after all, affected by the events. I was fast-tracked through medical school and honoured with my current post, but others weren't so courageous and chose to flee. Even a reclusive introvert like William had friends who left. People are affected differently by death and they react in different ways. After the Scare, many became depressed and sick just from trauma itself; some even developed symptoms of illnesses we had never seen before.

At the Public Health Bureau of Vancouver, we saw it as our duty, as the masters of the city's public health, to do something. We petitioned the federal government to extend the mandate of Special Decree 451 before it expired. The government agreed and the citizenry did not oppose. The scope of our mandate grew and the Bureau was finally given permission to set up the institutional and infrastructural means to remake Vancouver's citizens into ideal, healthy, twenty-first-century global citizens, and to return Vancouver to the model of Canadian progressiveness that it once was.

Shortly after, the first of our Health and Safety drones took flight to begin monitoring, and enforceable fines for public crimes against health were put in place. Today, if a Health and Safety drone or camera detects anyone's temperature is above 99 degrees Fahrenheit, the Syndics are notified and the person is whisked off to a hospital for treatment. To prevent further outbreaks, new measures have been implemented and are enforced. If anyone is caught littering, smoking outside a glass smoking room, drinking in public, or coughing; if a person appears pale or sick, if their eyes are bloodshot; if their health is seen as a danger to their fellow citizens in any way, the Syndics are notified, they're taken care of, and a crisis is prevented. The results of these measures have been outstanding, as evidenced by the shining new honour of being named "Canada's Healthiest City," but they haven't come cheap. All of this has cost money. Results need to be continually reproduced for us to continue.

Sickness is getting harder and harder to find. Life in pre-Scare Vancouver, though controlled and identical for most, allowed for a lot of outdoor public revelry, which has unfortunately since been lost. And with fewer people outside, we have less chance of finding the sick ones. While the right to freely associate was restored immediately after the Scare, Vancouver's citizens have had a hard time reemerging from indoors. What the Scare seems to have made justifiable is the avoidance of social contact altogether. People are asking themselves whether it is not easier, safer, better, to tolerate each other from the comfort of their own homes, on platforms like *Real*, than to go outside in social gatherings with friends. We hope that these anxieties will dissipate, or find new targets, after a time. The drones, the cameras, the Syndics—the tools actively combating illness, making sure public gatherings are perfectly safe—will, we are sure, wash away these fears and encourage people to come back outside where they can again be easily monitored. In the meantime, we have had to develop or borrow technology that can penetrate front doors, like the sophisticated computer monitoring that diagnosed William.

Much of this applies to William Potenco's case. What is different with him, and with others we are now only just discovering, is that he was sick even before the Scare. William's sickness, identified by our technology and which it is now my job to diagnose, is something special, since it emerged at the interstice of two colliding worlds. What we need to consider is that it was not the Scare that drove William indoors. He was there and sick already, with a kind of reclusive social disease that has gone too long undiagnosed. What the Scare did to people like William was something much more insidious—it created the possibility within him, around him, in his daily activities and pursuits, in his contact with people, in all of his innermost thoughts and desires, for future symptoms to emerge. William is a contradiction. Just as the rest of our citizens are getting used to the new order of things in the city and coming back outside, he is not. Just as every public place—every formerly dirty street, corner, crack and ally—has been made clean; just as crimes against health and hygiene are being curbed, William, it seems, is getting sicker, more reclusive. It's as if whatever was wrong with him before the Scare now has room to hyper-realize itself. William is reacting opposite to what we want, and we must find out why.

Report on William Potenco
by Doctor Officer Elias Degair

V

At the outset, it should be made perfectly clear that William is not depressed, not in the popular sense anyway. He does not mope around sad and gloomy, with thoughts of suicide. And this is no longer the early nineties, when throwing a good dose of lithium at someone would solve the problem. No, no. What William has is altogether a product of our unique time and place.

A day in the life of William Potenco starts early. His eyePhone Smartphone, the latest and most advanced, with all the most recent alarm clock apps, goes off at 6:00 a.m. William doesn't have to wake up so early. He doesn't have to be at work until 9:00 a.m., but habitually arrives ten minutes early to every shift, at 8:50 a.m., though that's not the point. The reason his eyePhone alarm clock app (programmed to play early morning radio wakeup programs from the 1920s complete with crackly news stories and popular songs of the day) goes off at 6:00 a.m. is so that William can complete the myriad daily tasks he sets for himself *before* he leaves for work. There is already an element of obsessive-compulsive disorder in this wake-up procedure—but let us continue.

William is efficient and skillful at multi-tasking and masterful at time management. By his own reckoning, he accomplishes more in the two or so hours he gives himself before finally getting in the shower and leaving for work, than most others do all day. Everything he does is carefully timed and planned. As his alarm clock plays some hit jazz tune from the 1920s, bleary-eyed William gets out of bed, fills his kettle and pours some medium grain coffee into his *cafetière*. He could travel down to Harmony's cafeteria, which opens at 6:00 a.m., but to William, even that short elevator ride is a waste of time (and besides, as he once wrote, "the coffee here tastes like burnt sawdust"), so he makes it himself in his room. The rooms in Harmony have a sink and cupboards, but no stoves, so upon moving in, William purchased a small refrigerator where he stores his coffee and milk.

As the water boils, William wakes up his computer and logs onto *Real*. William's first hour of the day is dedicated to his *RealJob*. When *RealEconomy* went live, William, Ryan and Mike pooled their startup funds and purchased a business in the hybrid sector of the technology division and, rather unimaginatively, named it RWM Solutions. They deal in the management and sale of small electronic goods, such as cellular phone accessories. Large producers of headphones, battery chargers, batteries, and so on, in China or Vietnam or elsewhere, who have overstock and want to unload their products on the *RealFlea Market*, send RWM Solutions their product lists and then William, Ryan, Mike and their five employees sort, catalogue, market, and sell these goods. All the services RWM provides are paid for by their clients in *RealDollars*.

William's job with RWM is product management, while Ryan and Mike deal directly with the customers. William believes that what makes RWM's clients happy is nothing more than getting their goods online and getting their profits quickly. He uses this attitude as a defense mechanism to mask what are actually some pretty serious general withdrawal symptoms. Ryan and Mike have tried to turn him around, tried to get him comfortable with personal contact. In one *Real* conversation we recorded, Ryan and Mike try to get William to read the *Analects* to teach him how to approach their Eastern clients. Typical of William and of his symptoms, he simply reverts to what he already knows.

(6:43 PM) Ryan Jeffreys: Will, you should read it, its [sic] very important. If you want them to come back you have to talk to them, hold their hand, and laugh at their jokes, otherwise they'll find someone new.

(6:47 PM) William Potenco: I watched [Michael] Cimino's *Year of the Dragon*, and I watched [John] Carpenter's *Big Trouble in Little China*. I'll be fine. Anyway, you and Mike are dealing with them directly, right? So if you've read it, it'll be fine.

(6:54 PM) Mike George: that's not really the point will, the book is more better [sic], and by the way big trouble in little china is stupid.

(7:00 PM) William Potenco: Mike, don't be a cinematic child. But if it makes you both happy, I will try to make time to read the book.

William never did read the *Analects* and remains firmly behind the scenes at RWM, contributing by doing what he excels at: focused efficiency. Mike and Ryan send him the inventory lists and he sorts the products: one list for headphones, one for batteries, one for chargers, and so on. After he sorts, he sends the lists to RWM employees, who then put the product up for sale on the *RealFlea Market*.

While he drinks his coffee, then—three cups, seventeen to twenty minutes per cup—this is what he does: he sorts. His talent for rapidly completing simple tasks like a machine on an assembly line is something to behold. When fuelled by strong coffee, William can usually complete, in the hour he gives himself, more than Ryan and

Mike could themselves do in three hours of their own time. On the days he can't—if, for example, like on Mondays, there is too much to do (William does not work for RWM on the weekends: he prefers to spend Saturday and Sunday alone in his room eating pizza and chain-watching television series and films), he'll finish the work later that evening. Most days this is not necessary. William is—and I have to be honest here, because it is so impressive—simply that good. If he were not so efficient and if it took him any longer at this work, the job would not be worth it. On an average morning, at the current exchange rate of one Canadian dollar to five *RealDollars*, William earns twenty dollars.

VI

When he's finished sorting, William, like many mentally ill people, prisoners, soldiers, and the confined in general, masturbates. This seems to work for William as a kind of coping mechanism, as if masturbating allows him to feel done with this part of his day. Physically and mentally, he explodes all over a stack of completed files or reports (if there were such a stack) as a way of punching out of RWM for the day.

Until recently, William masturbated every day. He has a few favourite websites that he regularly, but not exclusively, visits: www.triplexxx.com, www.porngurls.com, www.girlsxxxvids.com. In the past, according to our records, he would watch videos of young women and men doing, frankly, the craziest, perverted things. His browser history is both a shocking and penetrating catalogue of deviancy to leaf through: female porn stars getting stuffed, often violently, with dicks and every other damn thing in every hole, couples-fucking POV, gonzo porn, orgies, big black cocks, perfect-ass white girls, tribbing, pegging...the list of depravities is endless. Recently, it seems that this has gotten a bit too vulgar and predictable for William. Nowadays, his browser history is filled with searches for "real girls," "amateurs," "camgirls," and for women and couples who have nothing better to do than film themselves fucking. William must feel that these shows are in some way superior to mainstream porn. To be honest, this stuff is just as disturbing as the other—the women are often unattractive and unhealthy, old, ugly and fat with saggy, discolored skin, and most times look to be getting abused by steroid-pumped men with absurdly large penises.

An extensive examination of William's recent online search history suggests that he prefers solo female performers. Until a short while ago, William never once communicated with one of these camgirls. He fulfilled his perverted fantasies without engaging with them—he would just watch recordings of them posted by others on his favorite websites, or simply tune in for a free live show. But he's recently broken this rule—he saw someone that he had to talk to: Julia, whom he now sees. We'll deal with William and her in a separate report; for now, it's enough to say that his routine has recently changed, so that on days when he has arranged to see her, he doesn't always masturbate.

VII

Following his morning session and the flushing of his wad of tissues, William gets down to what he enjoys most, his online social life. He begins by opening his *Real-ID* page. He looks at his picture, smiling at it as it stares back at him. William's current photo is in black and white. It looks professional and depicts him with a slight smile that says, "I'm rather pleasant and maybe even optimistic." After this moment of self reflection, he opens his *RealDate Book* to check about upcoming appointments—other than Julia, and his mandatory three-month health examinations, his date book only contains his work schedule. Next, William updates his posts, and replies to conversations as needed—a happy birthday here, an "affected" or "unaffected" there, or a new composition, the standard catching-up things we all do on *Real*.

What can be said about William in his online socializing is that he is a proud and devoted communicator. When someone writes to him or addresses him in any form, he replies promptly, and his replies, unlike most in the social media world, are written carefully and in complete sentences. For if there is one thing (and there is obviously more than one, since he is borderline OCD) that William truly and obsessively hates, it is the short-form—what he calls "dumb"—language that people use on social networks (on *Real* it is called RealSpeak). While he has never openly defended the purity of the English language or maliciously chastised someone for their writing, his dedication to form means he does see a problem in abbreviating and converting into acronyms the whole of current communication. For most of us, this is just efficiency, something you'd think William would embrace. However, he is quite strict about it, and it explains why we haven't seen William on Blabber, despite that platform's appeal and potential for rapid communication. Ryan has tried to persuade him:

(12:34 PM) Ryan Jeffreys: IT's [sic] real cool, if you want to talk to someone famous you can.

(12:37 PM) William Potenco: You can talk, but whether they answer you is different, right? And I think I would find it almost impossible to say what I would want in so few words in a Blab.

(12:45 PM) Ryan Jeffreys: You have to learn to talk better and to use the codes, omg, and @ and such.

(12:50 PM) William Potenco: I just don't think that all those acronyms have any meaning. They seem so trite and empty, and when I see people use them I never know fully what they mean. I don't know if it's ever genuine.

(12:56 PM) Ryan Jeffreys: OMG! Will, its [sic] just for fun. Today I talked to three different Hollywood actors.

(1:00 PM) William Potenco: Talking to them? You mean blabbing, right? Did they even "talk" back? I mean, it is cool, I guess, but…

(1:03 PM) Ryan Jeffreys: Fuck ya, and it's not only that, you can stay updated, receive stories, alot [sic] of stuff. Anyway, you should think about it for business too.

(1:04 PM) William Potenco: Maybe.

(1:05 PM) Ryan Jeffreys: And also, Will, I wanted to mention about that job I told you about. Its [sic] still available at Bombardier, you should come, it would be sweet to have you here in Winnipeg.

(1:06 PM) William Potenco: Yeah. I'm not quite ready to leave Vancouver yet. Thanks though. Talk soon.

(1:08 PM) Ryan Jeffreys: later.

William has never tried Blabber. He seems, like the rest of the world, to prefer the format of *Real*. He feels that it gives its users the room to express their ideas more clearly. And he proves it too. William takes part in many *RealSeminars*, in the morning at home and on his lunch break, walking to and from work, in the bathroom or waiting for coffee, when he'll use the *Real* app to update his posts.

His priority is his own *RealSeminar*, which he established three years ago and on which he plays the role of chief monitor. In a subsection of the larger "film, film culture" category William's seminar is called "What's a dickfer?" and is dedicated specifically to 1980s North American comedy films. William watches these films over and over, almost obsessively. The title of the seminar is an obscure reference to the 1985 film *Spies Like Us*, starring Chevy Chase and Dan Aykroyd. It seems to be a particular favourite of William's.

It's not just comedies, but films of all sorts that William watches and loves. His strong relationship with films he connects to his childhood and an early close relationship with his now-estranged father. Jotted in his diary are memories of fond moments spent with his dad watching films. Every Friday night throughout his childhood, his father would arrive home from work with two or even three rented VHS movies under his arm and a bag of fast food for them to share in front of the television. William and his dad and mom would eat the fast food, then his dad would open a beer and William would be allowed to sip his fill of RC Cola. His mom prepared butter-soaked, salt covered popcorn on the stove. William remembers trying to stay awake until all the films were done, but more often falling asleep on the couch next to his dad, covered by a blanket. His dad liked old action adventure films like *The Black Knight* with Alan Ladd, *The Long Ships* with Sydney Poitier, *El Cid* with Charlton Heston, and *Spartacus* with Kirk Douglas. William liked the comedies like *Beverly Hills Cop*, *Revenge of the Nerds*, and *Porky's*.

William's diary says that his favourite Fridays were the ones when his dad would come home first and pick him up so they could go together to the movie rental store. On those days, William was so excited that he said he would nearly wet his pants in anticipation of walking through the aisles and aisles of films at the local Blockbuster. When he got old enough to operate the VCR, his father started to buy blank tapes so that he could record movies from the television. By the time he was ten, and despite the onset of DVD technology, William had a huge collection of more than a hundred tapes that he had spent hours carefully labelling, cataloguing and organizing according to an intricate personal classification system involving both genre and director. He took pride in his collection. As he watched a film on television, he would take the time to pause the recording during commercials so that there was no break in the story, for if there was one thing that drove his pre-pubescent head through the roof, it was having to fast forward through commercials. In one specific memory, William records that, realizing that he had forgotten to remove a commercial break, he threw a fit and whipped a cassette out the window where it smashed to black plastic bits and ribbon on the driveway. The film was *The Adventures of Robin Hood* with Errol Flynn, and the act of destroying it gave William such deep feelings of regret—it was rarely shown on T.V. and his only copy—that he cried for hours.

As William grew older, the technological superiority of DVDs, and then the Internet, along with the divorce of his parents and the end of his childhood, rendered his boyhood collection forgotten. Before leaving for Vancouver he had boxed it up. It must be collecting dust in his mother's basement, but who knows?

In any case, all those hours spent watching films have affected William enormously. His feelings are expressed occasionally with abnormal intensity because of his relationship with films. I don't think he wants to identify with the characters or their situations. He does not, for example, identify and thus *think* himself a hero or a romantic lead. That's not it—he has a healthy distance from that kind of delusional behaviour. What I think, rather, is that William, when he was young, experienced the emotions of the characters he watched so often, that he has come to convince himself that sadness, love, loss, hatred or other strong emotions are only really genuine if they are generated by watching a film. For William, then, the sadness he feels watching a hero die on the screen, is only possible by watching that hero die—otherwise, sadness doesn't exist. This phenomenon is not unique to William—it's a common feature of the modern coddled human condition in which emotional outlets are few and emotional outbursts are publicly unacceptable and ridiculed. What is unique about William, though, is how slight is the distance between the on-screen emotions and his own.

Eventually, he had to stop altogether watching films at the theatre, because he was simply too embarrassed by his public displays of emotional over-reaction. The last time he was in a theatre was at *Batman Begins* with his then-girlfriend Kim. William went only reluctantly, he says, thinking that with her there, he would be able to fight his emotions. But a few minutes into the film, at a sentimental scene where a young Bruce Wayne is rescued from a pit by his father and is told that when one falls down, one needs to be strong and to "get back up," William began to cry. Seeing him cry, Kim began to laugh and poor William, humiliated and heartbroken, got up and left. Later that day, Kim dumped him with the rather harsh last words, texted no less, that he was a "little crybaby bitch." William hasn't been back to a movie theatre.

On the surface, this aspect of William's condition seems significant, but medically, I don't think we should jump to any conclusions. It's not all gloomy. His crying doesn't indicate that he is melancholic *per se*, because his emotionalism works two ways: he bawls over trite sentimental Hollywood nonsense, but he also laughs like a lunatic at the terrible jokes and poorly written humour in crappy comedies. Taken together, of course—the uncontrollable sadness with the maniacal laughter—now *that* is sick; *that* is a kind of psychosis worth studying, since it indicates a level of volatile spontaneity that might, if left unchecked, pose a threat to others.

Until now, William hasn't identified these massive fluctuations in his emotional state as part of a condition. Rather, it seems that he stays inside to watch films because he feels embarrassed, and not because he thinks he's sick.

On an average morning, William stops socializing on *Real* at precisely 8:20 a.m. He has a shower, gets dressed in semi-casual attire —nice blue jeans and a dress shirt, untucked—and then takes the elevator down to the first floor of Harmony. Stepping out, he pumps two squirts of hand sanitizer into his hands and works it in while walking into the cafeteria. If the pretty young woman is not working, this trip goes smoothly; if she is, William's head is down and he's nervous receiving his small breakfast, which is usually just a couple pieces of organic fruit, maybe a free-range boiled egg, which he invariably takes with him to go.

William moved into Harmony shortly after the Scare. The former owner of the building, Chang, of "Chang's Chinese Import and Export," eager to get out after the Rampage, sold the building at a loss to the city and relocated to Richmond. The city then leased the building out to Maximilian Real Estate, who was responsible for its renovation. Harmony Cooperative opened soon after. Harmony's housing pamphlet reads: "A harmonious lifestyle begins with healthy living." To that end the Cooperative offers a diet regime consisting of a "total heath intake" menu of three, fully prepared, all-organic meals a day; a twenty-four hour gym for residents; and hand sanitizers on every floor. The building recognizes and strictly enforces the city's health regulations. Along with the city's cameras at the front doors, Harmony is equipped with many of its own, mounted outside the building, in the elevator, and on every floor. Further, "security personnel are always at your service," Harmony's administrators boast. Their video surveillance has been a great boon to us in observing William. It's their cameras that watch William as he exits Harmony every morning, usually tossing an apple into the air and catching it, ready and excited to start the day with a brisk walk to work.

William and I
by Thomas Vickers
II

I wait. It feels like a few minutes to be sure. I expect that he'll eventually find his words and say something, but he doesn't, and now he looks nervous, which starts to make me nervous. He's shifting around on his feet, his mouth is opening and closing, making these sort of smacking noises like he wants to say something, but the words just aren't coming. Finally I'm too uncomfortable:

"Hello," I say.

"…" He scratches the stubble on his chin and narrows his eyes.

"This is my first day," I say, trying to break the ice.

"Uh-huh. New here, then?"

"That's right. My name's Tom." I reach out my hand to shake his.

"Hi, Tom," he says, grabbing my hand. "I'm William."

"Nice to meet you, Will."

He gives my hand a good shake, but he still looks confused, shifting back and forth on his feet standing, eyes darting around, trying to get out whatever's on his mind. I think I understand what's wrong—I must be in his seat. I grin at him because it's kind of funny, this guy looking at me with these crunched up eyes, expecting me to know what he wants, but not wanting to be rude by telling me the get the fuck out of his seat. People are too nice these days.

"How long have you worked here, Will?"

"Ah, quite, quite a while," he manages.

"Nice place?" I ask, still smiling.

"Yeah, it's nice."

"That's good." I lean back and look out the window. "Nice view from here," I say. "You can see the entire square, hey?"

"Yes."

"Will," I say. "This wouldn't happen to be your seat, would it?"

At this he lowers his head, closes his eyes and lets out a deep sigh. I almost burst out laughing.

"It's not *my* seat," he says. "There are no assigned seats. But, it is that seat that I usually sit in. Actually, it's not so much even the seat. It's the computer."

"The computer? The computer's yours?"

He sucks his teeth and blinks and sighs again. I tilt my head like a dog would, screw my eyes up and make myself look puzzled.

"No, that's not it really. The computer's not mine, but it does have all my passwords and my search history saved, and all my day-to-day online stuff is saved on there, you know?"

I nod.

"It's a matter of efficiency."

"Efficiency?"

"Yes." He seems to be gaining his confidence. "I can be more efficient at my job on that computer." He smiles.

"I'm just having some fun with you Will. What about that computer?" I point to the computer next to his. "Does anyone sit there?"

"Not regularly." He sighs, thinking. "Nope," he says. "No one has sat there for a while."

"Okay, good then."

I stand up and he quickly sits down in my place. Before I even get resettled, he's taken off his coat and placed it over the back of his chair, put his bag under the desk next to his legs, and turned on the computer.

"I work full time here," he says as I sit down. "Everyone else, except Stu..."

"Curly-haired guy?"

"Right. Everyone else except me and him work part-time, so they change seats often." He seems distracted.

"Is something wrong?"

"No, no, it's just that I have this routine when I get here." His eyes dart around the computer screen, and he's shifting around, looking to see if I'd moved anything, readjusted the chair in any way. He leans back, rocks it a few times, looks out the window, and when he seems sure of everything, he says, "I just like to get signed in, get everything ready to go, and then get my coffee and get to work. I'm not used to seeing anyone here at this time and it's just thrown me off is all."

"I like to be early too," I say. "It makes a good impression to get to a new job early."

"I know that, I think so too." He nods and leans in close to confide. "A lot of the people here, they're pretty lazy—young and lazy."

"Stupid kids," I say. "So should I sign in too?"

"Umm, I don't think you can. Since this is your first day, you'll have to wait until Stu gets here. He'll set you up with a user name to login."

He's typing as he talks—logging in, I suppose. When he finishes, he stands up and asks me if I want a coffee.

"Sure," I say and stand up and follow him.

He turns his head to talk as we walk. "Sorry, it's just a routine is all," he repeats. "And, yeah, I've never seen anyone here before me. I

44

just got a bit weird I guess."

I follow him into this little kitchen with a sink, a small refrigerator, a few cupboards, a microwave, and an automatic espresso machine. As he's telling me about the kitchen, I'm noticing that this guy is pretty strange. It's not that weird to see someone in before you at work, so why so nervous and anxious? There's something peculiar about the way he operates, like one action or thought or sentence doesn't logically follow from the last.

"When does Stu usually get here?" I ask.

"He'll be here soon," Will says. "He never gets here at the same time, but usually shortly after me. He's unpredictable. In the meantime I can show you how this espresso machine works, because it's really terrible when someone breaks it, and a lot of new people are always breaking it. They don't know how to use it properly and when it stops working, you have to walk all the way to the other side of the floor where the programmers work to get a coffee, and those guys can be sort of jerks some times."

"The programmers are jerks?"

"They can be mean, yes. Usually, they just ignore you, because they think they're better than everyone else. They call us the bean counters."

"The 'bean counters'?"

"Yeah. I hate those guys."

"They sound like jerks. What else about this place?"

"The other department is Creative. They're okay. They don't seem to work much, but they're okay. Programmers think they're fags."

"Programmers think we're idiot bean counters and that the creative team are fags?"

"Pretty much. They're all men."

"Who?"

"The programmers."

"Oh. Not good."

Will nods, then gets down to detailing how the espresso machine works. For ten minutes, he explains the intricacies of its operation: where the water tank is and how its removed and refilled, how to open the front of the machine, how to clean out the old, used coffee pucks, where the fresh beans get loaded, how to change the size of the grind, what all the red and green lights mean, and which buttons and knobs to push to make a coffee the size and strength I want. By the end, I feel like an expert. Will then makes us both double espressos.

"The milk is in the fridge." He opens the mini fridge and points. "There's lactose free, soya, low fat, and normal."

"I usually don't take milk. Just a bit of sugar."

"Me neither," he says. "The sugar's here." He opens a cupboard and pulls out a little bowl of sugar with a spoon.

"There's other food here too," he says. "In these cupboards," he opens one and gestures, "there's chocolate and some gummy candies and stuff, which helps keep you awake. There's also some granola and other cereals on that shelf, and the milk in the fridge, if you want to eat breakfast, and free juice and pop and stuff is in the closet down the hall."

"Not bad," I say. "I guess I won't have to eat before I get here and I can save some money."

He looks at me strangely, like he doesn't understand.

"You know? The free food? The company food? You don't think it's better to eat the free food, than your own food?"

He half-shrugs and begins to walk back to his desk. I shrug too, but what a weirdo. When we get back and sit down, I ask him what I should do, but he just keeps deferring my question, telling me to wait until Stu arrives. Meanwhile, he gets right to work. As I wait, I decide that I might as well turn on the computer. Maybe, I can read the news or something. Problem is, is that I can't even get past the login screen.

"Hey Will, what's with this log in screen?"

He talks as he works. "With you part-timers—you're part time and not an intern, right?"

"Yeah, part-time."

"We haven't had an intern here in some time. Dana—did you meet him?"

"Nope."

"He fired the last intern. Anyway, with you part-timers, you're paid per hour, and you have to work four hours a day. I'm paid on salary now, because I'm full-time, so it doesn't matter for me, but for you, you have to login and logout so they know you worked your full four hours."

"Okay. So logging in is like punching in? I see! Man, it would have been nice to have punched in thirty minutes ago when I got here."

He stops what he's doing and looks at me curiously. "Why would you do that?"

"Because I'm here. I could have logged in. Then it would look like I've been working. Then I get to leave in four hours and not four and a half." I feel stupid explaining this, since it seems pretty obvious that no one would want to spend any longer at work than they had to, especially when you're not being paid for it.

"But you haven't done anything yet," he says back.

"Yeah, but how would they know that? It's just a number registered in a computer, right? No one's watching me. And now I have to stay a half an hour longer to get my four hours in."

"That's an interesting theory," he says and looks back to his screen. "But you have to stay for four hours after you log in, and you can't login until you get a user name. It's just how it goes."

"Yeah well, tomorrow then." I see Will shake his head. "You don't think that's right, do you Will?"

"It *is* a bit dishonest," he says as he works.

"I should be honest here?"

"They did give you the job," he says, not looking away from his screen.

"Yes, they did. Not paying me much though, are they?"

"Still a job."

He continues working and I decide to keep quiet and just think and wait. I didn't take this job for any reason other than the paycheck, so why wouldn't I think about that? It's almost 9:30, and I've been here for forty minutes of unpaid wasted time. What a fucking outrage. Finally, I hear voices coming down the hall. I see Stu, whom I met at my interview, and who calls to mind a kind of urban lumberjack— scruffy-faced and wearing flannel. He enters the room talking to a young, attractive woman, well-dressed in a grey fitted power suit and silk blouse that make her tits look great. When Stu sees me, he calls me over.

"Tom, it's good to see you're here," he says. "And you met William, that's good." He looks over my shoulder to Will and shouts, "Hey, Will."

Without raising his head. Will shouts back, "Hey."

"Anyway. Tom, this is Deirdre," he gestures. "She'll take you up to the front office to have you sign some paperwork. In the meantime I'll get you all set up in the system with a username to log in. Sound good?"

"Sure," I smile back, nice and friendly.

I walk with Deirdre to the front office. She asks questions and I answer: "Where are you from?"

"Alberta, originally."

"What do you do in Vancouver?"

"Not much. Read."

"How did you hear about Eureka!"

"Saw the ad online."

I give my answers in a friendly tone. I keep them short because I don't want her knowing that much about me—office assistants are the worst gossips—and because she doesn't seem all that interested anyway.

"I'm in charge of company culture," she says.

Company culture? That's a new one. "Oh yeah." I offer no follow-up.

We arrive at the front office, a small room with three desks, and we sit at her desk, me in front.

"As part of being Company Culture Coordinator," she goes on in a happy singsong, "I'll need to get a lot of information from you regarding your hobbies and stuff—where you like to hang out, what you do for fun, what movies you like, your other interests, all sorts of stuff. First then…" She reaches into a drawer and pulls out a piece of paper with questions on it and hands it to me.

"What's this for?"

"It's like a questionnaire. We like to have this information on file so we can plan our team outings, our event nights, and our other group activities. The information you give us helps me to plan and write up our newsletters."

"Uh-huh."

"You can look it over now, while I print off your contract. I don't need it back right away. Anytime within a week will be fine." She beams enthusiastically.

"Sure," I say and smile and begin to read.

It's a shocking document. Really invasive, to be sure. It's totally shocking what people expect from you for free these days.

"You absolutely need this information?" I ask.

"Yeah," she says, tilting her head and smiling.

How she can say that with a smile is beyond my comprehension. I'll never hand this form back. It's none of their fucking business what I do outside of this place.

Deirdre turns on her computer. In the meantime, I read over the form, fantasizing my answers. List three of your favourite movies: *None of your business what I watch.* List three extracurricular activities you like to do with a group: *I don't like groups.* List three hobbies: *reading alone, reading alone, drinking...alone.* Where do you spend your time off? *None of your goddamned business.* What sports do you enjoy? *Sports are stupid.* If you were to plan one night out with the people from work, where would it be? *Would never do that. Next question.* What is your *Real-ID*? *Fuck* Real. I accidentally laugh out loud.

"Something funny?"

"No, no. I was just thinking about something unrelated."

She reaches into another drawer and hands me another piece of paper. "Here's this week's Eureka! newsletter. I make these. She smiles.

You sure smile a lot. I think.

"You'll get one emailed to you every week. It tells you about company events, news, outings, whose birthday it is, our movie nights, pub nights, all sorts of cultural activities."

"Cultural?"

"Yeah, cultural. Our company culture," she smiles again.

"Right."

"Okay," she says to herself, "where is that contract file?"

I begin to read over the newsletter. The first announcement informs the "Eurekites"...

"I'm a 'Eurekite'?" I ask out loud. Deirdre just laughs. I shrug.

The newsletter informs all of us Eurekites that the company has just installed new ultra-hygienic water filters on all the taps and hand sanitizers in all the bathrooms. The second announcement is directed specifically to the part-time staff, reminding them to wipe down their computer keyboards before and after every shift with the alcohol wipes provided. The third announcement is about the upcoming *Star Wars* movie night: this Friday, some guy named Andrew will bring in his re-mastered high-definition copy of episode four, *A New Hope*, for the first evening of a planned month-long *Star Wars* retrospective.

"Retrospective?" I say.

"Yeah. Cool, huh?"

I keep reading. The last announcements tell me about the weekly pub night, a possible karaoke night in the future, and some other stuff that I just glance over. When I finish I put the newsletter back on Deirdre's desk.

"Oh, you can keep that," she says.

"Oh, thanks." I take it back and jam it in with the questionnaire.

"Anyway, your contract is printing now," she says. "It's pretty standard, just detailing the confidentiality agreement we have, your time off, your wages and stuff like that."

She hands it to me. "If you can get it back to me by tomorrow, that would be great."

"No problem," I say, smiling as best I can. "If you need anything else just let me know," I continue to smile. "I think it'll be very great to work here. I'm really looking forward to all of this stuff." I wave the sheets of paper.

I'm not planning to ever participate in any Eureka! activities, ever, but if there is one thing that I've learned from being in a university department it's that, no matter what, you have to be nice to the office assistants. This one, Deirdre, has turned company gossip into her job description and it's given her so much power. She has it in her capacity to ruin me and would have no problem doing it if she saw fit.

As I stand to leave, two other young women walk into the office. Everyone exchanges good mornings and hellos.

"Tom," says Deirdre, "this is Stef." She gestures to the short one with glasses. "Stef's in charge of payroll."

"Hi, Stef. Nice to meet you." I shake her hand.

"And this is Maggie." She gestures to the other one, Chinese I think.

"Hi Maggie." I shake her hand, thinking she'd probably look pretty good naked.

"Tom's new," Deirdre says to them both, smiling.

They nod and go about unpacking their stuff and settling into their desks.

"Well, anyways, I better get back," I say. "I'll have this stuff back to you soon. Thanks again." I leave their office, happy to get the hell out.

Report on William Potenco
by Doctor Officer Elias Degair
VIII

Between graduating in computer science and moving into Harmony after the Scare, our records on the details of William's life are unfortunately incomplete. What we have shows that he held various part-time jobs—in a grocery store, at a restaurant. He set up an online company with Mike George to build websites, which failed. He received financial help from his father when he couldn't pay the rent. Socially, he kept to himself. He rented a room in a house full of strangers and, as now, spent most of his time in his room on *Real*. Other than Mike and Ryan, he hasn't had other friends. None of his former dorm- or classmates knew him that well in university, and while today they do make up his contact list on *Real*, dialogue between William and these friends is minimal, consisting of sharing a few photos or an odd reminiscence now and then.

After the Scare, when William found his job at Eureka! and moved into Harmony, things should have gotten better, but they didn't. William's diary entries from that time indicate dark clouds looming on the mental health horizon. From his *RealDiary* a few weeks after moving into Harmony:

If the future were a bucket, mine holds no hope and no dreams. It's an abyss, an empty vessel into which I have nothing to pour. I have no imagination for the future. It's as though I've lost the ability to think about it. Now, I simply live the life that I've attained and nothing more. It's a good enough life, better than most by any standards, but all I do is live. I have no future, only a present.

My present is my friends Ryan and Mike. It's Eureka!, and it's my coworkers, the guy with the dreadlocks, the girl with the Rihanna haircut, the secretaries, Stu.... At work, in my 'fulfilled' present, I tap, tap at the keyboard buttons, punch the letters and words into the hardware. Software makes them appear on my screen. My mouse, the mice of us all, rolls over the surface of the desks in a monotone, having its buttons clicked into oblivion, a life and then a death. There are the endless cups of coffee, tea, juice, water, sipped by the same people out of the same Eureka!-stamped mugs that accumulate stains and chips until one day they break, crumble and are thrown away. Day after repetitive day—a entire life cycle of inanimate objects goes on around us inert human beings.

I sometimes feel a desire to get away. Maybe that is my future— to hold on to that desire to get away, to wish at least for a purpose, even if there is none yet determined. There must be something—I feel that something must happen, that time is running out. That instead of perpetually moving in a cycle forward, time is somehow counting down. I don't know why or how I know this, but I do. It's like those birds that know a disaster is coming. They fly away hours or minutes before an earthquake or a tsunami. It's an instinct, something that tells them to just up and fly off. I really want to know what that instinct feels like. I wonder if that is what I am feeling.

Perhaps William just had a bad day at work. Indeed, the entry that follows in his diary contains none of these themes. It's about the love he had for his childhood pets—two turtles and a lizard named Stampy —that he let run around his bedroom and fed worms and crickets. But nonetheless, what is expressed in this rather gloomy entry are

54

indications of precisely the post-Scare symptoms of hyper-realized loneliness and hopelessness that our software found, and that we're now tracking. This diary entry is an access point of sorts; it forms part of a sequence and a puzzle. In it, we see William spiralling downward, and we also see the whole of William's illness beginning to take shape.

For not everyone sees the world as William does. People in Vancouver today go about their daily routine happy to have survived and be alive as healthy citizens. They do not ruminate over their sad, nonexistent futures. The problem with William, as we continue with him in his daily routine, walking out the front door of Harmony carelessly tossing his apple, is that he's come to think his lonely reflections as normal, when they're not.

Most days as William walks to work, he keeps his head down as he passes the city cameras at the entrance of Harmony and again at the intersections of West Pender, Abbott and Cambie. We do have an incident from one of our health and security drones, however, that warrants mention. It happened quite recently. William was recorded by a mini-helicopter drone. It came up behind him and stopped, hovering like a dragonfly for a fly-by health check. William turned to look at it. He stared for a second into the camera before a look on his face of puzzled disgust appeared. He looked right and left to see if anyone was watching, and then, as if the drone were a rat or other vermin, William, with unexpected agility, angrily attempted to kick it. The drone easily evaded the kick and circled around in front of William, at which point he shouted "shoo" and tried to smack the drone out of the air. The drone fell back, and William, clearly frustrated, screamed, "Fuck you!" and lunged viciously at it with a look of murder on his face. Evading once again, the drone flew off, but the footage is there, it's all been recorded: William was clearly temporarily insane.

We also have Syndic footage of William on other occasions, usually when he stops to observe them perform their regular cleaning duties or as they put up my city beautification and health posters. It's hard to say from this footage what exactly William thinks of the Syndics. Recently, he seems to just laugh at them, so I can safely assume that his opinion is growing in negativity. Like most of us, William refers to them by their rather pejorative colloquial name, "the Syndics," instead of their official title, Health and Safety Officers. We do have one recorded instance when William had a direct conflict with a pair of Syndics. It happened one day on the way home and William wrote to Mike about it on *Real*:

(6:43 PM) William Potenco: A pair of Syndics tried to give me a ticket today for littering. I'm so mad. I want to smash their fucking faces in.

(6:44 PM) Mike George: what happened? you didn't lose your temper, did you?

(6:46 PM) William Potenco: No. I wanted to, but the problem got resolved.

(6:48 PM) Mike George: what happened?

(6:50 PM) William Potenco: They thought I threw a piece of paper on the ground, but it just fell out of my pocket. Fucking Nazis!

(6:52 PM) Mike George: they probably just felt like they needed to prove something. dont [sic] worry about it, it was a misunderstanding.

(6:53 PM) William Potenco: I just don't see the point of them, damn potheads. I wish they would get out of here. They've been plastering up all these "No Spitting" posters around Harmony all week. What the fuck!?

While William's frustration might be justified, he should know by now that the Syndics are necessary—they're there for his and everyone else's safety and they ensure the general health of the city. Despite their colloquial name, the Syndics are in fact not government officials.

They're more of a proxy police force employed in private firms as a preventative force—a deterrent. They were created in a crisis to save the city money. The Syndics patrol and monitor the environmental and hygienic integrity of Vancouver. They're closer in function to the private security firms hired by the wealthy to patrol their neighbourhoods.

After the Scare, the city needed to see things more pragmatically. Vancouver was broke; there were many more crimes, new crimes and new criminals, and we needed more people to patrol it all. When we started recruiting Syndics, it wasn't hard to fill the ranks. Plenty of people were interested in lending a hand to keep the city healthy. The first recruitment campaigns were held at the big summer festivals: the Vancouver Folksy Festival and the Cheakamus River Music Festival, where eager recruits, wanting to enforce the environmental and hygienic health regulations of the city, lined up by the dozens. The city filled its quota of a thousand recruits within a month. Since then, the number of Syndics has grown to around five thousand.

Nowadays, the Syndics wear green armbands and work in pairs, patrolling all of Greater Vancouver. Their first duty is more or less the beautification of the city. They're not refuse collectors, but they're paid to keep things clean and to report any unclean areas to the proper authorities. Their second duty is to make sure that Vancouverites are aware of, and follow, the new health and safety codes. They hang posters and put up stickers where they patrol. For example, during the campaign against smoking in public places, they put up posters that read, "Clean air is public. Smoking is not." In the campaign against body odour, especially on buses, the stickers read "To smell good is to be good," and in the campaign against littering, "Only trash throws garbage on the streets." In each of these campaigns, my direct poetry on the posters combined with the visible presence of the Syndics has proven to be an effective deterrent against the new health criminals.

Another duty of each pair of Syndics is to mete out justice to those committing health crimes. In most cases, punishment comes in the form of a ticket: from $20 for spitting or stinking, to $100 for littering and $200 for smoking outside the designated, outdoor, glass smoking rooms. In case the situation gets out of hand, if someone tries to resist or run away, Syndics are armed with mace, a flashlight, and a Smartphone. The latter has proven to be their best weapon. A Syndic's Smartphone forms a three-way connection among the Syndic, the drones and the police. Their Smartphone notifies the Syndics when a drone has recorded a possible crime. The phones are also used to video- and audio-record all Syndic interactions with the public, and to call the police if needed. The Smartphone is the Syndic's best friend.

IX

Assuming he hasn't dawdled, it takes William fifteen minutes to walk to Eureka!. Billed as "the social network for academics," Eureka!, according to *PediaPedia*, was "founded as an Internet startup," with the explicit and admirable purpose of "bringing together the academics of the world on an accessible platform where open, free, and equal discussion is encouraged in a global effort to foster new and otherwise unattainable social and intellectual bonds in the continuing and ongoing cultivation of the garden of knowledge." William was hired in Data Management in the summer after the Scare. By then, says *PediaPedia*, Eureka! had already gone through two rounds of financing. Notably, in the second round, they received significant financial backing from Harold Brinks, a long time Sydney Rothsteen collaborator and venture capitalist. When William was hired, membership at Eureka! was close to three million users and William was thrilled to have landed the job. In an excited and rambling message to his mother on *Real*, he wrote enthusiastically about being on the cutting edge of modern business, how "data mining," "big data" and data management were going to be the future and centre of both the on- and off-line economy, how this new position was his "dream job." William also predicted that in a few years' time, Eureka!'s membership would leap over the ten million member hurdle, Eureka! would be bought by *Real*, and he, William, would then be working for Sydney Rothsteen. William's mother responded encouragingly, but she didn't seem to know much about it.

William's job in Data Management was a monotonous one, often requiring nothing more from him and his co-workers than to click and drag information from column to column or box to box, minute after dull minute, hour after dull hour until the shift was over. Other tasks have included writing the word "yes" over and over in a spreadsheet for four hours a day. William's willpower, his perseverance, his strange affinity for monotonous labour, saw him succeed at this job where others, so many others, had failed. Aside from his team leader, Stuart Fraser, not a single other employee from when William was hired has managed to last in Data Management. The fact that William has been there so long is admirable.

But then again, William is different from most. He's able to dedicate himself to his work—not that others don't, but William's dedication, even enthusiasm, for the boring, brain numbing labour they do there at Eureka! is a source of genuine pride for him. It is work he looks forward to. Six months after he was hired, William was made full-time. Since then, he arrives early and has never missed a day. When his early morning arrivals became a problem—he would wait outside for ten, twenty, thirty minutes before someone would show up and let him in, or he would disrupt the work of the cleaning staff by trying to buzz in—Stu persuaded Dana Burrows, their department boss, to give William a set of keys. This, too, he was so proud of that he wrote to his mother on *Real* about it:

(7:32 PM) William Potenco: Mom, they finally gave me a set of keys today! Dana didn't seem so happy about it, but Stu stood up for me. It feels better than a raise.

(9:00 AM) Margaret Potenco (MOM): I'm so happy for you Willy, keep working hard. Love mom.

There are three owners at Eureka!, corresponding to the three departments. The CEO and founder is Professor Brian Fogel, a former history of technology professor at Simon Fraser University, who runs Creative, and in practice is Eureka!'s face and brains. William has never spoken to Dr. Fogel and remains anxious about the possibility of running into him at work. The head of Programming, also a former professor, is Frank Belfour, a short, unhealthy man and long time friend of Dr. Fogel.

Dana, William's department boss is the third owner. Dana is a constant source of anxiety in William's life. William has written on at least five different occasions about witnessing Dana fire an employee from Data Management. Each time, it's almost the same: In front of everyone in the Department, Dana calls an employee, who William might know as the "guy with the hairdo" for example, to come into his office. Shortly thereafter, the employee, now an ex-employee, emerges, gathers their things, and leaves in absolute silence or softly sobbing. A few minutes later, Dana himself emerges to announce to the Department why "the guy with the hairdo" was let go. Here is an excerpt from William's diary. It's hard to tell if this is paraphrased from William's memory, or if William is now somehow actually recording Dana speaking:

Today, Dana not only fired the girl with the Rihanna haircut in his normal torturous way, but he also subjected us to a gross display of his megalomania. She, like all the others before her, was called into his office. Moments later she emerged, crying pathetically, and left in shame. She must have been humiliated to cry like that. And then, to have to leave in front of us all. It's so sad. A few minutes later Dana, the dick himself, came out and with a cold smile said, "As some of you may know, we have had to fire Jessica. Yesterday, she made a mistake in judgement, which turned out to have consequences far beyond what she knew and which cost the company some valued reputation. It was not so much her mistake, but the fact that she did not confess to it, that got her fired. Fortunately, our programmers were able to track down who was using the computer at the time the mistake was committed and that is how we knew it was Jessica. I wanted to inform you all of this in person so that you know why she was let go and because I believe in open communication between myself and all of you." And then he turned, walked back into his office and closed the door.

But what I don't understand is that if it was a mistake, how could she have known she made it? And why did he have to fire her in front of us all, and why the speech? Dana is nothing but a modern-day tyrant. He enjoys generating fear in us all. It's as if he can feel it coming from us, he can smell it in our sweat and it gives him power, like reverse kryptonite...

Although William never takes the time to learn his co-workers names, and never vocalizes his feelings, what we see here is that he is clearly capable of great sympathy for them. What is also clear, but again never vocalized, is William's readiness to question authority. In practice, William has trained himself simply to steer clear of Dana. When he's at work he keeps his eyes on his screen and rarely goes near Dana's office. But then again, William tries to avoid everyone. He says hello when it's expected—in the morning in the communal kitchen, at the coffee machine, in line for lunch—but as is typical of his reclusiveness, he'll sit alone for lunch in the cafeteria with his eyePhone, or bring his mid-morning coffee promptly back to his desk and his work.

But for all of his outward reclusiveness, William is a keen and perceptive listener to, even eavesdropper on, other people's business. On his lunch break at work he eats and watches, and relays to his friends Ryan and Mike what he overhears from his coworkers. Without actually saying anything at all, William finds himself silently taking part in their conversations. From just a few days ago, for example:

(12:05 PM) William Potenco: I just sat down to lunch. Some smoker is talking about the outdoor smoking boxes and how humiliating they are; how people watch him and stand ready to report it if he steps outside for a smoke. He also said that they cost a fortune to ventilate them. He's probably right that the money could be used to fix things elsewhere.

(12:07 PM) Mike George: yeah.

(12:10 PM) Ryan Jeffreys: He made his choice. And where should that money be used? He's lucky to have those boxes. It's the taxes on cigarettes that pay for them, that's why the price went up. Smokers should pay for their own upkeep.

(12:12 PM) William Potenco: The guy with the dreadlocks just said that exact same thing.

(12:15 PM) Ryan Jeffreys: He sounds smart.

(12:17 PM) William Potenco: The smoker guy's pretty pissed off now, says that people like him have had enough of this crap.

(12:18 PM) Ryan Jeffreys: too bad for them.

(12:20 PM) William Potenco: Anyway, they're talking about [Quentin] Tarantino now.

(12:22 PM) Mike George: have you seen his new film will? it's awesome!

(12:24 PM) William Potenco: These guys seem to think so too. To be honest though, I think Tarantino is overrated.

(12:27 PM) Mike George: what!? you can't be serious.

(12:30 PM) William Potenco: Yeah, well, Mike, sometimes you just need to think a bit harder. Look at what Tarantino does; he just replaces affect and sentiment with shock and awe. He's no Sydney Lumet. With Tarantino it's all just boring dialogue separated by stupid splatter violence and crude, seriously unfunny humour. He hasn't been good since *Pulp Fiction*.

(12:34 PM) Ryan Jeffreys: He may have a point their [sic] Mike…

(12:40 PM) Mike George: you guys don't know shit. who is sydney lumet?

(12:43 PM) William Potenco: *Serpico*, *Network*, jeez Mike, sometimes you amaze me… Anyway, I have to get back to work. Talk to you later tonight.

(12:44 PM) Mike George: you're crazy will. talk later.

X

William's work at Eureka!, aside from his minor complaints, is his pride. As I've tried to indicate, William is very good at what he does.

Since he's begun, his main task at Eureka! is what is known as "structuring." When a member joins Eureka!, he or she is grouped together with others depending on which institution, usually a university, he or she associates with when signing up. From there, depending on the information they choose to provide, members are slotted into their departments, research labs, study groups, and so forth. Similar to an online dating service, where people designate themselves as straight, gay, male, female, trans etcetera, or a professional network where people indicate what skills they possess, on Eureka! the group you affiliate with determines how and to whom you will be connected. For example, if user A is from the University of Delhi and studies microbiology, he or she will be linked with user B who is from the University of Calgary and studies microbiology

For this to succeed, for Eureka! to work and to create new, worldwide, academic relationships, depends on a huge database and taxonomy of global institutions and their internal structures. Research into the internal departmental structure of each university the world over, and the task of uploading the structures into Eureka!'s database, constitute "structuring," and William excels at it. He's likened the job to "building a skyscraper."

> You begin from the blueprints; work up the metal framing; erect the scaffolding; install the window frames and windows, door frames and doors as you go; make room for the plumbing and the electrical wires; and finish it all with the drywall, paint, carpet, and trim. Each floor is then numbered and made ready, until finally the day comes when the doors open and new members pour into their new online home.

It's a rather beautiful picture he paints—one that reminds me of my own work here at the Bureau and of my own efforts in building what we have today.

Intermittently, William does other tasks at Eureka! such as, "sorting" (putting new members into their respective institutions), "gatekeeping" (determining who gets to join Eureka!) and "institutions" (deciding which institutions are worthy of being listed on Eureka!). Of all the tasks, though, William takes the most pride in, and is best at, structuring. He wrote this rather metaphysical reflection on the job almost two months ago:

> Today, at the end of a long and frustrating month, I finally finished, uploaded and activated the structures of all ten campuses of the University of California. On days like this, I wish I could see as a computer sees—watch the 1's and 0's as they build my structures. I wish I could see them come to life, as I watch a new building come

64

to life. I wish, too, I could experience, as a new user to Eureka! does, the ease and comfort of sliding into one of my structures. It must feel like sliding into a warmed bed or a bubbly bath [...].

No one, according to Stu, can structure like William. He's become one of Data Management's greatest assets and the other employees of the team, those who speak a second language and are responsible for structuring in places like Japan or Germany, for example, have started looking up to William for advice. This, from a three-month-old internal online Eureka! discussion:

vickywong31: Hi William, I'm structuring the Chinese Academy of Social Sciences. It's so big! Do I have to include all of the research labs for all of the different subsections all over China? It's gonna take me weeks!

William01: Hi, Vicky. Yes, you should include the labs. And don't worry, it doesn't really matter how long it takes. If you were to finish the Chinese Academy of Social Sciences you would just have to move on to another. The point is that we want as much detail as possible, for the users to select from when they sign up. Make sense?

vickywong31: I suppose. It's just so boring…Anyways, thanks for the help :)

William01: No problem, and boring is the nature of this work. It's something we need to accept. Anyway, good luck in China ;)

We see clearly again William's confident, proud, even happy online self in this dialogue. And we start to recognize a pattern. William is confident when he socializes on *Real* and online at work, yet in the rest of his actual day-to-day existence, he remains distant from everyone else, as if he wants to keep unseen. At work, he has slipped comfortably into the role of an authority figure, yet he doesn't seem to realize it, for he never uses his position to push over anyone else. He probably doesn't even know what vickywong31 looks like. She could be sitting right next to him, but beyond referring to her as, maybe, "the Chinese girl," he wouldn't pay the least attention.

There is, then, this enigma with William—a contradiction or reversal of normal, that is driving him inward towards implosion. We can only suggest that his recent infatuation with staring at the rain is a symptom or a coping mechanism he's using to fend off the coming catastrophe. Take this diary entry from only a week ago:

If I could compare my life to anything right now it would be to the rain. In Vancouver, when it rains, which is always, there is never any thunder, never any lighting, but just a monotonous, unimaginative drizzle that at times quickens, at times almost stands still, as if a cloud itself is sitting on the ground and I'm forced to walk through it.

Today, it rained all day, and at work, like a neurotic counting the seconds of the day, or a prisoner counting the flies in his cell, I counted the streaks of water running down the window. I must have been at it for quite some time, because Stu had to come over and wake me from my trance. I smiled and pretended to be back in the here-and-now for his benefit, but after he left, I went right back to counting. It seemed important, to give my attention to the streaks of water. Besides, it was a temporary respite from structuring Kansas State University.

The weather lacks any definition whatsoever. Like my life, it plods on in a slow routine, day after long, boring day. The endless rain, like my life, could do with a bit of a smashing, crashing thunder and lightning every so often. Some days it feels like it might come. The air feels heavy, the smell of thunder is strong, and the clouds grow big and evil, but then it fizzles, the clouds disperse into an indefinite grey—a monotony that parallels my life.

No one else seems to mind. I heard the guy with the dreadlocks say he doesn't care about the rain, and Stu, who rides his bike to work every day regardless of the weather, must not care at all. Do they just ignore it? I have no idea how that's possible. Maybe it's not hard for them, but for me, it feels heavy. A thunder storm, that would sure be something.

There's little to gain right now from further describing the minutiae of William's everyday life. What we need for a preliminary diagnosis is right here in plain view, if you know what you're looking for, as I do. With William, it's challenging because he plays a very good game; he wears a tough shell that first had to be cracked. But let's look at the facts: there is William's surface, his strangely fulfilling life guided by his routine. He wakes, works, eats, works more, goes home, eats, watches films. In between, he socializes. It all sounds almost normal, like a routine that I or anyone might have. William, too, thinks it's mostly fine. He thinks he's healthy. And compared to some of the unhealthy fat people around the city whom we have to treat for fat crimes, he is physically fit. On the weekends, he moves from his room to Harmony's cafeteria and back, and during the week he walks to and from work. It's not much, but it's more than most. And he's young. When he looks in the mirror or sees his profile picture on *Real*, William sees a youthful, handsome, healthy exterior.

But this William, this outwardly normal-looking man, is, I assure you, not healthy. This exterior is but one of his masks covering a long list of symptoms, including but not limited to the following: He's delusional—he thinks he's normal, but he is emotionally unstable, verging on a bipolar, perhaps even a tri-polar disorder; he's borderline obsessive compulsive; he is a pervert who can't control himself; he is withdrawing further and further from reality; and he is disrespectful and has emotional issues with authority. There is also, of course, the diary, in which he is constantly brooding over his unhealthy thoughts.

William's Disease is all of these, but more. I beg you to consider this: on top of these rather traditional symptoms of delirium, dementia, depression and so forth is a new dimension: William's Disease is both outward and inward. It is the projected mask of normalcy that covers

67

the symptoms listed above, and it is also an inward mask. It's this inward mask that is new and troubling. The inward mask makes William think it's okay to live a life opposite to what we want for him. When he should be confident and out engaging in the real social world of people, he is inside, online—socializing and confident, yes, but in secret. And when he should be alone and in private, he is on the street, walking around in the world, or at work. It's this second mask, this deep layer of William's Disease, that's our concern. We must tear it off.

William and I
by Thomas Vickers
III

When I get back to Data Management, I see that more people have arrived. In total it looks like about twelve now. No one looks up from their computers when I walk in, except Stu who stands when he sees me.

"Come with me, Tom," he says. "Did Deirdre get you all set up? She's nice, hey?"

"Yeah, she's great."

We walk around the semi-circles of desks to where I was before, next to Will. I sit back down and Stu says to Will, "I just don't have the time today, Will, so I'm gonna need you to train him."

"You want *me* to train him?"

"Yes, Will, you're senior staff, and you know this stuff better than anyone."

"*I'm* senior staff?"

Stu just laughs and walks off, but Will's not joking; he looks genuinely confused, or else just downright modest, it's hard to tell. In any case, he takes to the role immediately and seriously.

"Well, I guess I'm training you, then," he says.

"I guess so."

"So, you already know a bit. And now you have your login name…"

"Actually, I don't yet."

"Oh, well, just let me ask Stu, then." He types something.

"You ask him on there?" I ask. "Wouldn't it be easier for me to just get up and go ask?"

"No, not really. Here we communicate on the computer. It's faster and not as noisy."

"Okay." I shrug.

"This is your login name." He turns his screen towards me so I can read it. "The first thing you do when you arrive for a shift is log in. When you leave you have to make sure to log out by clicking on this button." He demonstrates on his screen. "You also need to specify the task you worked on all day. You have to do that so they know how many hours you worked and what you did. A lot of people, they just get up and leave and forget to punch out and it all gets messed up, and Dana, he's in charge of the hours and that, and he hates that when people mess it up." He pauses. "So, then, why don't you log in? I just gotta do something here, so let me know when you're ready."

When I'm ready, I look over at his screen. He has his *Real* page open. "I'm ready, Will," I say.

"Just a second," he says. "I'm telling my friend Ryan in Ottawa that I'm senior staff." He keeps writing, but explains at the same time. "Just open up Eureka! and start to set up an account."

"Okay."

Will waits two minutes and then asks. "You got it open? Are you in? For now, you can speed through the new member profile and fill in your details later. It's similar to *Real* in a way, but geared towards academics. You know what Eureka! is, right?"

"A bit, I read a few articles online, and the *PediaPedia* entry."

"Okay, so you know the basics, that it began a few years ago, that it's a social network for academics..."

"Yeah, that stuff, I know…"

"That today, it has around five million members, but the goal is to reach ten million…"

"I didn't know they had a goal. Are there even ten million academics?"

"…"

"So, ten million."

"The ten million member hurdle. When Eureka! reaches ten million members, chances are they get bought by *Real*."

"Right."

"You don't sound so enthusiastic."

"I don't think *Real*'s all that great is all. And Rothsteen seems like a total slime bag. Have you read "The Secret History," that article that came out last year?"

Silence form Will.

"Have you?"

"That rant written by that Osama whatever?"

"Rant? If anyone said it was a rant they're an idiot. And that obviously wasn't his or her real name. No one knows who wrote it. But have you read it?"

Nothing at all.

He obviously hasn't so I change the topic. "Why is it so important to be bought by *Real* anyway, and why do they need to have everything?"

"Is that a real question?" he asks.

I laugh, but he looks serious. I stop laughing. "Yes, it's a real question."

"Well, Tom." He rotates in his chair to face me. "Let me ask you something: What is it that you want out of this job?"

"Not much, I suppose. I'm just here for the summer to make a bit of cash is all, and then I'm back out."

"Hmm. Okay then, but that's not really normal, is it? Most people do jobs looking for some kind of upward mobility. Unlike you, I don't want to leave. This is my career, so that's why it's important that Eureka! gets bought by *Real*. Because I, Stu, that guy there with the dreadlocks, Dana, the owner of Eureka!, Dr. Fogel, all of us—we all want to work for *Real*. I want to move up in this place, move up in life, make money and be happy. Do you know where the employees of Netzle, or of Joisty, or Bouncepic, or Nifty, or Clicmap, or any of those startups are right now? Do you know where their owners are?"

"I don't, Will. I don't even know what those are, to be honest."

"They're startups, based now in California and their owners are all rich. They were all bought by *Real*. They all reached the ten million member hurdle and were bought by *Real*."

"You make it sound like it's a destiny, but it seems like an old-fashioned business monopoly to me."

Nothing from Will.

"Don't you think?" I press.

A sudden look of desperation comes over his face. He rotates back to face his computer. I don't want to upset him, but I can see the lines on his forehead getting deeper as he strains for words. His head drops, he sighs and looks helplessly down at his keyboard. He crosses his arms, leans back in his chair and looks out the window. Finally he lets out a long sigh and looks back at me.

"I don't think about that," he begins calmly. "I mean, I just don't know what to think about that. I don't know why people get criticized for just wanting to work and have a career. I also have a job on *Real*, you know. I'm just trying to get by and it's fucking hard. You have to make money, right? It's what you need to live. And I like it here, and I'm good at what I do. So what's the big problem!?" His eyes have grown big and his face is red. He's definitely not calm anymore.

"Okay," I back away from the conversation. *This guy is nuts.* "It's not a problem, I was just making conversation," I say.

"Sorry. I'm not mad. I just don't need a hard time," he says, exasperated.

I understand. The guy's serious about what he does. It's good to know. "I get it," I say. I change the subject. "Look, anyway, what should I do now? I'm all set up here with my account."

"Right. So go and click on that administration tab." He gestures. "There you'll find all the subsections and links to the tasks that we do here. Just let me ask Stu what it is he wants me to train you on. Eventually you'll learn everything, but... just wait a sec."

"Asking him on there again?" I ask.

"Yes. Actually, why don't you set up your account for that too. You can do that now, if you want. It's how we communicate here. It's quick —that program in the corner of your screen." He gestures with a finger.

"This one? Called Speaka?"

"Yes," he says without looking.

A few moments later, I have my Speaka account set up. I'm Tomman21.

"So many passwords," I say quietly to myself.

"What?"

"Oh nothing."

I glance around the office, but there's not much to look at. I can see Stu's face past the two rows in front of me, but otherwise, all I get are the backs of people's heads. No one has sat next to me on the other side.

"Where did you say you were from, Tom?" asks Will.

"I didn't, actually. I live up north. I feel like I was driven up there by this place. I'm not really from anywhere. I mean, I moved around a lot. I was born in High Level, Alberta. Ever heard of it?"

"No."

"Well, it's a real shit hole, home to murderers and thieves, right near the border between Alberta and the Northwest Territories. Anyway, my dad is English, from England, you know? And my mom is French, but France-French. They were living in England, but my dad wanted to leave and so he took a job in High Level as a history teacher. We only stayed a couple years. After that we moved a lot—Brandon, Manitoba, Thunder Bay, Ontario. I did my undergrad in Edmonton, and then a Master's in Toronto. After that I went and lived in Russia for two years and then came to Vancouver to start a PhD in Russian history. It's my Russian that got me this job. But then I started to hate Russia and Russian history and the PhD. And the professors started to hate me, and I them, and so I dropped out and left Vancouver. Now I spend my time up at a friend's farm in a small town called Rolla. My parents live in Montreal."

"I was born in Kitchener, Ontario."

"Oh yeah, hey. I know where that is. I had some friends from Kitchener when I lived in Toronto. I never went there myself, but they all seemed to like it."

"Yeah, it's okay. I haven't been back in a while. My mom still lives there…. Anyway, Stu wants you to start with sorting. That's when you deal with the people that have already been accepted to Eureka!. They've already made it past gatekeeping, which is another task you'll learn later, but because they didn't properly identify which institution they belong to, or their institution doesn't exist, they need to be sorted into the appropriate place. That part is pretty easy. The harder part is when they say they belong to an institution that isn't in our system yet —then you need to use your judgement, based on our guidelines, to make a decision."

"What exactly are *our* guidelines?"

"Stu didn't say? Well, if it's an academic institution, we will always set it up, but if it's not, then you need to make the call."

"Okay. It sounds a bit confusing."

"We'll do a few together so you can get the hang of it. So go into the new users list, there." He gestures.

I do what he says and I see a list of names and other information, but Will changes the subject again before we start.

"Wow, so you speak Russian? That seems hard."

"*Konechno*, of course it was, but I needed it for my research. It's sort of expected that you speak a second language when you do a PhD in history. What did you study?"

"Computer science."

"At UBC?"

"Yep."

"So you were here during the Scare?"

"Yeah. It was bad."

"I bet. I was in Moscow at the time. I thought it was a police state there, but my friends said it got pretty bad here too."

"A police state?"

"Yeah, like cops everywhere, with no freedom to go anywhere."

"Oh that. Yeah sure, but that was necessary."

I keep silent. I can't agree, so I change the subject again. "Why aren't you programming, Will? You have the degree. It must pay more."

"I could, I guess, but I don't want to. I find programming boring."

"And this isn't?"

He laughs, finally. "Yes. But big data is the future. They call it the new oil, you know? I want to get good at how it's managed. Anyone can program, just like anyone can pump gas, but it's the managers who have the real control."

I don't fully understand his analogy, but I nod anyway. "What about the owners? Don't they have the power?"

"I'll never be an owner. I don't have the money or the people skills for that. I have to think within my limits. So," he changes the subject, "look there on that list you pulled up. You can see there what we deal with. See that first entry? Marion Guttari: CUNY DEE. The reason she wasn't automatically sorted is because she just typed in acronyms instead of the full name of her institution and department. You'll get to know the acronyms as you go, but for now you can trust me because I know: she's at the City University of New York in the Department of Electrical Engineering. Click the "sort" button. It works like a drop-down search bar. Type in the word 'city'." He pauses while I do it. "You see?" He points at the screen. "There it is: City University of New York. Click on that." He pauses again. "And there she goes." Her name vanishes. "She's sorted. You don't have to worry about the department, that's a different task that gets taken care of later. For now just get them into their proper institutions."

"Seems easy," I say.

"That one was an easy one. If you don't know the acronym, you just search for it online. Most of them are very common and you'll catch on fast."

"So what's a hard one then?" I ask.

"Let's find one. Scroll down on the list a bit."

I scroll.

"There, that one." He points. "Beth Finkner: WAGI."

"Do you know what that means?"

"I have no idea, but let's find out. Cut and paste her name and the acronym into a search," he says with growing excitement.

It might be that he's enthusiastic to be training me, happy that he's senior staff, or maybe he's excited to discover something that he didn't know. Maybe it's all of that, who knows, but whatever it is, it's infectious and I get excited too. I never expected this emotional reaction. It's the element of investigation that's so invigorating. Examining, delving into the details of a complete stranger's life, discovering something once hidden from you is thrilling, for sure. It's like a chase. I haven't felt like this since I this was in the archives in Moscow searching out old information on fallen members of the Communist Party. The circumstances were different but the experience —the thrill of discovery, knowing who did what to whom, finding the information that would crack the case and close the file—that is the same. The difference, of course, is that those old fallen comrades I was researching in Moscow—they were dead. Beth Finkner is alive, and Will and I are investigating her like cops do criminals.

The open case of Beth Finkner is quickly closed. We find her, and what WAGI means, in less than a minute; in one search, actually. It's an acronym for Women Against Gender Inequality and they have a website.

"Okay," says Will, "the first thing you need to do is check whether or not we already have them set up. In this case, because the website seems quite junky and their organization is obscure, we probably don't. If we do, it's great, you can just drop her in. If not, we have to investigate a little more what the organization does, and decide whether we should make them an institution on Eureka!."

"So, it's not just universities and colleges, then?"

"Not anymore. It used to be, but Eureka! wants more members— they want the private sector as well, so people doing research in any institution are now considered academics."

"What does that mean?" I ask.

"It means that any institution that conducts research of any kind: pharmaceutical companies, hospitals, think tanks, mining companies and so on. And anyone who works for those places and is doing research can get on Eureka! Understand?"

"Yes, unfortunately I do. It's fucked up though."

"Why?"

"Because those places do research, but a lot of it's harmful, and they do it for money."

"But this isn't a question of morals. And some are NGO's."

"Bah, whatever." I don't want to argue with Will. I don't think I can. A guy either gets it or he doesn't.

"Anyway," he says. "Search that women's site and see if they qualify."

"Okay," I sigh and go in.

"Does it look like they do research? Do they have a research department, or research subsections, or anything like that?"

"It doesn't seem so, not specifically. It looks more like they disseminate information, more like activism, I think. It says they write reports, third party assessments—but no research, specifically."

"Okay, so you just drag Beth Finkner into that "Independent Academic" category, there." He points. "And then you move on to the next name."

"So we don't set up the WAGI?"

"No we don't."

"Fuck that, man!"

"Why?"

"Because they look like they're doing good things in the world. They're fighting for a good cause. And so what? They're not doing *research* according to Eureka!, so they get no representation? In the meantime, you set up pharmaceuticals?"

"Tom, it's just not part of the job to debate that. It's based on Eureka!'s guidelines." Will starts to laugh, but I really don't think it's funny.

"I'm going to set up them up as an institution anyway. Show me how, please."

"I wouldn't do that if I were you. If Dana finds out, you'll get in trouble. He's fired people for less."

"Well, fuck him. I have to live with myself, you know. Show me please." I stare at the screen.

I hear a sigh. "Suit yourself," he says. "Just because I'm senior staff now, doesn't mean I tell you what to do. That's up to Stu and Dana."

So Will shows me how to set up an institution, and I set up the Women Against Gender Inequality. I give them their representation on Eureka! and it feels good, like I've actually won a small war, made a difference, like.

After that, though, the training on sorting was over. Will, either disgusted with me, or happy that he had done such a good job training, left me alone to work.

It's pretty slow going at first. I have to spend a lot of time searching for acronyms, but that's really the only learning curve—rapidly as possible cutting and pasting into the search engine.

As for the rest, for my crusade, after I set up WAGI, I make a conscious decision, as a kind of crusade, to simply ignore Eureka!'s guidelines and use my own heavily critical moral-based criteria. I set up lots of institutions over the course of the shift. I don't give any representation to big business, pharmaceuticals, mining companies and the like. They're responsible for more harm than good. They keep people in Africa sick for a profit, they pollute rivers and lakes, and they're run by world-class assholes. Nope, every time I see one that day, I think *Fuck you, go to hell*, and pass over them and their asshole employees who want onto Eureka!.

Just before my shift ends, Stu comes over and stands between Will and I.

"So," he says to Will, "how's Tom doing?"

Will looks at me and smiles. He hesitates a second, like he might rat me out. He stops smiling, winks at me, and looks up at Stu. "He's doing fine, Stu," he says. "He's caught on real quick."

Stu turns to me. "Good. How many pages do you think you went through, Tom?"

"Maybe four—four or five, I guess." Each page had about thirty or so names to be sorted.

"That *is* good. For your first day that's great." He turns to Will. "You'd better watch out, Will, he might get to be as good at sorting as you." He smiles.

Will shrugs without looking away from his screen. "I doubt it," he says.

For the rest of my first week and into the second, I sorted. It was insanely boring work—and I know insanely boring work. During my Master's degree, I worked at the campus photocopy centre at the University of Toronto. You want to talk about boring, how about watching a machine make copies, hundreds of thousands of them? And when the machine gets angry and jams up, you have to pull the paper out of it to make it happy again. That was fucking boring, but at least I got to stand up and walk around. Another job I had, I worked summers planting trees—tree after tree, thousands of trees, 10 cents each, all summer long. That was boring too, but at least I got healthy, and there were horny women around, and my friends were there, and you could get real drunk, that was fun. I also worked in a mail centre stuffing envelopes and sticking stamps. Fuck, *that* was boring. But this job at Eureka!, man, this might be the all-time worst. Maybe, if it was a good day, one out of twenty names was as interesting as Beth Finkner of the WAGI—someone who works for an obscure organization that I have to track down online. Otherwise, it's just a long string of names of idiot academics who can't follow Eureka!'s simple instructions, and are too stupid to fill in their institution properly when they sign up. It's up to me to put them where they belong—you here, you there. It was a bit funny to me—finally I was in charge of these dickhead profs. Anyway, I got real fast at it. I mean real fast. By the middle of my second week, I was clearing six to seven pages a day. Stu was pretty damned happy with me.

I also got to know Will pretty well during that time. When we worked mornings, we both arrived early and I sat next to him. It got to be a bit of a game for us—who could arrive earlier. I knew he had a key, so I'd get there early, login and sit around, read the news, check my email, and drink coffee until Stu arrived.

Will's attitude towards my record-breaking speed at sorting was— well, I think he was a bit pissed off that I was faster than him. He didn't show it, of course, but that says something, too. He's a modest guy. There's no question that he's far more careful and dedicated at what we do than I am. He actually cares about his job, whereas I just see it as a paycheque. Regardless of that, though, I'm still a good worker. I may hate my job, I may complain constantly while doing it, and I may undermine the rules at every chance I get, but that doesn't mean I won't be on time and work hard and fast when I do actually get down to it. I won't take long breaks, or slack off, either, at least when people are watching. I don't know what it is. Maybe it's some kind of Protestant work ethic, but I've never been to church once, so I doubt that.

I think I was working like I was at Eureka! because they were a quota company. They needed to see the numbers. Every day they had thousands of people signing up, and those people had to be processed. Part of what makes you a good worker at a place like that is just making the quotas. They tell you to do a thorough job, but what they really mean is, hit the numbers. It's like in Stalinist Russia. What made you a good commie? The number of traitors you could denounce in a month. It didn't matter if they were traitors or not, they just had to be denounced. I was good at making the quotas.

One morning, a week or so after I started, I decide to tell Will about this theory on work.

"Hey, Will," I say and look over. "I'm just flying through this shit here. I think I must be breaking records for daily output."

"Yeah, and are you being careful?"

"Not so much. But if Eureka! wants to hit this ten million member hurdle, shouldn't we be getting the members processed as fast as possible?"

Nothing from Will.

"It's just quotas, right? That's what the ten million member hurdle is, right? A quota?"

Still nothing.

"With quotas, it's the one who gets the fastest results who gets rewarded, right?"

"Maybe."

"I'll give you an example," I say. "I studied Russian history, I told you that, right?"

"You did."

"I focused more or less on Stalin and Stalinism, and there was this guy, this simple worker; a miner…"

"What was his name?"

"His name was Stakhanov and he was just a simple young guy who, one day, mined so much coal, a hundred tons in a one day he mined…"

"Obviously impossible."

"Well, whatever the number, it was more coal than anyone had ever mined, ever, they said. And it didn't matter if it was impossible, because it happened and that was that. So after that, he could do no wrong: he was praised by the government, by the people, by just about everyone. He became a fucking hero of the people. They named a day after him in the Soviet Union, and in the US he was on the cover of *Time* magazine. A commie on the cover of *Time*. It's crazy. Look what we have now." I gesture to the poster on the wall. "Mindless drones, mere reflections of real people."

"So, what's your point?"

"My point is that when you produce the quotas you get the praise."

"So you think you're like this Stakhanov guy?" he asks, finally turning from his screen to face me.

"In a way, yes."

"The difference, Tom, between you and him," he says, a smile coming to his lips, "is that *he* probably did a good job." He laughs.

"You're a funny guy, Will. But, whether he did a good job or not is not the point. The thing about smashing coal or punching data into a computer is that you have to be like Stakhanov and just hit the numbers."

"You can do what you like, Tom. Be that Russian guy or whatever, but the point isn't just the quotas. You aren't really doing a good job, are you? You have to be fast *and* follow the rules or the whole thing gets screwed up."

"Man, you make this so un-fun."

"You think you have it figured out?" he asks, kind of pissed now, it seems.

"With this type of job, more or less I do."

"If everyone worked like you, bridges would collapse, buildings would crumble," he says.

"Actually, it's funny you say that. That's what it's like in Russia with the buildings and bridges built during Stalin's time. But Will, this isn't a bridge or a building, this is a stupid social network. And besides, I think like Marx: 'All that is solid melts into air.' It's the nature of this system. It's all just built to be temporary."

Will shakes his head and turns back to his screen. I hear him mumbling under his breath. I could try to explain further, but the guy's just too damn proud. I guess, too, I wasn't quite honest. The other thing that makes me work hard is knowing that if I became the best employee, meaning the fastest, they won't fire me. Even if they do catch me setting up the so-called wrong institutions, they might reprimand me, of course, but I'll just lie and say it was a mistake, and then move on and do it again. They won't fire me as long as I'm smashing quota records.

As far as company culture went, which I worked out just meant being social, this was my first job in an office and it was severely weird. When I worked the afternoon shift, I tried to sit next to someone besides Will to see what would happen, but no one ever talked to one another or to me. Even with Will it was hard. They all preferred to type-communicate on that ridiculous Speaka software. All shift long, the other employees would try to be funny with one another by posting Eureka! member profiles and pointing out some stupid detail to get the others to laugh, or waste time by talking about the last episode of some crappy, American sitcom. The conversations were a stream of continuous useless blabber, a total waste of words. No one ever spoke out loud, at least not until they got out to the little kitchen and coffee machine in the common area, and then it was pure gossip. The background noise at Eureka! was just that: snippets of gossip heard over the constant whir of the espresso machine, keyboards being tap-tapped, mouse buttons being click-clicked, and sighs, I mean a lot of sighs, which made it clear to me that everyone hated their jobs. I don't know if these are the familiar sounds of every office, but in Eureka! those combined noises were the sound of fucking nature.

Anyway, I did strike up a few conversations. There was the dude Will called "the guy with the dreadlocks," who, it seemed, showed up and left whenever he wanted. He was okay. And there were a few cute girls, who were nice to smile at. The only real exception in the bunch was Jen, whom Will referred to as "the girl with the green-framed glasses."

One morning I'm bored as hell sorting, and Will's pretty unresponsive, working hard and not talking, when Maggie, the sexy Chinese office assistant, walks into the room. She's trying to speak over the hum of keys and buttons tap-tapping.

"Some new furniture," I hear, and "needs to be assembled … looking for volunteers …"

I look around the room, but nobody raises their hand—only a handful even look up. Putting furniture together sounds pretty fucking amazing compared to what I'm doing, so I shoot my hand up. Jen, "the girl with the green-framed glasses," raises her hand too, and the two of us stand and follow Maggie into a room with four big boxes. We're given some tools and told to put together four new desks. Maggie leaves.

I'm not sure why Will picked up on Jen's glasses as a way to identify her. They are green, sure, but it's her hair that I would say is her most notable feature. It's like fire. For reasons that are a total mystery to me, I find red hair severely alluring. I want to bury my face in its waves. I can hardly take my eyes off it.

Jen and I had only talked briefly before this—once at the coffee machine and one time when I sat next to her for twenty minutes during a shift change. I didn't get much out of her. But here in this room, away from everyone else, she seems to ease up.

"Where are you living in the city, Tom?"

"I'm staying down by Jericho beach in that old hostel there. Know it?"

"I do, yes. It's a nice old building."

"A former army barracks, they say. It still feels like that a bit."

"So you're here just for a short time, or …?"

"For the summer. What about you? Where do you live?"

"East End."

"Oh, nice. Is it still more or less inexpensive to live there?"

"More or less, yes. Prices dropped a bit after the Scare, but that just made it more crowded."

"All the DINKs, hey?"

"Dinks?"

"Yeah—dual income, no kids …"

"Right. Yeah. I don't know much about that. A lot of young people, a lot of gentrification."

"Gross."

"Yeah."

"So what do you really do? Outside of here, I mean," I ask.

"My real job, you mean?" she smiles. "I write. Plays and poetry and stuff. My two roommates—our place is more like a studio. The other two are visual artists, but the three of us work together on the same themes, and try to get shows."

"That's amazing."

"We're trying. This place is falling apart and it's hard."

"The city?"

"The city and more. The planet."

Now we're talking. "Totally."

Jen's quite handy with the tools and teamwork and, so we're moving quickly, putting together the desks.

"What do *you* do? Your real job?" she asks.

"Here in the city I do nothing much. I read and drink and try to think about maybe writing. When I leave, I'll go back up north to work with my friend Erik. Erik Matheson, you heard of him? He makes documentaries."

"No I haven't."

"You should check him out. Anyway, I help him with what he's doing and I help around his place. It's a big farm and there's always work to do."

"Sounds okay."

"I can't live down here anymore," I say. "It just got so sad."

"I can't give up yet. I grew up here," she says. "The place is messed up, but it used to be something else. At least kind of, right? I mean people came here to get away from the crap elsewhere. My friends did."

"I suppose so. I never really saw it like that, but you would know better than me."

"It used to be genuinely open here before, before all these health and safety codes. People liked it here and you could do a lot."

"I guess."

"You probably have a hard time seeing it. It sounds like you never really lost anything after the Scare."

"Just my hope in humanity."

"Don't be so dramatic. I mean real things—freedoms. You just left, right?"

"Yeah, I did. But, regardless, we've all lost out on this one. Not just here, but in the rest of Canada and the world. It's been a huge step backwards."

"Yes, but in real terms, here in the city, some lost out more than others, Tom."

"Yeah. Sure. You're right. The Chinese, the homeless, the sick." Of course, she's right. Men like me lost the least.

"It's not just them now. It could be anyone. What happens when the healthy are made into sick? What happens when you or I start to be *defined* as sick?"

"I know. It's fucked. And you're right. It's happening right now. So —fight back?"

"I don't know. It's scary. I've lost hope too. I think everyone has. Me and my roommates, we try to live in opposition to the rules if we can. I write about it. I'm plotting the Public Health Bureau's downfall through poetry."

That really makes me smile. "I thought everyone in this office was a total loser."

Jen laughs. "I see that you and Will get along."

"Will's a bit strange, but he's super interesting."

"He always helps me when I ask. Otherwise, I don't know, he keeps to himself. I don't blame him, You never know who's watching you."

Jen's great and she even has a healthy dose of paranoia. We finish putting together the rest of the desks chatting away like old pals. I even ask her out for a drink and she says yes. After we finish and I get back to my seat, I still have an hour left in my shift. I tell Will about the work putting the desks together and about Jen, but he seems uninterested. I ask him if he ever does anything but work and he sort of laughs. I ask him, joking, if he's ever taken a vacation. He says that he has, but at the time, he couldn't leave Vancouver because of his

RealJob, so he just stayed home and chain-watched *Oz*, the HBO show about prison, and listened to old jazz on the Internet.

"Old jazz? Where did that come from?" I ask.

"My grandfather."

"Do you like new jazz?"

"Nah. I don't even really like the old jazz. It's more like the atmosphere it creates that I like."

"How was *Oz*?"

"Okay. A lot of men though. A lot of cock scenes."

And that was the end of the conversation! Fucking weird.

Addendum to the Report on William Potenco
by Doctor Officer Elias Degair

The case against William is progressing. In the last two weeks, our twenty-four hour on- and offline surveillance has continued, and I've also contracted with a third party to do an assessment and diagnosis of the intricacies of William's online perversions: his relationship with his parents and with women, specifically to his so-called girlfriend Julia. Technology willing, this report will be completed and submitted within the next week and will further validate our observations. Other measures have also been put into play. Most importantly, however, is that William has been given space and time. He needs to keep believing that nothing is wrong, that he's a normal man living an unobserved normal life. This natural state is the only state in which we'll ever learn and understand how his disease progresses. William's Disease is infinitely complex. In any case, I suspect that very soon— very soon indeed—there will be real results. What we've seen in these last two weeks is already outstanding.

Take this recent *RealDiary* entry:

I know I have a temper. I know it's often the smallest things that send me into a rage, when all I want to do is smash peoples' faces in. These same small things can have the opposite effect...make me feel sad and small, so that if I could, I would dive head first into the cracks between the keys of my keyboard. Naturally, I try to avoid these things. Is it so hard to want to live a good life? Is it wrong to just want to go to work, enjoy one's hobbies, aspire to excellence, make more money, and then enjoy more hobbies? I don't have a problem with people minding their own business, so why do they feel it's necessary to get into mine? I just want to be left alone.

Today, it was as if I had a sign on my head that read, 'Please make sure to bother me all day and make me feel bad about myself.' Everybody around me felt the urge to make my life more difficult. It began early. At work, a new guy started. I know he didn't know any better, but he was sitting in my seat when I arrived. I should have just said to him outright, 'Excuse me, please can you move? You are at my desk,' but that would've been dishonest and maybe rude. I wish I'd handled it better. Confidence with people is something I struggle with, I know I do. But this guy. He was sitting there and I was looking at him, and it was almost like he knew that I was nervous. That is what is so angering—he knew he was in my seat and he wanted to just toy with me. Why would someone want to do that? Is it funny to them? All I wanted was to get to work.

I guess in the end it sort of worked out for the best, since later in the day, I got a kind of promotion, but not really the one I was looking for. I don't really want to train all the new employees, but knowing that Stu has that kind of confidence in me feels good. Ryan didn't seem to care, though. He hasn't cared about what I do for a while now. I told him about it and he just laughed, he said I should never have gotten so comfortable working for a startup, since they always fail. 'Always?' I said. I mean, is he that dumb? *Real* was also a startup at one point.... Anyway, the guy I trained won't last long, which is good. I give him a month before Dana calls him into his office. If he would just follow the rules, he would be fine, but he wants to change things—he's a radical and he's going to mess up Eureka! and I'll probably be the one to fix it all.

91

He was very critical of *Real*, that same old 'Secret History' stuff. I really should read that article. Ryan says that it's a lunatic conspiracy rant written by a coward. That's impossible to know, I told him, but he says he knows it. Mike doesn't seem to care. I don't know if I care. I don't think it would change anything for me. I know what it says anyway—Rothsteen is a spy and we're all being spied on, blah blah. Everyone knows it and it's all been denied, and we all know by now that they can spy on us if they want. Why would they, though? My life is as boring as the Vancouver rain. It is utterly ignorable.

Outside is dead, black night. There is no sound but the clacking of the keys I'm hitting, and there is no colour except for my monitor and the neon sign across the street: fake illumination in a noiseless night. Nothing has changed—merely a shift in the contours. My life is as it was. Tomorrow, I will get up and do the same thing as I did today, and I'll be content. Everything is fine.

"Everything is fine"? Not quite. William is overcompensating here. He's lying to himself. His subjective account of this day contradicts an objective account of my facts. Let's look closely at William's conversation with Ryan on *Real*, referred to in his diary.

(9:43 AM) William Potenco: Ryan! Are you there?

(9:45 AM) Ryan Jeffreys: Just finishing up some RWM stuff. You got alot [sic] done today. Good work.

(9:46 AM) William Potenco: Thanks. Anyways, Stu just told me I was senior staff and he put me directly in charge of training a new guy. I told you I would go places here.

(9:47 AM) Ryan Jeffreys: hahahahahah, that startup. You know startups always fail and that that's gonna fail, right?

(9:49 AM) William Potenco: I have to get back to work.

That's the full conversation, but there's something missing. Where is William's "Always?" He claimed in his diary to have retorted to Ryan with the word "always?" as a sort of rebuttal to Ryan's dismissal of William's job at Eureka! In the actual conversation, though, this does not appear. This small detail may be insignificant—or it could signal a shift in William's online behaviour; a loss of confidence in his online presence. He may be lying to himself as a way to compensate, constructing a new past in which that confidence existed and is confirmed by his recording it in his *RealDiary*. What this actually indicates is a further breakdown of his mental world: his confidence is disintegrating further, he's getting sicker.

A few days later, in another dialogue with Ryan on *Real*, more alarming indications of William's disintegrating mind appear and are worth mentioning. He had just gotten home from work. The cameras at Harmony saw him enter the cafeteria and approach the dinner counter, head lowered. The pretty young woman served him food and he left. Shortly thereafter, he was back in his room talking to Ryan on *Real*:

(7:03 PM) William Potenco: Hey Ryan, have you ever read the "Secret History"?

(7:06 PM) Ryan Jeffreys: What!? That piece of conspiracy bullshit. Will, everyone knows that's a lie. Rothsteen denied it, the press denied it. Why would you want to know?

(7:08 PM) William Potenco: This new guy at work keeps mentioning it. I thought I would read it.

(7:10 PM) Ryan Jeffreys: New guy, huh. You don't need to waste your time reading it. Just *PediaPedia* it.

(7:12 PM) William Potenco: Yeah. The new guy—his name is Tom —he also says that *Real* is just another monopoly, that it's bad.

(7:13 PM) Ryan Jeffreys: This guy sounds like some fucking commie. You get all sorts of freaks out there in Van, huh. *Real* might be a monopoly, but that's how it works. It shows our economy is healthy again.

(7:15 PM) William Potenco: It just got me thinking.

(7:16 PM) Ryan Jeffreys: I'd stay away from that "new guy." Will, you should really just come to Winnipeg. You can stay here and work with me at Bombardier. It'd be cool.

(7:17 PM) William Potenco: Yeah, I don't know. I need to think about it. Anyway, I think I'll watch a film now to cheer me up.

(7:19 PM) Ryan Jeffreys: Okay dude.

From his *Real* browser history, we know that after William finished this dialogue he watched the 1989 comedy *Bill and Ted's Excellent Adventure* with Keanu Reeves. The film began at 7:45 p.m. and ended at 9:15 p.m. William then wrote in his *RealDiary* at 11:00 p.m. From the end of the movie to his diary entry, William was on his *RealSeminar*, extolling the virtues of *Bill and Ted's Excellent Adventure*. William claimed that the real "excellent adventure" was not Bill and Ted's, but the one undertaken by Socrates, Billy the Kid, Napoleon, and so on, when, towards the end of the film, they experience modern life at a shopping mall. William goes on to compare the encounter between man and shopping mall and consumer culture with Frank Romero's *Dawn of the Dead*, in which human zombies attracted to a shopping mall are gunned down by a group of heroes. After discussing it, members of the seminar concluded that both films are terrific examples of the role of the shopping mall in contemporary life, but that *Bill and Ted's*, since it's a comedy, is much more effective in getting the message across.

This sort of pseudo-academic nonsense is of little concern. It's in his dialogue with Ryan where we see William exposed. He's exhibiting symptoms of suspicion and paranoia. We see this most clearly in his questioning of his friend, who has nothing but William's best interests at heart, and in his questioning of *Real* and Rothsteen.

There is also William's relationship with Thomas, which is of some concern. Thomas is not the type of person William needs in his life, now or ever. Over time we'll see, but for now, we just hope that William's introverted character traits prevail, and that, as his friend Ryan advises, he'll keep Thomas at a distance.

Thomas himself is hardly worth mentioning. His full name is Thomas Rudolph Vickers—thirty-five years old and, as Ryan says and as his reading material suggests, likely some kind of communist. We've known about Thomas for some time. CSIS knows about him. He has a short, pathetic file. A few years ago, he was back and forth to Russia on several occasions. He speaks Russian, and was working on a history PhD at the U.B.C. entitled "What it Meant to be Red in Stalin's Russia." But he didn't finish. He dropped out and dropped off the radar. He's a quitter who ran away and now spends his time attached to one Erik Matheson, a radical documentary filmmaker out of Rolla, B.C. who makes films critical about issues no one cares about. At best, Thomas Vickers is a kind of armchair radical, a nobody—a fellow traveller on a meaningless trip, with a big mouth and no guts. His false consciousness keeps him in the past and in the dark about his own failures. If only we could designate "poor loser" as a disease, Thomas and all those who failed to understand the end of history would be rounded up and forcibly treated. His phoney radicalism is from a bygone age and William will surely ignore it. William is too attached to his job and his dreams to listen to radicals, communists and paper iconoclasts like Thomas.

"The Secret History of Sydney Rothsteen and *Real*" by Osama Hussein Dot Com

Real. The name is as ubiquitous as the Internet itself. As fast as people are connecting to the Internet, they are joining *Real*. From the smallest village in the remotest corner of India, to almost every household and Smartphone user in greater New York City, *Real's* tentacles extend everywhere, envelop everything and constrict everyone. *Real's* global servers and databases collect, filter and store more data in one month than all other Internet data ever collected. Ninety percent of its user base is said to never log off. Instantaneous and open communication, affect and acquaintance, and user control are *Real's* hallmarks and the features that have turned this once weak startup into the single most successful capitalist phenomenon to date. Yet these features, designed to lull individual *Real* members into a false sense of happiness and security, make them all the more subservient, all the more a slave, all the more the raw material for someone else's dream. Behind open communication is confession. Behind so-called user control is obedience. And behind all of this is the *Real* users' master, Sydney Rothsteen, a modern-day King Leopold, and sole proprietor of the largest army of willing slaves in the history of mankind.

In a sycophantic chorus ringing out from the highest mountaintops in every corner of the globe, praises for *Real* are heralded out. "This is the American Dream!" the voices chime. It's the story of the humble upstart startup, RealFriend—just another hack operation that entered the fray of cutthroat social networking. It managed to survive and grow on a clever marketing strategy geared to an older, mature audience, and on an advanced user interface that seamlessly combined the best features of its competitors into one tight package. In its first years, RealFriend grew by introducing a seemingly endless and flawless variety of features and software that attracted disgruntled emigrants from other social networks and pioneers looking for something new. RealFriend's user base surpassed 500 million, just when the U.S. and global economies crashed in 2008. In that same year, RealFriend introduced *RealEconomy*. A game to all but Sydney, *RealEconomy* has since been called the saviour of global capitalism and may force the most major global financial readjustment since the end of Breton Woods.

But it took more than that for *Real* to become the most popular and profitable Internet based business ever. It also took members. In 2009, after his competitors failed to reach a deal, Rothsteen announced that RealFriend was going to China. A month later he dropped the "Friend" and became *Real*. Since then, India, Russia, Indonesia—the numbers have been staggering: of the close to three billion global Internet users, some 2.5 billion are on *Real*. They create six billion "compositions," listen to thirty billion songs, and produce two exabytes (equivalent to 500 million DVDs) of data a day. Sydney Rothsteen is now the Big Man of Big Data—a warlord in the global theft of the data of our lives.

On *Real*, by the time a new identification page (the infamous *Real-ID*) is set up, the information voluntarily given—favourite films, authors, musicians, sexual preferences and so forth—have been reduced to a few lines of data, which, when combined with other lines of similar data, generate social trends that advertisers want to know. What you just gave up for free, as the price of entry into the fiefdom of Rothsteen's *Real*, is now profitable; you no longer own it nor control it nor have a say in what happens to it. Now Sydney owns it. It's his personal property and it's aggregated and sold to the highest bidder. At this new frontier of capitalism, Sydney Rothsteen, much like Cecil Rhodes did in Africa, steals and tricks and lies to acquire his space and resources. As Kurtz traded his ivory at the Inner Station, so do cyber-imperialists like Sydney traffic their resources on the new frontiers of capitalism.

For capitalism must adapt or it will die; it must find a way to get the money that is in people's pockets at the beginning of the day out of their pockets by the end of the day. It doesn't care how, it simply must. Commodities are created out of nothing, then monopolized to make them scarce and valuable. Personal information is just such a commodity.

Unquestioning obedience is a hallmark of this system. Today's teenagers—the future generations of lawyers, doctors, teachers, and politicians—are now posting more personal information onto social media sites than ever. They don't even care who is collecting their information or how it is being collected. The kind of obedience this requires, the kind of docile citizen that is produced these days, is not an overnight phenomenon. It is not a trend; it is a social psychology, which has been learned and is enforced. Teachers, parents, doctors, professors, lawyers, CEO's, team managers, social workers, and bureaucrats all teach obedience. The major institutions—the school, law enforcement, the family, the courts, the church, the corporation, the business, the hospital, and the state—are structured to produce and reproduce subservience. And to make sure you comply, you are watched. Your obedience is guaranteed by omnipresent and perpetual surveillance, keeping you in line, recording what you say, what you do, what you think. The thousands upon thousands of mechanical and digital eyes are like so much anesthesia; they make you weak enough to accept all kinds of social experimentation and social control.

Social networks have proven how effective this training is. *Real* asks you for your information, and because you've been trained and they have asked, you give it to them. Some information is termed private, some public, but this distinction matters little. Everyone can use public information. Advertisers use it to sell you commodities, but just as your census information is used not just to count you, so your *Real* information is used not only to sell you a Coke. Government agencies and institutions like the NSA, MI6, CSIS, departments of heath, universities, social scientists, researchers, think tanks, the police, and just about anyone else who wants can also access this information. It is used to devise better means of taking care of you, making sure you are healthier so you can work harder and longer, making sure you are patriotic enough, that you are operating normally, buying the right stuff, spending your money and going into debt like you are supposed to. In short, your information is being used to adjust you accordingly, so that you operate as a perfect citizen—you go to work, you salute the flag, and you spend all your money.

For the enemy, for the terrorist and for those who don't want to obey and who are disobedient, however, there is something else. In the U.S. it's called the Patriot Act, in Naples it's called a state of emergency, in Vancouver it's called Special Decree 451, in China it's everyday life. Whatever it's called locally, it is the paradigm in which we all now live—what the philosopher Giorgio Agamben calls the State of Exception, in which the individual has no legal status. If a person is accused under the Patriot Act, for example, she or he is not thought of as a prisoner, or even as a person charged with a crime according to American laws, but simply as a "detainee," an object of a detention that is indefinite not only temporally, but also in its very nature, since they have been removed from law and from judicial oversight, completely. The concept of freedom needs to be entirely rethought in such a place. For in the state of exception, governments can do what they want, when they want and to whom they want, without worrying about right or law, local, international, or extraterrestrial.

The proof of the complete removal of rights in this country is clear. In 2011 it was revealed that the U.S. Department of Homeland Security, in conjunction with the military contractor General Dynamics, was illegally monitoring U.S. citizens' emails and phone calls. In May 2013, the U.S. Department of Justice was caught illegally spying on the *Associated Press*. In June 2013, the NSA was caught illegally collecting phone records and tapping the servers of leading Internet companies to read emails, look at photos, and track people. These revelations, unprecedented in scope, are now normal in the state of exception. What is abnormal is a society that allows this to go unchecked. From 1920 to the mid-1930s, German society descended into acceptance and support of Nazism. In those same years, the Soviet Union normalized the Gulag. At present, so too has U.S. society become like the camp. What is different is only the form. The U.S. government does not need to build a gulag like in the Soviet Union. Every house in the U.S. has become a potential jail cell, because every house can be listened into. Every person carries, in the form of his or her Smartphone, a tracking device. What we have is a voluntary gulag. All the measures are now in place, the democratic safeguards have been rubber-stamped, the technology is available, and the people have bought it freely. What is modern American freedom? It is the freedom to purchase your own incarceration.

But modern ideology tells us that this is not so. Smartphones, the Internet, Facebook, Blabber, and *Real* are not means of incarceration. According to the best copywriters money can buy, they are means of communication. Open and free, instantaneous communication. "Helping a couple billion people connect is something I find myself proud of," said Rothsteen. The corporation, however, is not, and has never been a friend of the people. The old truism that big business and government cooperate with each other is more obvious now than ever. When government asks, business bows and yields. Is it surprising that the heroes of liberal capitalism—Bill Gates and Eric Schmidt, the CEOs of Microsoft and Google and the voices of global charity and morality—didn't even raise a finger when accused of their compliance with the NSA? When they simply handed over your personal information to the government? It shouldn't be.

The connection between big business, the military, and the U.S. government is well known. What is not so well known is Sydney Rothsteen's personal family involvement. In him, the connection between business, government, and the surveillance state is closer than in any other individual. In him, the concept of political economy reaches its apogee. It began in 1919, when Sydney's great-grandfather, Witold Rothstein, a German munitions manufacturer and importer of American-made weapons into pre-World War I Germany, immigrated to Canada. In 1926, Rothstein purchased Canadian Vickers Limited, an aircraft and shipbuilding company. In 1944, Canadian Vickers Limited was absorbed by the Canadian Government and became Canadair, the primary supplier of aircraft to the Royal Canadian Air Force. Two years later, Canadair was sold to the Electric Boat Company. In 1952, Canadair and the Electric Boat Company officially merged and became General Dynamics. The Rothsteins are on the original merger contract as ten percent shareholders.

Sydney's grandfather, Diederich Rothstein, continued the family business. In 1953, he was the leading figure behind General Dynamics' purchase of Convair, an American aircraft manufacturing company. Sydney's father, George Rothstein, dissatisfied with just producing weapons, trained as an engineer and was lead builder of General Dynamics' most successful aircraft to date, the F-16 fighter jet. He was also behind the purchase by General Dynamics of Chrysler's entire defense division in 1982. George Rothstein died in 2002, leaving thirty-year-old Sydney the family's fortune of some $15 billion.

Poised to follow in the family business, Sydney organized General Dynamics' purchase of General Motors' defense division in 2003. However, just two years later, in a move that shocked only the naïve mainstream media, *Real*, then known as RealFriend, went live with Sydney at the helm. For the record, in the official biographies, and in the made-for-TV movies, this is the beginning, the origins of Sydney's career. In these quaint retellings that fawn over business and power, Sydney comes off as a man of money, a venture capitalist and daredevil, who leapt into the maelstrom of online social networks only on a whim or because of a bet—or as some have it, the result of a psychic reading. In these fictional examples of mass amnesia, Sydney's background with General Dynamics and his connection to the manufacture of some of the most horrific and deadly weapons ever made is said to have ceased or is not mentioned.

But Sydney never did stop. In the same year that RealFriend went live, General Dynamics purchased MAYA Viz, a little known technology design firm commissioned by the U.S. Department of Defense to develop a software and military communications network known as Command Post of the Future (CPOF). Rothsteen consulted MAYA Viz Ltd. in his development of RealFriend. The result is that the advanced drag-and-drop features that enable U.S. military commanders to conduct more efficient and deadly warfare on their enemies are the same as those used by a user of *Real* to combine songs with video and animation on their Canvas.

After purchasing MAYA Viz, General Dynamics bought the software producer Mediaware; two months later, *Real* rolled out its intuitive advertising technology. In 2010, the same year that membership on *Real* passed a billion and a year before General Dynamics and Homeland Security got together to spy on U.S. citizens, a program called Net-Enabled Command Capability (NECC), another brainchild of the U.S. Department of Defense, was cancelled. General Dynamics bought NECC's resources: a global network of information nodes with fixed stations in the US, transportable stations abroad, and "mobile nodes," or floating data centres at sea and in the air. What happened to these "resources" after their purchase is unclear. What is clear is that *Real*'s capability to accommodate its rapidly expanding global user base and its ability to collect and store the kind of information that those users generated doubled.

When Sydney Rothsteen brags that *Real* is the largest country on earth, he's not joking. It is a country. It's his country, and in it, the line between economics and politics is all but erased. The line between the product—free communication—and the motivation behind it—ceaseless government surveillance—simply does not exist.

Today, Sydney Rothsteen has made *Real* into the fulfillment of the Wagnerian dream of the *Gesamtkunstwerk*—the fusion of all the arts—political and cultural—in one work. From atop the holy mountain, *Real* and its creator shine in a glittering blinding gold. So captivated are we, so blindly do we insist on the very technology and ideology that enslaves us, that we do not see it for what it is: mass deception.

Real and Rothsteen, the political economy, are not the tools of salvation, they are the chains that bind us. *Real*'s First Reality Lenses, the next tool in the wholesale collection of data, are right around the corner. They guarantee us reality as *Real* wants it to be. A kind of perpetual escapism and imprisonment in the world of *Real* forevermore. In a wild reversal of John Carpenter's *They Live*, we will not put in the lenses to see the truth, but rather to escape into the lie of a *Real* world, where apps will exist that further camouflage our collective incarceration. There will be apps that make it always sunny; that add holograms of celebrities to the mix of everyday life; that block out homelessness, mask dirt, grime and clouds and make rain disappear, that shelter us from nasty third world-violence and terrorism, and block out the Other completely; that make everyone feel rich, successful and happy. Courtesy of Rothsteen and *Real,* deception will soon be available at the flick of an eye.

Report on Will Potenco and Julia Singer Commissioned by the Vancouver Public Health and Safety Bureau, Doctor Officer Elias Degair submitted by the Women Against Gender Inequality (WAGI)*

The following report, commissioned by Doctor Officer Elias Degair of the Vancouver Public Health Bureau and compiled by Women Against Gender Inequality (WAGI), is a chronicle of Will Potenco's relationships with women. It begins with a personal history of his childhood and adolescent years, before discussing his current relationship with Julia Singer. The purpose of this document is to present the contours of Will's relationships with women, detail the main historical and psychological features, and then offer our opinion on what Doctor Officer Degair has termed the "illicit" elements in

---

*A note on sources: All information has been provided by the Vancouver Public Health Bureau under Provision 9a of Special Decree 451. They include: Will Potenco – complete browser history and *RealDiary* entries; Will Potenco, Julia Singer— complete catalogue of online conversations; Julia Singer—complete recorded online performances with The Girl Next Door; provincial court and government records and police records.

those relationships.

Will Potenco was born on April 4, 1984, the only son of Margaret Potenco, née McCoy and James Potenco. William is tall and thin, has short brown hair, is unmarried and currently resides at the corner of Carrall and West Pender in a bachelor suite at Harmony Cooperative in Vancouver, British Columbia. Will graduated from the University of British Columbia with a degree in computer science. He currently works two jobs: one in the data management department of Eureka!, "the social network for academics," and another in the hybrid sector of *RealEconomy* with his two partners, Mike George (Ottawa) and Ryan Jeffreys (Winnipeg), at a company called RWM Solutions. Will is financially stable with a minimal student debt of $18,500, which he is working towards paying.

Julia Singer was born on July 20, 1990, the only daughter of Gail Singer, née Dixon, and Jim Singer. She is of medium height, has shoulder-length, light brown hair, is unmarried, and currently resides on Chester Avenue in shared accommodation in Montreal, Quebec. Julia graduated from the University of Montreal with a degree in sociology. She currently has two jobs: one as a waitress at Le Chien Bleu, a late-night pub catering to students at the University of Montreal, and another as a self-employed, professional webcam performer, colloquially known as a "camgirl," for the Montreal- based website The Girl Next Door (www.thegirlnextdoor.com). Julia has a student debt of $23,000 which she has not paid back and which she thinks she has managed to dodge.

Will's history of relationships with women begins with his mother. From all that he has mentioned of Margaret Potenco née McCoy, it's clear he places her in an important position in his life. It wasn't always like this. When Will was fifteen years old, his parents divorced. In a masculinized country like Canada, it's typical in a divorce to see the woman blamed for ruining the marriage. Will's father, James Potenco, accused Margaret of an extramarital affair and, among other things, of being "unfit to mother," "dishonest," "disloyal" and "unfaithful," as if seeking happiness in the arms of another man disqualified her from being a mother. It's as if her act of unfaithfulness called into question her ability and capacity to love and care for Will. The court's decision, after a round of harsh character assassination by an all-male court that sided with the humiliated and revenge-seeking father, was to punish Margaret, who was uneducated and at the time unemployed and unable to afford an attorney. As we see it, Margaret fell out of love with an unloving man, and for seeking warmth in the arms of another, was punished by having her son taken away.

In compensation, Margaret was granted a small alimony, pitiful by anyone's standards. It was ordered that if she wanted to see Will again, she was to establish a "healthy and honest home." This was difficult, given that she was financially and emotionally ruined and placed in a perpetual cycle of debt to pay the court costs. Yet, despite all odds stacked against her, Margaret did secure a "healthy and honest home." She found a low-wage job at as a bank teller and was able somehow to get a mortgage on a small two-bedroom Edwardian. To the surprise and likely dismay of James Potenco, she was eventually granted visiting rights to her son.

That Margaret fulfilled the court's demands is a testament to her strength and her love for Will, but it made life no easier for her. Unbeknownst to her and her son, James had already begun further legal processes to have himself absolved of paying even the small amount of alimony. Based on a ludicrous stipulation set out in the original divorce proceedings that she pay for her own upkeep, Will's father charged Margaret with breaking the court's rules by receiving money from a third party, a man—the so-called "home wrecker" who was "responsible" for James's divorce. James won, and six months after the divorce, the granting of alimony was revoked. Three months later, Margaret was forced to file for bankruptcy, give up her home and move into a spare room with an old family friend. Will had only been twice to see her and the home she had worked so hard to give him.

Will was not aware of what his father was doing or of what was happening in the courts. Whether a mother is fit or unfit is not something that enters a boy's mind. At the time, Will was doing what many children from broken homes do—getting into trouble. Thanks to his newfound sense of freedom, Will rebelled against the external world that he perceived had let him down, and in the year after his parents' divorce, was caught by the police twice. Once was for vandalism. He had destroyed a church nativity scene at Christmas time —smashed the three wise men, dropkicked baby Jesus, broke the heads off farm animals—and was required to apologize to the ministers and to do forty hours of community service shovelling snow from the church's walkway. The second time, he was caught drinking underage; his punishment was being brought home to his father in the back of a police car.

It's easy to identify what was going on here; this kind of delinquency in children from broken homes is not exceptional. Will's destruction of the nativity scene was his way of saying "fuck you" to the church, which symbolized all institutions and power he could not reckon with. It was his response to his feelings of abandonment at being stripped of the right to see his mother. He violently tore the heads off papier mâché sheep as he would've liked to have destroyed his feelings of sadness and desertion. The drinking, on the other hand, was simply an escape mechanism to avoid confronting his sadness.

At the same time, the relationship between Will and his mother was dark. James Potenco's malicious accounts of Margaret, his constant reinforcement of a fictional bad image of her, his descriptions of her as a bitch, whore and home wrecker, caused Will to neglect his mother. Not until he was eighteen, shortly before he left Kitchener for Vancouver, did he begin to understand his parents' divorce.

What remains unclear is just what led to his new understanding. We can only speculate that he found something—a document perhaps, or (with Will this is always a possibility) a film that made him reconsider. Whatever it was, when he was eighteen, Will developed a deep feeling of empathy for his mother's situation. By that time, she was living with a man named Frank, an electrician and divorcee with two young sons of his own. Will's new closeness is seen in his diary recollections of that period when he speaks of frequent happy visits to Margaret and Frank's place and the fun he had "hanging out" with Frank's kids. At the peak of these feelings, he packed his things, left his father and went to stay with Margaret for his last six months in Kitchener.

A boy's decision to go and live with his mother could be read in a naïve, pseudo-Freudian way as a boy punishing his father, killing him by leaving him, and marrying his mother by staying with her. Hollywood likes to see things this way, as do governments, courts and official institutions, because this interpretation exonerates them from responsibility for creating socially troubled people. It places blame solely on the subject, who is then seen as "obviously just Oedipal." It would be ridiculous to think of Will this way. We prefer to see things not as prescribed but as empirically proven. It is not evident that boys are conditioned to reject their fathers and live with their mothers, as laid out in some 3,000-year-old myth. In Will's case, he became self-aware of his mother's plight and decided to exercise his agency by choosing to leave James and live with Margaret. Will's empathy was genuine, guided not by mystical or mythical forces, but by real emotional understanding.

A couple of important points regarding Will and his parents need to be mentioned. One is that since arriving in Vancouver, it's Margaret, not James, whom Will has since communicated with most often. When he set up his RealFriend account, it was Margaret and not James in his list of first five friends. Furthermore, after the Scare, when Will finally got a chance to go home for a visit, he got into a terrible argument with his father. He recounted the entire episode in his diary. He writes that he had booked a flight and his father had agreed to pick him up at the airport. Will says that he arrived happy, looking forward to seeing his dad after such a long time. James had remarried and Will had not yet met his new step-mother. Will waited at the airport, but James did not come. He waited longer, still nothing, so Will called.

"Hey Dad, where are you? You said you'd pick me up."

"Sorry, Bub, but me and Carol [Will's stepmom], well, we decided not to come and get you…"

"I can see that! I've been waiting here for two hours. Why didn't you come?"

"Well, Bub, we just feel that you might still be infected and we don't want to take that chance."

"Infected! What are you talking about!?"

"They say on the news that they don't know if H8N—whatever—is entirely gone. They say everyone coming from Vancouver should be quarantined for two weeks before contact. Just to be safe, you know? We just don't want to get sick, Will, you know?"

"But, Dad, it's fine. I'm not sick. They wouldn't have let me fly if I was sick. We all get scanned now. There are scanners at all the airports. Even here in Toronto."

"But they say on the news…"

"I haven't seen you in so long and now you're telling me that you won't see me while I'm here. I'm only visiting for two weeks!"

"We're sorry, Bub, but, you know…"

"Actually, I don't know. You're kidding, right? You must be kidding!"

"Don't get upset, Will. We'll just wait and see you next time, that's all."

"…"

"Will?"

"Dad, I don't think there can be a next time."

"Will—Bub…"

"You're a real self-centred asshole, you know that?"

Will hung up and went home to his mother's on a public bus, where he stayed for the two weeks. True to his word, there hasn't been a next time with James. They haven't spoken and their bond seems to be permanently broken.

Aside from Margaret, Will's relationships with women after he left home have not been so successful. At least, not in the sense we usually understand, where two people meet, get to know each other, form an emotional bond, explore their feelings for some time, and then either happily move along together, or go their separate ways, both emotionally stronger. No, we can't say they were successful in that sense.

His first relationship, his first recorded feelings of love, and his first sexual encounter, were with a woman named Beverly, Bev for short. According to Will, Bev was pretty and smart. He met her one night shortly into his first year at university, when they were both drunk at a bar on campus. Afterwards, like many horny young students in their first year, they went back to Will's residence and jumped head, penis- and vagina-first into bed, and only then into a relationship.

What came after was somewhat predictable and formulaic. The young couple did what they thought they should do—what Canadian society and culture teaches young straight couples. They went on dates to dinner, movies, walks, concerts, and so on, mimicking the trappings of "normal" dating couples. They copied the image of an ideal relationship as expressed in every date movie and television sitcom they had ever seen. With no experience of their own they imitated as best they could.

The problem was that this image contradicted reality. Will's reality, given his past broken childhood, was that the bond between men and women is fragile. Despite the date-night movies and sitcoms, Will had seen first hand—especially through the actions of his own father—that men are fickle. Far from the stereotypical strong, rational men often portrayed in popular media, men can be erratic, capricious and petty, little boys who sometimes base decisions on the mentality of the schoolyard rather than on careful self-reflection and considered thought.

This is what Will knew and how he began to act, so that after the so-called honeymoon phase of his relationship with Bev, things began to break down. Will began to complain about her, likely first to his friends, then publically on *Real*'s Canvas, where even Bev could read it. He complained about what she liked to do, what she wore, what she ate, the details of her everyday life that didn't suit him. Some relationship experts call this behaviour normal: Will didn't feel strongly about Bev, so he was gathering reasons to reinforce his desire and strengthen his resolve to end the relationship. The thing about Will is that he's not able to act "normally." He's a young man from a broken home with a terrible male role-model. His behaviour, far from normal, signals a form of social pathology—a disease passed on from father to son. A pathology has a way of becoming first a trait and then a permanent defense mechanism used almost instinctively when circumstances are perceived to be absurd or unjustified.

Will saw as unjustified what Bev did one day on a public bus. There was only one seat left, Will recalls. He offered it to her but she declined so he sat. She then sat on his lap, which he says "horrified" him. He found her actions to be "violent," "bewildering," "ridiculous" and "unfathomable," not because he was embarrassed, but because he felt she intended to make him uncomfortable. There is nothing to suggest that this was Bev's intent. Most likely she thought she was making an affectionate gesture. When he reacted as he did, walking off the bus, she went after him and he exploded. The truth became clear: Will was terribly uncomfortable not just with Bev, but with the entire relationship they'd constructed. It simply did not fit with what he knew, so he acted out. Will read her action as an affront because he wanted it to be. He needed an irrationality to end the relationship, because he'd been shown first hand by his father that relationships don't end in rational discussion, but in absurd arguments.

They separated shortly after. Not even a month later, Will rebounded with Kim. It's unfortunate that Will met her, as Kim was not good for him. She was cruel. We've read in his diary how manipulative she was and how she preyed on Will's weaknesses: his sensitivity and increasing desire for solitude. She forced him to take her out to social gatherings, hockey games, parties, clubs and bars with people he did not know or care about. She kept him up and out late and pushed him to his emotional limits until he broke down one day in a movie theatre and began to cry. She saw his behaviour—natural given the kind of abuse he was taking—as a weakness, and they broke up. That was nine years ago and Will has not been in another serious relationship until now.

It would be simple to say that Will was more emotionally deformed than ever after these experiences. But Will's response to Kim's cruelty was only natural, just as his subsequent withdrawal from women was only a smokescreen. After Kim, what might look like Will's withdrawal from women was actually just a different form of interaction with them. Rather than attempt another relationship, Will chose to objectify women, not out of malice, but more as a coping mechanism—a way to feel comfortable and connected with women without being near them.

Will's objectification of women occurred during a period of ongoing objectification of women by our society as a whole, paralleling the explosion of Internet porn over the past fifteen years. The proliferation of online porn began when Will and his generation were most susceptible to it, when the Internet became a substitute for all sorts of communication, including sexual.

However, Will's use of women as an object to get off on is not so typical. The clearest expression of Will's complicated attitude toward women comes from his first description of Julia:

> She is beautiful: her brown hair, short and bobbed; her medium-sized, perfectly shaped breasts and rosebud nipples; the small dimples above her ass, matched by the dimples on her face when she smiles; her full red lips; her demure demeanour; her ocean-blue eyes I wish to swim in; her hair that smells like lilacs I will never smell; her lips that taste like sweet chocolate I will never taste; and her skin so smooth like an ivory I will never touch. Julia will never be a burden to me. She will not be hanging around, forcing me to do things that I don't want to—she won't call, she won't demand...

Cutting through the overwrought sentiment, we can see that Will's objectification of Julia is unorthodox: she is the object of his sexual fantasies, the perfect woman described only in her physicality. But she is also, in her real physical absence, a kind of non-object—she is not near Will, which enables him to be with her in the first place. In a positive way, Will's image of Julia enables him to form a stable

114

relationship. This may seem unconventional by some standards, but what he is expressing in the diary entry above are strong and healthy emotions.

Will and Julia met by accident. While Will was surfing porn one day, Julia literally popped up in front of him. The Girl Next Door, the website company Julia works on, employs the popup tactic to get business. The unsuspecting viewer is looking at porn and all of a sudden there is a real woman or man staring at just you. This is not unique to The Girl Next Door, but is employed by many camgirl websites. We know from the detailed records of Will's browser history and his Internet search record that he is usually quick to close these windows. But something made him hesitate that day; something about Julia caught his attention—the flutter of an eye, the nibble of a lip. She would not have been naked; most camgirls don't work like that. We've watched her and we know she doesn't get her clients by sitting on a bed inserting sex toys and jumping into the performance. When a viewer first encounters Julia, she's sitting at her desk at her computer, seemingly looking at the viewer, but the camera is set to catch her on an angle, in profile. The viewer watches her as she looks at the screen. And she is pretty. According to his browser history, Will spent a full five minutes staring at her before clicking back to his usual porn. But he left her on in the background—a clear image of her to go back to. Her big blue eyes drew him in, he says. They captivated him, as "the clear blue ocean water." Will kept her there behind his other windows, going back to her now and again. He watched the slight movements of her eyes, head, lips. She would have been smiling, laughing, typing to other men like Will whom she'd perhaps caught in mid-masturbation and whom she was now pulling in with her quietly enticing act.

Will had never talked to a camgirl before. He liked to watch, not talk. Julia was his first. She impelled him to type in that first "hello."

Eventually she replied with a brief but cute, "hi."

"You're very pretty," Will wrote back.

"Thanks," she replied, smiling just enough to reveal her dimples.

"What's your name?" Will asked next.

"I can't tell you that," she said, looking coy, "but how would you like a private show? Maybe I'll tell you after that."

With most horny men wanting a quickie, this tactic would probably have worked, but Will wasn't interested. He didn't want to watch this girl do whatever it was that she did privately, at least not now. For now he was more interested in looking at her as she was, sitting and looking beautiful, paying attention to him. It's as though he wanted to have a conversation with a woman who was interested in what he had to say. Finally he did ask, "How much would that cost? A private show?"

"$50 for 20 minutes," she typed.

"Oh. That's a bit expensive. I have to think about that. How would I find you again if I wanted to?"

"It's not so expensive. I gotta live, too, right? But if you reconsider and want to find me again, I'm on at this time every day. You just need to come back to the website and search for me: jewels."

"That's your name?" typed Will.

"No. Are you crazy? That's my name here, for the website and for you."

"Right, no. I didn't mean it like that."

"Relax, Mr. Sensitive, I'm playing with you. But come back, okay."

"Okay."

"For now though," she typed back, "there's no free shows...."

She vanished, the screen refreshed and there was a Filipina woman in front of Will, whom he quickly got rid of by closing the window.

In fact, after meeting Julia that day, Will closed all his sites. She'd obviously got to him and he couldn't stop thinking about her. For two days, he thought about her, about spending the money to see this woman for whom he was developing some kind of feelings. First he tried to get her to pop up again—he clicked through porn sites trying to find her, but she wasn't there. He went to The Girl Next Door and tried to see her again for free, but that's not how they work. If Will wanted to see her, he would have to make an appointment; he would have to pay for Julia.

The first time, Will woke up earlier than normal. He went to the website, set up an account, found Julia, clicked on her for an appointment, and there she was in front of him again.

Will-i-am84: Hello. Do you remember me?

jewels: Of course I do, Will-i-am84. Can I call you Will? Are you Will?

Will-i-am84: Will. Yes, that's my name, Will Potenco.

jewels: Okay Willy, you're going to be prompted to another screen right now, where you'll have to enter in your payment method and then you'll see me again in a private room. Okay?

When he saw her again, the setting had changed slightly. She was in the same room, a typical room in the upstairs of a shared house, small with a pointed ceiling, double bed, desk, wardrobe, night table, wallpaper. The lights had dimmed and she was lying on the bed. The camera was on the desk; the desk chair had been moved so as not to obstruct the view; her laptop was next to her on the bed so she could continue to type. There was a song playing in the background. She was wearing only a red lace bra and matching underwear.

Will-i-am84: Will you tell me *your* name?

jewels: I barely know you, so I don't think I should. What if you're some kind of creepy stalker, Willy? [She smiles.]

Will-i-am84: Okay, I understand, it's just weird thinking of you as jewels.

jewels: I know, Willy, but we're going to have to get used to that.

Will-i-am84: How about where you're from? Where do you live? Can you tell me that?

jewels: You seem real sweet, but I can't tell you that either, silly Willy. Let's just say I live in a big city, with lots of people.

Will-i-am84: Hmmm, well, can you tell me how old you are? I'm almost 30.

jewels: I'm old enough, if that's what you mean. Older than old enough, actually.

Will-i-am84: That's not what I meant. I trust you.

jewels: haha you're funny. [She takes off her bra.]

Will-i-am84: What's that song in the background? It reminds me of some movie.

jewels: You know this song? That's funny. It's on *Real*. They have these premade playlists of sexy songs that I use.

Will-i-am84: It sounds familiar.

jewels: you're funny Will. It's just a song.

Julia then began to touch herself. She started by massaging her right breast with her right hand. With her left hand, she reached down beneath her underwear and began to rub herself. Will interrupted.

Will-i-am84: Hey jewels. I'm not really interested in that today. I mean you're really attractive, I think you're so sexy, but you don't have to do that today. I'll be back another time. I just wanted to talk a bit. I wanted to see you again and chat.

jewels: ???? Umm. That's kinda weird Willy.

Will-i-am84: Really?

jewels: Yes, really. I mean it's up to you of course, but there is time left, and you did pay for it.

Will-i-am84: Yeah, maybe next time though. I mean, I know about the time, but I think I might just leave now anyway.

jewels: What? Before the time's up? But Willy, no one does that! What's wrong?

Will-i-am84: I'll come back in a couple of days. Nothing's wrong. I figure I can see you twice a week. What do you think?

jewels: you can come back, of course. But are you seriously leaving?

Will-i-am84: Yes. I should go. I have to work. I'll see you again. You're very beautiful. Bye.

jewels: ? bye.

Will waited almost a week before seeing Julia next. He was excited about meeting her. In a short message to his mother on *Real,* he mentioned Julia as a "new nice girl I met," and "one that I can talk to." Margaret encouraged him by telling Will to be himself.

That's exactly what he did. The next date, again taking place early, around 6:00 a.m. PST (3 a.m. AST), went much like the first. Will began by asking her about working for The Girl Next Door.

jewels: If I can get two shows a night, that's a hundred bucks. Well, almost a hundred, because I have to pay the website, but that's pretty good for less than an hour of work, don't you think?

Will-i-am84: Not bad, I suppose. I make about 150 a week on *Real,* and I only have to work an hour or so each morning.

jewels: You have one of those *RealJobs*? I thought about doing that, but they sound real boring, and I can make more doing this.

Will-i-am84: Yeah. My friends and I, we have a factory, a few employees too. I use the money I make to see you.

jewels: You should work more then, haha, jk. But I guess I'm thankful you spend that on me. They seem a bit screwed up to me though, those *RealJobs*, that *RealMoney*…I don't know, I guess as long as it can be turned into actual money, I don't care.

Will-i-am84: You're on *Real* though, you said?

jewels: I am.

Will-i-am84: I won't ask you for your username, since I know you won't tell me. But if you want to find me I'm #Ten-Two-Twenty-Two or you can find me on my 80s comedy movie forum called "What's a dickfer?"

jewels: You're funny.

Will-i-am84: Why do you work so late?

jewels: I have another job too and it's late at night. Besides, as a camgirl it doesn't really matter when you're on. There are always people on the Internet from all over.

Will-i-am84: I have another job too. I work for Eureka! do you know them?

jewels: nope. What's that?

Will-i-am84: It's a social network for academics. It's like *Real* for professors and stuff.

jewels: sounds boring.

Will-i-am84: The job, or Eureka!?

jewels: haha. I meant Eureka!. But I'll look it up. Look, Will, your time is almost up. Do you want to watch me?

Will-i-am84: No, not today. I just wanted to talk. Do you like this— What you do?

jewels: I like to masturbate, so yes. Sometimes I don't feel like it though, so then I don't work, but for me I always seem to feel like it. And anyways, I'm not having sex for money am I? I'm not a prostitute, or some cam-whore.

Will-i-am84: I know. I didn't mean it like that. Don't take it the wrong way. I'm sorry. I have to go now.

jewels: Will, I'm not offended, I was just saying. Sheesh, you are sensitive.

Will-i-am-84: Yeah. Anyway, I just have to go to work now. I'll see you again next week, umm, maybe Tuesday. Okay? I hope you're on.

jewels: For you, of course I'll be.

On their third date, because he felt he had courted her enough, or because he just wanted to see her perform, Will didn't talk much.

jewels: Willy! how are you? I missed you!

Will-i-am84: I missed you too. I think today I want to watch you.

jewels: Finally! [she smiles].

Julia's routine for Will began with her turning up the music. Then she stood up from her desk and began to slowly pull off her top. It was tight; she let it slide up to reveal the bottoms of her breasts. With a quick tug it was up and off and with a slight bounce her round, small breasts popped forth into view. With her top off, she began to dance slowly to the music, slightly swaying her hips; she massaged her left breast with her left hand until her small brown nipple got hard. With her right hand, she unzipped her skirt and let it fall to the floor. Underneath, she had on black lace panties and black stockings held up by a garter belt. She unclipped the garter belt and sat on the end of the bed. She brought one leg up and with slow methodic motions peeled down one stocking, then repeated her actions for the other leg. The black panties were off next—she pulled them down with her thumb. Except for the garter belt, she was naked.

Will was extremely turned on, and he typed: "I'm so turned on right now."

Without responding, Julia stood away from the bed and kept dancing; slow supple movements, curving, slowly twisting up and down, rotating, turning now and again to show Will her ass and smooth moon-white back. She returned to the bed for a second time and lay on her back with her knees up and legs spread. She was still using her left hand, playing with her left breast, but now with her right hand she began to rub between her legs.

Will was beyond himself, and he typed: "!!!"

She stood up again and leaned forward into the camera, continuing to play with her breasts, rubbing them, squeezing her nipples. Finally, she turned around and got back on the bed on her knees with her ass facing the camera. Her hand came through her legs. She began to make slight pelvic movements; she inserted her fingers; breathing heavily, moaning, she made herself climax for Will. She fell forward, time ran out, the screen went blank, and there was nothing more between them.

Since then, almost two months ago, little has changed in the pattern of their relationship. They've seen each other a total of sixteen times, and although Will has not asked, Julia has still not given him her name. Will has not yet heard her voice, for, although she turns on the microphone for Will to hear her moan and climax, she turns it off again right afterward. As to their conversations, they're quite banal—they mainly talk about films (Will), the "Quebers" (Julia's word for the Québécois. She's an Anglo and did eventually tell Will she lived in Montreal), friends and work. Julia has performed for Will four more times, but on all other occasions they have just talked. Sometimes she talks half-naked on the bed, other times she sits at her desk fully clothed.

Some patterns in their relationship that bear mentioning: Will has never asked Julia to perform twice in a row, and the level of communication between Will and Julia has become relaxed and comfortable, displaying a growing sexual and emotional openness. In one recent conversation, Julia was wearing glasses:

Will-i-am84: You wear glasses?

jewels: Sometimes if I'm tired, or if my eyes get sore from staring at the screen so much. Do you like them?

Will-i-am84: I do. With your hair pulled back into a ponytail like that, and those glasses, you look like one of the secretaries at my work.

jewels: sexy?

Will-i-am84: Yes.

jewels: You have a thing for the sexy businesswoman look, Willy?

Will-i-am84: I guess I do.

Predictably, for their next date, Julia dressed as a "businesswoman" and stripped down from a power suit into nothing but her glasses before getting onto the bed and climaxing for Will.

Perhaps the final thing we need to mention about Will is that he's been acting strange and erratic recently in his conversations with Julia, abruptly switching subjects according to no recognizable thought pattern. We can't account for his behaviour based on his relationship with Julia, and suspect there's something else going on, some external pressure outside of his love life. It's good for him that he now regards Julia as someone who listens. He needs her, and it demonstrates Will's level of trust and the degree of importance he places on her. In this final dialogue, the most recent we were given access to, we can see how affective their bond has become:

jewels: Willy, how are you!? I'm happy to see you.

Will-i-am84: I'm okay.

jewels: not so talkative today? You want to watch?

Will-i-am84: How are you? What have you been doing?

jewels: Just getting by Willy, working a lot, but spring is coming. Montreal is so beautiful in the springtime.

Will-i-am84: Yeah. Vancouver is pretty gross right now.

jewels: raining a lot?

Will-i-am84: Yeah, but that's not it. I like the rain.

jewels: haha

Will-i-am84: I don't know what it is exactly. My new friend at work, Tom, he thinks this place is a dump, and he thinks *Real* and Eureka! are a kind of a quasi-spy network, or something.

jewels: what do you think?

Will-i-am84: I don't know. I don't know anything about that. I hate thinking about it.

jewels: oh, Will. I'm sorry.

Will-i-am84: I've just been feeling strange lately, naked or something. I don't know. I think everything will be fine, but I feel really strange, like I'm naked in the doctor's office and he's staring at me. It's an awkward feeling.

jewels: It'll be fine, Will, everyone gets a bit down now and then. You'll see. Try not to think about it all so much. Watch a funny movie, like you like.

Will-i-am84: I haven't been able to laugh at them recently. It's even been hard to write on my *RealSeminar*. It's not because I'm down. I feel just as though I'm losing touch with that part of me somehow.

jewels: it's just a phase, Will, don't worry, we all go in and out of phases like that. Don't make me worry about you. I like you too much, okay?

Will-i-am84: I like you so much. It'll be fine, I'm just stressed maybe.

Their relationship has obviously come quite far. They're close friends and they're engaged in a form of sexual relationship. But Will has not once brought up any kind of normal relationship topics—the future, visiting her, moving in together and so forth. He's never mentioned meeting her in person, for example. What this means is that he holds no illusions about Julia. He knows exactly what he wants from her, and part of that is to keep her, mysterious, where she is. For Will, Julia will never materialize.

So is she a sexual object, then? In her relationship with Will, is she being objectified? The short, uncomplicated answer is yes. He pays for her sexual services, so regardless of the form, she is a sexual object.

She relies on her beauty to make a living—this is the truth of her life, one she has chosen. Yet with each man, she makes a new choice. Julia does not need Will's business; she is quite popular online with other men and women as it is. But she lets Will come back—she wants him to. She has made the choice for him because in many ways, the relationship goes beyond money and serving as his object.

The more complicated understanding of the question is that most people are objectified, but they just don't know it. When we work for a wage at a demeaning job that doesn't make use of our true talents, we are being objectified. Julia has chosen her profession, but she is a sex worker who, to make a living, is forced to be billed as "jewels." She is exploited for profit by a greedy and sleazy Montreal-based website, as Will in data management is being exploited for profit by a Vancouver-based startup. The economics behind both situations are identical. It's only our collective moral sense that makes one seem worse than the other.

When we took this assignment from Doctor Officer Elias Degair, we assumed that there was some kind of illicit and/or illegal activity going on with Will, since that's what our organization normally looks into. We want to make it clear that there is nothing illegal about Will and Julia's relationship, or about her terms of employment with The Girl Next Door. She is not a child, she is not a sex slave, she was not kidnapped from a poor country and smuggled here to provide sex for her freedom. These are the cases WAGI is normally concerned with. Julia is over eighteen. She is alluring and nubile, and she tantalizes, but she also takes steps to ensure that her audience is over eighteen. What she does is perfectly legal. In any case, it is the website that would have to bear the burden if something went wrong. The Girl Next Door has to ensure that its viewers and members are legal or they are liable, not the other way around.

In conclusion, we must emphatically state that there is no criminal offense or victimization in the relationship between Will Potenco and Julia Singer.

Truly,

Women Against Gender Inequality.

William and I
by Thomas Vickers
IV

I'm sitting next to Will, who's focused and working hard to be sure. I'm bored as hell, sorting again, but it's not all that bad. I've already set up three institutions: Equal Voice Equals Progress, the Animal Welfare Board and the Congress of Labour in Canada. None of them do any research whatsoever, but since I say they deserve a place in Eureka! they get in. In the meantime, I've also denied three other companies that most definitely do research and should have gotten in: Vital Health (a pharmaceutical company), Sifter Co. (a mining company), and Fourier Chemical Co. This clandestine activism may not seem too radical, but I'm pretty sure that it's small acts like these, by people like me in the remotest corners of institutions, that really make a difference. It's that old story: the pebble dislodges and rolls down the mountain and causes a landslide. I'm dislodging pebbles like a motherfucker.

Jen and I have been on opposite schedules, so I don't get to see her much. Today, though, I'm working a full shift, so maybe she'll be here in the afternoon. I decided I wanted a day off to get drunk on the beach. It's a risky thing to do, drink in public in Vancouver. I know that, but I'm willing to take my chances with the stupid Syndics. Anyway, to compensate for the day I want off to get drunk, I have to work this double shift. The good thing about working a double is that you get a free catered lunch; the bad thing, of course, is that for eight hours instead of four, you're stuck doing the most fucking boring, mind-numbing work. Will's a regular superman for enduring it day in and day out.

Around 10:00 a.m., Stu walks over. There was something different about him that I hadn't noticed until then.

"Hey guys," he says, "how goes it?"

"Good," I say.

"Okay," says Will without looking away from his screen.

"Stu," I say, "you're wearing pants. What the hell?"

"Yeah," he says looking down, looking them over, "I put them on when I got here—new rules from Dana that Management have to wear pants. They're really uncomfortable and ride up into my balls."

"Next you're going to have to comb your hair."

"Never!" he says. "Anyway, Tom, you're in for the full day, so I think that I'd like Will to show you gatekeeping." He turns to Will. "Will, do you think you can train Tom on the Fence?"

Will looks up. "Sure, Stu, no problem." He smiles.

Stu leaves, and Will, smiling, eagerly starts to explain gatekeeping, which sounds pretty fucking ominous.

"Eureka! doesn't let just anyone in," he begins. "You already know most of what I'll say, but just to reiterate: To get in, you need to have an academic or approved institutional domain name as an e-mail address. If you have that you're in automatically. If not, you have to be able to explain that you do research. It's at that point that gatekeeping comes in. Gatekeeping is verifying that the new users without a proper domain name actually are who they say they are, and do what they say they do. Get it?"

"So far," I say suspiciously.

"Okay. So then," he gestures, "you can go to your admin page, and down to new users." He pauses as I do it. "Yep, there," he points.

I do as he says. The page opens to a list of people. Under each name is a brief statement written by that person as to why they want to be on Eureka! and what kind of research they do.

"That list, we call the Fence…"

"Are you serious?"

He looks at me like *I'm* crazy, but continues without flinching. "Basically, what you have to do now is a bit of research to try and verify what these people claim. It doesn't have to be extensive. Just find out if they're part of the organization they say they are, if they have a degree and publications and so on. If they pass, you hit that button at the bottom, 'candidate processed'…"

"Are you kidding man? This job is so fucking unbelievable." I shake my head and flap my arms.

"What do you mean?"

"The fucking 'Fence?' Does it have barbed wire, this 'Fence'?"

"What? No, it's just a name."

"It's not just a name, Will, and this is not harmless, so stop acting so stupid." I pause because I want to see if it's sinking in, but when he says absolutely nothing like normal, which leaves me even more confused about him, I go on. He's not getting off the hook this time. "Data management, Will? It's like we're fucking spying. It's barbaric. I mean, 'gatekeeping?' We're fucking border guards, damn immigration officers guarding a 'Fence.' Listen to the language, man. Eureka! sounds like a fucking country here. It's a country and we, you and me, are at the border with our AKs. The data—that's not data, that's people. The research into 'who they say they are,' that's a background check. Then what happens? They get in and we start sorting them, slotting them, moving them in and out of categories? It's fucking crazy." I start to laugh it's so absurd. "It's a good thing I hold academics in such low regard," I say, shaking my head. "The fucking morons; if anyone does, they should know better than to trust their information on the Internet."

Will looks back and forth quickly between his monitor and mine as though verifying that we're seeing the same thing. I wonder if he's ever thought about this. Does he see this "data" as peoples' lives; that what we do is to manage lives? I don't raise the direct question. Maybe it's just easier for him to see it as an abstract numbers game: McNamara, Eichmann, I get it. I just can't fathom how someone who's done this job for so long and who spends as much time on *Real* as Will, could not have thought about it. But then again, maybe that's the point.

"Anyway," I say, "is there anything else to this shit, Will?"

Nothing.

"Will!?" I turn to him.

He's staring down at his hands on the keyboard. "Yeah, umm, no," he says. "Only, if they aren't who they say they are then you click the 'fail' button."

"Okay. They fail. For sure. Great." I laugh, shaking my head.

For the rest of the morning I'm a border guard at the US/Mexican 'Fence' kicking out the illegals and letting in the worthies. Will and I don't speak much more. He seems aloof—maybe he's clueing in, or he might be just lost in thought or in his work. I don't know; he's just real quiet.

At 12:30 p.m., after letting a ton of illegals cross the Fence, I get up and walk down the hall to the large common room for lunch. The room has about a dozen big tables, and it's pretty full of people, most of whom I've never met. I can pick out the programmers—they're all men

130

and for some reason they all have some kind of facial hair: a soul patch, or sideburns, or a moustache, or a goatee or a combination (never a full beard). Most have thick-framed glasses on, they're all in blue jeans and golf shirts, and they look like assholes. There are others, too, who look aloof from the world and who I take it are from Creative. Regardless, I don't talk to any of them and they don't talk to me. While I'm standing in line for food, I see Will, who left just before me, but he's sitting alone at a table in the corner engrossed in something on his eyePhone, so I don't disturb him. I get my lunch—the sign says penne all'arrabbiata—and look around for a seat. At a table in front of me are Stu, Deirdre and the guy with the dreadlocks, so I go over and sit there.

"Hey," I say, as I sit.

"Oh, hi. How are you, Tom? Are you having a good day?" says Deirdre in her friendly singsong.

"Not bad," I say. I look at the guy with the dreadlocks, whose name is actually Greg, and I say, "Aren't you part-time too?"

"Yeah," he says, "but sometimes I come and eat anyway."

"But part-timers aren't given a free lunch."

"Meh." His mouth is full of pasta and red sauce. It's falling out there's so much. It's actually pretty fucking disgusting.

"Whatever. So, what are you guys talking about?" I ask.

"People," says Stu.

"Yeah, people and money and stuff," says Greg, mouth still full.

"People and money and stuff?" I echo. "Like what?" I take a bite of my pasta and it's fucking spicy. "Fuck, this is spicy! How can you eat it like that?" I ask Greg.

He laughs with a full mouth. Gross.

Deirdre laughs. She is pretty. I have to give it to Stu. I assume he's fucking her, since they're always together.

"I was explaining," says Stu, "that this morning on my ride to work

131

I accidentally splashed a women with mud and she got so upset she said she would report me to the Syndics."

"What did you do?" I ask.

"I apologized as best I could, and tried to help clean it— it was only one spot—but she was going berserk. I just had to leave."

"One time an old man on the bus said he would report me for my dreads," adds Greg.

"We're already at denunciations, great," I say.

"Anyway," says Stu, "I was saying before that, that since the economy is good again, I can start up with my RRSPs."

I laugh.

"What?" says Stu, grinning.

"Stu, you're a bit young to be talking about retirement, aren't you?"

"You gotta think about that stuff, man."

"You do," says Greg, again talking with a mouth full of penne.

"I suppose," I say.

"I'm just happy about *RealEconomy* and the Rebound," says Stu. "It was looking pretty grim there."

"Yes, yes," says Deirdre, "it was."

"Do you have a *RealJob*, Tom?" asks Stu.

I laugh again. "Ah, no man, I don't. I'm not on *Real*."

"Really?"

"But how do you function?" asks Deirdre, in real disbelief.

"Same as I always have."

"I've never met anyone not on *Real*," says Greg.

"That's funny, Greg, since it's only been around for less than ten years."

"You know what I mean," he says, shovelling more penne into his mouth, lips covered in sauce.

"Yeah, well… do you actually think the economy is better?" I ask.

"That's what I was saying," says Greg, chewing. "It's *not* better."

"Obviously," I agree, thinking, and I don't think I'm alone here, that anyone with dreadlocks must be a radical of some sort.

"I was saying that we still need to cut back more," he says. "We spent all of our money. My uncle says we should have cut welfare completely, and that it was a bad idea to begin with." He finally wipes his mouth.

"What!? No, no, not that," I say.

"Yep, the Scare gave us the chance, but we didn't take it. My uncle also says we should be cutting all that 'environment-friendly' shit. He says it's a huge waste of money and that we should be going for full nuclear power since it's better and cheaper."

I'm nonplussed. Stu and Deirdre seem to be enjoying their food.

I don't want to get into a fight. "Okay, that's really stupid You've sort of totally mixed up your argument there, but yeah, I guess nuclear can be a good form of energy as long as it's kept clean and safe. But to say cutting back on the other forms of energy production is a 'waste,' man that's stupid."

"Yes and there are the accidents," says Deirdre. "Japan, for example."

"Right, there's that. That was tragic, nuclear needs to be made safe."

"That was good what happened," says Greg, mouth full to capacity again.

"What did you say? What was 'good'?" I ask.

He looks up from shovelling pasta into his stupid maw. I guess I look like I'm about to shove my fist in his face because he kind of pulls back. My face must be red from the fucking spicy pasta.

"I mean." He wipes his face with the back of his hand getting sauce everywhere, and continues, "that it's stuff like that in Japan, that's how

133

we learn."

"Learn what exactly, dipshit? That earthquakes and tsunamis destroy nuclear power plants?"

"Take it easy, guy. Don't call me a dipshit," he says. "What we learn is that Japanese stuff is garbage and that we shouldn't trust it."

"Are you a fucking idiot?" I say. "Are you joking?" I really want to punch him square in the face. Instead I look at Stu and Deirdre for some support, but they don't even nod or acknowledge or back me up at all.

"Don't call me that. It's true."

I glare at him and shake my head. "You're just dumb, right? You're repeating things your uncle, whoever the fuck that is, says…"

"I'm not dumb. I'm going to med school."

"At U.B.C?"

"Yep."

"That hollowed out shell of a program. That doesn't impress me, you fucking stooge."

"Okay guys," interrupts Stu, "that's enough. I think we'll have to pick this discussion up another time."

"I have to get back now," says Deirdre, looking at me sympathetically as she stands.

"Yeah," says Greg, "I should probably get to work too."

Fuck you is what I want to say, but, "Yeah, whatever" comes out. "I'm going to finish this obviously overly-spicy arrabbiata. I'll see you in twenty minutes, Stu."

When I get back to the office, I guess my face is still red and Will asks me what's wrong.

"Nothing much, Will, but that guy with the dreadlocks, he's a real piece of shit."

Will laughs.

"What's so funny?" I say.

"You know he's Dana's nephew, right?"

"Dana's his uncle? Right. Great. I almost just got in a fight with him."

"Oh no," he says. "Why?"

"It's not so important. He's just a dumb fucking idiot is all. I guess it runs in the family."

"You better be careful," he says. "If the guy with the dreadlocks tells Dana anything bad about you, Dana'll just look for reasons to fire you."

"Ah, fuck them both," I say. "They're a bunch of cocks, fucking cock-family." I turn back to face my screen and shake my head. "Assholes."

I don't like Dana and Will doesn't either. With me it's automatic: he's the boss and I hate bosses. It was pretty evident, just from looking at his asshole face, when I first saw him, that Dana's a vicious bastard. His approach to worker relations is what anyone in animal training knows as the dog theory: you beat a dog once, and afterwards all you need to do is show him the whip; you rub the dog's face in its piss once, it stops pissing on the rug. It's fucking brutal. It's an approach to humans that would get you lynched in a revolution. Unfortunately, it works just fine in a dictatorship, or a complacent, apathetic place full of docile muppets like an office building in Canada.

With Will, though, it's a bit more complicated. Will's big problem is that he thinks Dana's unpredictable. I get that. No matter how hard you work, no matter how good a job you do, you just can't be comfortable around a boss or any guy with power over you who's unpredictable. A guy who bases his decisions and his actions on feelings, rather than any kind of professional or reasoned understanding is never easy to be around. Will thinks that's why Dana fires people—because he doesn't like the way they look one day, or because his coffee tasted like shit, or because his wife didn't make him breakfast. He might be right, who knows, but after working this job even as short a time as I have, I really don't see how anyone could fuck up data management. To get fired here, you must really have to shit the bed. But I never really see Dana. He goes into his office in the morning, closes his door, and only comes out for a piss or a shit or a coffee. Sometimes he yells at Stu; other times he reorganizes something that doesn't need reorganizing. He spends a lot of time in the kitchen. Jen told me that he hits on the women. Lascivious scumbags with power like him, they know no fucking shame. Dana, that short, squat, greasy haired, wet-lipped, fat-fingered, chubby little pervert, waits in the kitchen to hit on the female employees. As Jen described it he leers about, eating food meant for the employees, waiting for the opportune moment to graze against a female body, rub up against an ass or a tit and brag about himself, or invite the female employees out for "business drinks" to talk about their futures. I've never seen him do this, the pervert stuff anyway, but I do see his way of standing next to the coffee machine, licking his lips, then leaning against the counter at an angle that enhances his paunch, preparing to deliver his routine. I imagine it goes something like this:

Dana: "You know when Brian, Frank and I started this company, it was just a dream we had. We had no idea that we'd change the world."

Uninterested Female Employee: "Oh?"

Dana: "Yes. And you know something else, our ambitions, Brian's and mine, are limitless. He thinks we'll win the Nobel Prize for what we're doing."

Uninterested Female Employee: "Really?"

Dana: "Yes, yes." He leans in, she leans back. "Eureka! is now *the* platform, *the* tool, that enables scientific and academic research to

136

move forward. Before us, it used to be academic journals, conferences: all very formal. What we've done is we've gone around these, and around all the pomp of academia and the publishing world to create a new kind of utopia where academic research can go on, free and uninhibited."

Uninterested Female Employee: "Crazy."

Dana: "It is, I know. And just think, now you're part of that. It may not seem like it, because you don't see the forest for the trees, but you're helping to create this."

Uninterested Female Employee: "Wow, I never saw it that way."

Dana: "It's amazing. And if you want to talk about your role here, my office is always open, or we could get a drink one day after work."

Something like that. I don't know. Maybe I haven't done the uninterested female employee justice in my imagination, but that's the picture I have. Jen's convinced he has a really small penis, too. She says, "You can just tell with guys like that," but who knows. Anyway, my hatred is natural. Will's is convoluted, but I get it, because I know he's got such a strange way of seeing things.

I brood over the lunchroom incident for the next couple hours while gatekeeping. I won't get fired. There's no way. I'm just too good at this shit. But, still, it drives me nuts, these idiots, these dickheads like Dana and Greg that think like they do. Finally, I turn to Will and ask him what *he* thinks about the economy. I expect that he'll probably stay silent, maybe grumble and deflect my question and just keep on working, but he doesn't. He tells me that he actually thinks about it a lot. He says he knows his role: with his *RealJob* and at Eureka! he's just an employee, a worker.

And he says to me, "There's nothing wrong with that, Tom, because for society to work you have to have ranks of some kind to provide incentive. In this society we have so many ranks and positions;

workers, managers, and so on upwards. Eventually, I want to be a manager, so I'll have to be a worker first. I've accepted that. The problem is that some of these CEOs and executives, they didn't go through the ranks and they don't understand what it's like to be on the lower rungs of the ladder. I would love it if Dana did what I do once or twice."

"Or go shovel shit for a day," I say.

"Have you seen that 1980s film, *Trading Places*, with Dan Aykroyd and Eddie Murphy?"

"I think so, maybe when I was a kid. Jamie Lee Curtis shows her tits, right?"

"Yes, you perv, but that's not my point. The point is you need to have people like Dana trade places with a poor person once in a while to create empathy. It's kind of like on *Real*."

"On *Real*!?"

"Yes. On *Real* it's your *Real-ID* Number that gives you a kind of alternative status."

"*Real-ID* number? Fuck man. And?"

"And so, I can be someone I'm not when I'm on *Real*. I can be someone with power. That feels nice sometimes."

"It does, does it?"

"You know," he continues, "on *Real* I moderate this *RealSeminar* that's dedicated to 1980s comedy films…"

I laugh. "Really?"

"Yes," he says. "You know what those are, right? The *RealSeminars*?"

"I have an idea."

"Then why are you laughing?" he says in earnest. "There's real important dialogue that goes on in those. Probably better than in your PhD classes, up in your ivory tower." He's getting angry.

"You're probably right. Relax, man."

"Anyway," he calms down. "To make my point. I found out a while ago that Stu was a member in my seminar. I also found out that he has a higher *Real-ID* number than me." He pauses for effect. "And so on *Real*, and especially in my *RealSeminar*, it's like I'm his boss!" He's grinning wildly.

What a fucking nut. "You're a crazy guy, Will," I say.

But *he* has to listen to *me*." He's still grinning ear-to-ear. "Do you get it?" he nods to himself and I wait, because I know he wants to answer his own question. "It's like *Trading Places!*"

"Oh, I get it," I say sarcastically. "It's really just not the example of class war that I had in mind."

"Why aren't you on *Real*, anyway? You never talk about it. I mean, everyone is on it," he says.

"That dickhead with the dreads at lunch said the same thing. I can't believe the shock people get just because I'm not using the fucking thing."

"Well, it's hard to believe Tom. *Real*'s innovative. And with the *Real* Lenses coming out soon. It's pretty amazing what they'll do."

"Yeah, I'm not so sure. But, look, I was on it. When I first started my PhD, most of my friends and I were on it. I mean, how could you not be? Everyone was talking about it. It was like a new car, all shiny and bright and smelling fresh, promising freedom. And you had to join, right? Man, all those grad students, the real critical ones, the professors, everyone was joining up, they jumped right on. 'It's good for our networking,' they said. What fucking idiots. Anyway, so yeah, I was on. It looked great and the pressure to join was too much."

"So how'd you leave then? Why did you leave?"

"Will, it's not crack. It's not so hard to leave. Maybe I was helped by circumstance. After I dropped out of my PhD I realized that most of my so-called friends on *Real* were just self-serving colleagues from my department. Parasites. They were never my friends to begin with. I didn't talk to them outside of class, and after I left Vancouver, I didn't talk to them at all. I stayed on *Real* for a while, but I realized that all I was doing was reading their Canvas posts, more to laugh at how dumb they were than talk to them. Anyway, I started to feel gross. So there was that sort of personal side of it, but I mean, there was all the other stuff, too, Will. You must have an idea why someone would leave *Real*? It's not a secret what's going on there. It's well reported. I mean, first it was the advertisers who preyed on you. But okay, that was kind of fine, since they've been doing that for years and *Real* was just a new tool for that. Then it was all the privacy stuff: we had no privacy, we wanted better privacy settings, we supposedly got them, but then we find out that they meant nothing anyway, and that *Real*, Blabber, and all the rest were handing over our information to the government all along. It's unbelievable. I asked you before if you've read the 'Secret History.' Have you?"

"I want to. I mean I've read about it. My friend Ryan says that it's just a waste and a crappy conspiracy theory, and the guy who wrote it is a coward…"

"Your friend Ryan is an idiot, Will. I'm sorry, but he says that because he probably read one of the hacked up versions, or he just doesn't want to confront what it says."

"There's more than one version?"

"There are plenty. The original was a well documented forty page piece of investigative journalism. It called Rothsteen out for being in compliance with weapons manufacturing for the U.S. government and for being an American and Chinese spy. Later the whole document was removed, pretty much erased form history, by Rothsteen who filed charges of libel against any media source that published it. The chicken-shit editors all fell in line. Any version you see today is going to be edited to shit."

"Really? Why ?"

"Things and people, and people's voices—they're written out of history all the time. It's how it goes."

"So why should I read it then?"

"You just should. Look, have you ever clicked on a link or a news story on *Real* that was about a protest or a riot or the poor, or any kind of socially progressive, maybe anti-government demonstration? Have you ever written on your Canvas or in that *RealDiary* about any negative feelings towards the government?"

"Maybe."

"They have technology that picks up that stuff man, and if they pick it up from you, then they have every reason to look into your information and make judgments about you. The point in the 'Secret History,' that 'communication is confession,' is pretty persuasive. I don't see how that can be denied."

"In Canada though?" he says, actually surprised. "All that spy stuff is in the States, and all my privacy settings are at the highest. I … I just don't understand why they would …"

"They do it because they can. Think of Trudeau's War Measures Act, but permanent. In Vancouver, Special Decree 451 has not been revoked. They can do anything they want now for no reason at all. And the States? Are you serious? They're probably spying on us right now. They fucking spy on everyone. They're fucking nuts."

"But it's good."

"What's good?"

"*Real*'s good," he says with conviction.

"Well, it is a remarkable piece of apparatus, to be sure," I say. "When you look at it in its individual parts, when you break it apart into its elements, it's not all that evil. There's the mail, the video, the news, the information, the Canvas and so on. But, you can't build up a full picture of someone when you break them into their individual components—you can't understand *Real* unless you take it as a whole. That's also what makes it so hard to leave. You maybe don't like one small thing, but you won't leave just because you don't like one thing. I know it takes a lot for a person to leave *Real*. But they're fucking spying on you man. End of argument. Why do you like it so much, anyway?"

"It enables my entire life to function."

"That's crazy. You're dependent on it."

"I am," he says

"That's just not good, Will."

He pauses to think. "Well," he says, "I guess not entirely. It's hard to tell. I don't talk to my girlfriend on it, but everything else—well, not here of course, but—well here too—so everything, almost."

"Girlfriend?"

"Yes, my girlfriend."

"She's not on *Real*?"

"She is, but we don't use it to talk."

"Hmmm. Okay. But look, that's not really important. The point is that your whole life is on a platform for anyone to see. You're in bed with that snake Sydney Rothsteen and with all his friends. You're naked. They're probing you and taking samples, and you can't do anything about it."

"Sydney Rothsteen is an amazing person. And actually, he rebutted all that stuff in the 'Secret History,' by the way. I did watch that interview, and that was on *Real*."

"Yes, we all saw that, it wasn't just on *Real*. I mean, Rothsteen isn't interviewed often. It was a pretty big joke. The questions were scripted; the woman, Cheryl Dean, who interviewed him, she used to be so critical when she was independent, but her interview… she's just another corporate hack now. But look, forget about that, because Sydney Rothsteen *is* a snake. What is it called when you sign up to *Real* again?"

"A compact?"

"Right, a compact with a snake and a thief. You know what Solzhenitsyn said?"

"Who?"

"Alexander Solzhenitsyn, the Russian author. He said, 'You'll not get fruit from a stone, nor good from a thief.' Rothsteen is a thief, plain and simple. And those numbers, my god, Will, those *Real-ID* Numbers that you're so enthralled with, don't they remind you of something? The numbering of people in a concentration camp maybe?"

Will laughs. "Students in university have numbers too, Tom."

"Not pinned to their chest or tattooed on their arm, and that doesn't make it better, Will. That just shows how much we've all come to accept being numbered. And it's not fucking funny. Prisoners in concentration camps used their numbers for status too, just like you say they do on *Real*. And what about the *Real-ID* page? 'Each profile is unique,' right? That's what Rothsteen said. Sound like a fingerprint? And how can they be unique when you all have them? It's ridiculous. You're all identical to him. You're a means to a profit."

He sniggers again and I can't believe it.

"You're missing the other side of it," he says. "*Real* also enables people. People can make money on *Real*. They can organize on *Real*. Those revolutions in the Middle East and all that…"

"You got me there, Will," I laugh. "*Real* and Blabber said they made those revolutions and then everyone on *Real* and Blabber believed them. In fact, everyone who thinks this kind of communication is setting us free believed them. But if you actually looked into it you might find a different story—a history of revolt in those places that goes a bit further back then fucking *Real* and Blabber and their so-called revolutionary credentials. And look now at the tragedy of those places, like Egypt—they're run by the military, in a state of emergency too, and all those people that used *Real* and Blabber during the revolution they've all been questioned, arrested. Some imprisoned, some executed. Real fucking progressive! And you know why? Because their information was given to governments by *Real* and Blabber. Will, these are not tools used *by* us, they are tools used *against* us."

"So, what then?" he says. "It can't be so black and white."

"Frankly, some things are, and if you actually care, you have to do something."

"Like what?"

"Well, you can give them everything you are and all you have for free, or you can leave. It's called boycott. It's an old strategy, but it can be effective. And it's a start."

"You'd have to boycott the Internet completely."

"Well, no, Will, you don't. Don't make it so difficult. You just have to be smart and careful."

"That's stupid."

"No it isn't."

"You're full of shit, Tom."

"Pardon me? You're being real stupid right now. If you don't want to leave, fine. If you think you have nothing to hide, that's great. But why does your e-mail address have a password? Why does your bank account have a PIN number? Why does your fucking apartment have curtains? For Christ's sake, everyone has something to hide. Everything you think about, all your desires, your little dark fantasies

144

and impulses, all the things you let leak out on places like *Real* without even knowing it, are not hidden. And trust me man, innocence and guilt are relative terms. One man's terrorist is another man's freedom fighter. And look, I wanted to have this talk with you about *Real*, and we did, but if you think I'm full of shit, or if you think I'm just making this up, you can go fuck yourself."

"Okay. I'm sorry. I didn't mean it..."

"You know, where I live, in northern B.C., far from your fucking *Real* and your Sydney fucking Rothsteen and the video games that you call jobs, the government is busy fracking—pumping liquid underground to force gas out. It comes out all over the place, into the air, into the fresh water, onto people's land. My friend who has a farm just delivered a two-headed cow. For real. His six-year-old daughter has to live there. At any time, the place could go up in a huge gas explosion. That's real. That..." I start to stammer, "I mean what the fuck man, that..."

"I said I was sorry. I didn't know about that," he says.

"No, of course not. How could you? Why would you want to? Do you think *Real* reports on things like that? Do you think anyone does? Vancouver has become so disconnected that they think smoking is a problem. The people here care more about not eating meat than humans going mutant. It's fucking shameful. Tell me something, Will, when was the last time you saw a crowd of people gathered freely here in Vancouver to protest anything?"

He shrugs.

"Okay, any old crowd then?"

"I don't know. Canada Day, I guess."

"So, the last time you saw a crowd was when the government sanctioned it?"

"I suppose so, yes."

"You don't think there's something wrong with that?"

"People are afraid to. I never thought about it more than the Scare."

"Exactly! That's the goddamned point!"

Just then there's a sudden BANG—a sharp, terrifying thud against the window next to Will. Both he and I are practically thrown from our seats from the shock of the noise. It sounded like someone took a baseball bat to a pumpkin. I look around the room; everyone in the office is staring at the window. Will acts first. He gets out of his chair, opens the window, and looks down towards the street.

"It's a bird," he says. "Look."

I stand next to him and look down. On the sidewalk below is a mass of black twitching feathers, jerking around in circles.

"Looks like a raven," I say. "One time up north one flew into the windshield of a car I was driving—scared the shit out of me and nearly drove me off the road."

"Why the hell would it fly into the window!?"

"I don't know Will. Maybe it heard what you were saying."

Others in the office start to gather at the windows. I hear murmurs of "how disgusting" and "that's so sad." On the street below, too, some people are gathering, staring at the bird as it jerks and jolts and flops around.

"Someone should step on its head for Christ's sake," I say. "It's clearly suffering and going to die."

"I'm going down." Will turns and rushes to the elevator.

I follow him. By the time we get down to the street, two pairs of Syndics have arrived and are standing, just staring at the poor bird. It's barely moving.

"Aren't you going to do something?" Will screams angrily at the Syndics as we arrive. "Put the thing out of its misery, you shitheads!"

"We can't." The tall, skinny one shrugs.

"It likely has rabies," says the short one.

"And probably fleas," says the fat one.

"Are you getting all this?" says the last one to the tall one.

"Yes," says the tall one, who is using her Smartphone to film the poor bird as it dies.

Will's watching their lips move, but he's not listening. "You're a bunch of fucking animals!" he screams.

He tries to push through to the suffering bird, but they block him. The tall one pans her Smartphone over and points it at Will's face, while the fat one holds Will back. At that moment, the bird stops moving. Will pushes the Smartphone away and clenches his fist, and for a very brief second it looks like he's going to punch the fat one. His eyes are red and his lips are twitching, but instead of swinging, he turns and walks off. I want to follow, but decide to stick around instead to see what'll happen.

A couple of small drones have arrived and are hovering, doing circles overhead, and it's not long before a white van with the Vancouver Public Health logo on the side shows up. Two men in white masks, white plastic coveralls and blue rubber gloves step out. They open the back of the van, take out a plastic snow shovel and a garbage bag, shovel the dead raven into the bag, throw the bag and shovel in the back of the van and drive off. The whole unceremonious operation is over in less than two minutes. They hadn't said a thing.

When I get back up to the office, Will's sitting at his desk with his head in his hands.

"You okay?" I ask.

"Yes, I'm fine now," he says.

I can see that he's not. "What are you doing?" I ask. He has *Real* open.

I'm trying to compose something on my Canvas, but I can't."

"Why are you doing that?"

He's not paying attention to me. "You know in those old cartoons," he says, "the dead crows with crosses for eyes lying on their backs with their feet in the air…I used to think those were really funny, but now, I, I …" He stammers.

"Will, you need to try and relax. Stop drawing and go get a glass of water and sit down in the common room, or tell Stu you have to go. You only have thirty minutes left in your shift anyways."

He's lost. "Do you like The Smiths?" he asks.

"The band?"

"Yes."

"They're okay, I suppose. Why, what's that got to do with it?"

"I always thought their music was sad, but now I think I'm wrong."

"I'm sorry, Will."

"I've never seen anything die. I don't want to see anything die."

He gets up and walks towards the bathroom. I sit and I think about the raven. The stupid bird didn't see the glass window and flew right into it. It's pretty obvious. Maybe its brain was fucked up. It's just that in these parts, a dead raven is a like a bad omen. It has to do with Raven and the first men. It's Raven, say the Haida, who first opened and coaxed Man out of a clam shell. Raven is responsible for humankind. Raven's the trickster. Cunning Raven, he opens the shell so that he can have someone to laugh at and play with—Man—and now he flies into a window and kills himself. Are you kidding? That's just not funny.

Will comes back and starts to gather his things.

"You okay?" I ask again.

He doesn't hear me.

"Will" I say louder. "You okay?"

"Yeah. I'll be fine. Thanks."

"Look, I'm off tomorrow—what are you doing tomorrow night?"

"Tomorrow night?"

"Yeah."

"I usually see my girlfriend."

"Can you see her another night? I have a couple friends showing up in town. We're going out to drink. You should come. It'll be good for you."

"I don't drink often."

"That's all the more reason for you to come. You know, there's this old Russian saying that goes: 'The hard times brace you, and the soft times drive you to drink.' I'm not really sure how it applies, but you should come out and have a drink anyway."

"I'll think about it," he says. "Let me get back to you."

"Well, you have my number so call or text. Don't e-mail though, okay?"

"Sure," he says.

He puts on his coat and walks to the elevator. A few minutes later, I grab my things and make for the exit. As I'm passing Stu's desk he says, "Do you think Will's going to be okay?"

"He seems pretty resilient," I say, "so I hope so."

Stu shrugs. "See you tomorrow?"

"I'm off tomorrow, pal."

"Right, right. Have a good day off then."

RealNews Interview with Sydney Rothsteen
originally aired September 3, 2013

Host: To all our viewers around the world, from China to Chile, I'm Cheryl Dean, and welcome to this very special episode of *RealNews*'s award winning talk show *Hotseat*. Today, we're joined by multi-billionaire entrepreneur, philanthropist, inventor and founder of *Real*, Sydney Rothsteen, who's here to discuss the success of the social networking site *Real*. He'll answer questions ranging from the rise of *Real*, to privacy and surveillance, to controversy, to *RealEconomy*, and he'll maybe even reveal just what's in store for *Real* and us eager *Real* users in the future.

CD: It's very nice to have you here, Mr. Rothsteen.

SR: Good to be here, Cheryl.

CD: Since we're constrained by time, I'd like to jump right into it. Tell me, Mr. Rothsteen, did you know that *Real* was going to be such a huge success? Looking at the numbers, *Real*'s meteoric rise seems almost fated: from one billion to 2.5 billion users in less than ten years; from generating no revenue to growing into the third largest economy in the world in the same time...there simply has never been another story quite like yours.

SR: Fate had no part in it, Cheryl, I can assure you. It was a superior product, and a population that was ready to use it. In our post-social world, the old social as it had been did not give enough. People were unfulfilled in their actual lives and felt alienated from one another. What was needed was a new and better means of communication that would not only connect people to each other, but also to the information they wanted. That is what *Real* did. That's what it is—it connects people to each other and connects those people to information. More and better information and communication furthers the development of society. So, fate? No. I—we—*Real*—that's who did it. It had noting to do with fate.

CD: Let's talk about those early days of *Real*, when you called yourself RealFriend. Why did you change the name?

SR: Well, RealFriend was a product of its times. We were all friends back then, weren't we [laughter]? Initially what was obvious was that not everybody is, quote, friends, with everybody else. The Room feature was meant to solve this problem, which it did, but then the category Friend just stopped serving its function altogether. *Real* outgrew the simple social network function of *just* connecting people and became so much more. It also grew quickly globally. 'Friend' doesn't mean the same here as it does in China or India or Russia. Dropping the Friend bit was part of growing up...so we just went for *Real*.

CD: You mentioned China. Going into China was a key moment for *Real*, and something that other social networking sites before you had struggled to achieve. How do you think going into China helped *Real* best its competitors?

SR: *Best* my competitors? We didn't best them, Cheryl, we destroyed them [laughter]. We saw where and how everyone else had failed and we went there. One way was going into China. The other was our superior product. We won because we're a better product. We stamped that pedigree with China.

CD: Well, do you want to talk about China first, or the product, *Real*?

SR: You're the interviewer.

CD: Okay, let's leave China for a second, and talk about some of those features that make *Real* such a better product...

SR: Sure.

CD: ...some of which have generated some controversy...

SR: Controversy is good. Eminem said it: We need a little controversy.

CD: Okay. Good then. Eminem. So I wonder if you can comment on, for example, *RealNews*, the platform we're on right now. It began as another aggregated news source; a ticker at the bottom of the user's screen that compiled and displayed the headlines from many different global media sources. But this changed, and *Real* began to report its own news, both user-based—what *Real* calls "Hands On News"—and stories reported by *RealNews* professional journalists. Why did you make this change? And why can't users turn off their news ticker?

SR: We made the change because we could. One reason I wanted *Real* to have an official news agency was because I was tired of seeing the crap news reported elsewhere, and I was tired of being pushed around by other media sources. The other reason was that, with so many users walking around globally with video cameras on their phones and filming every terrifying act they see, there's no reason not to provide a platform for them. And now look. We have some of the best reporters in the world and more coverage than any other news source. Rupert Murdoch would love to be me.

CD: And why can't users turn off their ticker, or view other news channels?

SR: Because I say so [laughter]. No, honestly, it's because they should be forced to read the news and stay informed, that's the reason behind the ticker. Why can't they view other sources on *Real*? That's pretty self-evident, don't you think? You can't watch Fox on CBS, can you?

CD: But Fox and CBS don't reach 2.5 billion people.

SR: No, no they don't [laughter].

CD: I guess what I want to get at is whether or not you see a danger in this—for instance, since there's only one news source available to your users, this controls what they know...

SR: Not at all. They can go elsewhere for their news if they want, and *RealNews* is not some kind of mind-control device. It's objective reporting.

CD: And what about what happened two years ago, when a reporter posted false details on the price of crude oil, and global markets panicked?

SR: Shit happens [laughter]. No, but honestly, that was a mistake and it was corrected and after a bit of a financial merry-go-round, things were back in order.

CD: Except in Qatar.

SR: Except in Qatar. Oh well.

CD: Okay. So. Speaking of financial merry-go-rounds, *RealEconomy* is about to be tabled at the U.N. Governments and economists around the world are saying that *RealEconomy* has provided the quote final nail in the coffin of the U.S.-dollar-based global economy. What do you have to say about that? How did that come into being? In 2012, *Real* and *RealEconomy* were even called the quote saviour of global capitalism, the main reason for the Rebound. How did that happen?

SR: *RealEconomy* began as a game. I, we, had no intention of turning it into what it became. It was more of an experiment: if Adam Smith could be god and play out his perfect system, what would happen? If his hand, my hand, could actually be the invisible hand—that's what we wanted. Then *RealEconomy*, when combined with our *RealBanking* service, took off and *RealDollars* became like a new resource, a new gold [laughter]. It was really amazing to behold.

CD: So why was this seen as the saviour of global capitalism?

SR: Well, you have to understand the history of capitalism. Capitalism had to begin somewhere. It began in what Adam Smith called previous accumulation—Marx called it primitive accumulation. In either case, *RealDollars* inexplicably fuelled a new round of accumulation and gave the capitalist system a bit of a boost. Just in time, I'd say.

CD: I don't really follow you.

SR: You haven't read your Marx [laughter]. It's the kind of accumulation you get before capitalism can start. Capitalism began when a number of merchants—at first merchants, then monarchies, states and so forth—got a lot of some kind of valuable resource, gold, for example. They used that gold to generate more money—capital—by investing that original resource into factories, industry and so on. *RealDollars* served this function when they began to be worth actual money; they too began to be used for investment, and to generate capital and growth.

CD: I don't quite understand.

SR: Neither do I [laughter].

CD: No, I mean I don't see why this wasn't stopped.

SR: Who could stop it? After it started, I wanted it to continue. It was amazing to see and at first it was all self-contained on *Real* where no one but me could touch it. The *RealDollars* were sold on the *RealFlea Market* for actual money that was transferred through our

RealBanking system. Since then, it's been out of my hands, but initially anyway, no one but me had control over it.

CD: It sounds like it was quite unstable.

SR: Perhaps.

CD: Critics have called it rigged. Is it true that when the game *RealEconomy* first began, certain members were given more initial start-up cash than others?

SR: Yes, of course. What is it they say? Membership has its privileges. This is how you reward your longtime users. And, honestly, this is nothing new. The global capitalist system is rigged as well. Its longtime players—the very rich—they don't worry. Their children don't worry. The world economy is not fair, and neither is *RealEconomy*. You have to work hard to make it, otherwise, don't play.

CD: And is that what you did?

SR: What?

CD: Work hard to make it?

SR: [laughter]

CD: And today? Do you feel at all threatened by the kind of money people are making on *Real*? I saw online last week that one Chinese user had just surpassed $500 million profit.

SR: Who's to say he or she or all the others aren't all me [laughter]? But, honestly, no, I'm not worried, the Chinese are good at making money.

CD: Turning to China then, what did *Real* have to give up to get into China, as you earlier put it? I mean, the issue with Facebook and Google was that they felt they and their users would be compromised and lose their privacy if they went into China. So what did—what do —you and your users, especially your Chinese users, have to give up to use *Real*?

SR: Look, this is a big myth, and it stems from a big lie. We did not have to give up anything. *Real* users who are not living in China, they don't have to give up anything. Anyone—*anyone*—who knows anything about modern China, and I know a lot about it, knows this: whatever business activity you want to participate in, whatever operation you want to run on their turf requires that you give them—in *Real*'s case, *them* is the government—it requires that you give them a cut. They want what's theirs, just like any business. So we gave them their cut of the information and of the profits. That's what they wanted and that was that. The fact is, Google made a huge blunder when it pulled out of China.

CD: Due to censorship, right?

SR: Right, but the problem was they took it personally; they made it into a question of morality. So [Eric] Schmidt or [Larry] Page, I don't know which one, or maybe both, they say, [mocking duck-voice] "We're Google, we're not evil. The evil Chinese, they're evil, they wronged us." They cried a bit and then took their ball and went home when they should have just given in. And look what happened: China's number one search engine now, after *Real*, is Baidu, not Google. Facebook, too, they didn't want to comply with the PRC's [People's Republic of China] regulations on content filtering and they were shut off. They should've just given in. Now look at them. [laughter].

CD: Why didn't they give in, do you think?

SR: It's quite simple. They let their provincial American moral righteousness trump their business sense. They thought in terms of good and evil and let their Enlightenment sentiments dictate their actions in a country that never had an Enlightenment. It was a fundamental misreading of the situation. One that I read correctly and pounced on. Their petty provincialism, their nationalism even, it stands in stark contrast to my globalism, and to the internationalism that's built into the world economy. It's a shame really, but I'm not complaining.

CD: So can you talk a bit about how that worked in China? Did you have to give over your software, or...

SR: No, no, of course not. Despite what everyone thinks, the Chinese respect intellectual property rights. What we had to do was simply hand over majority control of our commodity in China.

CD: Your commodity? You mean the information you gather on *Real*?

SR: Yes, the Chinese government gets a 51 percent share of the profits from the sale of that commodity.

CD: And what about the information itself? How does it work on *Real* with privacy in China?

SR: I can't really answer that. It's not the same as it is in the U.S. The clear-cut line that we have here between what is private and public, a line that is fading anyway, never existed in China. In any case, users of *Real* in China do have privacy settings. How they work, though, that's up to the government of China. Whatever they've decided has so far not affected growth.

CD: And the allegations that you're a spy working for the Chinese government?

SR: Absolute rubbish. What a predictable smear. I mean, what can I say? It's just so absurd...

CD: And so now? What about Google? What about your other competitors?

SR: What about them? They lost a long time ago. People nowadays, they may still visit Google, but they live on *Real*. As far as the rest? Amazon, eBay, YouTube, their services became redundant, didn't they [laughter]? Why would anyone want to have so many windows open on their computer when they can have just one? Why would anyone want to enter their personal information into all those separate websites when you can log into just one? We streamlined everything, made it easier and more efficient. The best middleman is responsible for two things: facilitation and organization. That's what we've done better than anyone—ever.

CD: Let's talk more about privacy.

SR: Let's.

CD: I wonder if you can talk about how privacy works on *Real* here in America? I mean, it's a big topic these days.

SR: Look, there are two parts to it. One is the government side, which I would be happy to talk about, since it's been blown way out of proportion. But there's also the business side of it, which seems to get lost in all this conspiracy, whistle blowing bullshit.

CD: Yes, well, maybe we can talk about the business side first. It is well known that every setting on *Real* is set to public when a user first signs up for an account.

SR: Yes, that's true.

CD: Why is that?

SR: Well, we do clearly state that to all our users, so it's not a surprise or a trick or anything. In fact, it's the first thing that a user encounters when they log in, not only the first time, but all subsequent times after that.

CD: But why not have everything set to private to begin with?

SR: Well, that would sort of defeat the purpose of a social network, the whole sharing and communication component of what we're trying to do at *Real*, wouldn't it [laughter]?

CD: But could it not work either way? If it is indeed the first thing a user encounters when she logs in—the privacy settings—could she not just change the settings from private to public for those things she wants shown?

SR: [laughter] No, not really. It doesn't work that way on *Real*. And this is the big point from the business side of things. Please remember that *Real* is a free product. We do not charge users a thing to join; we gain all our profits from advertisers. Once users come on, they can join *RealEconomy*, spend money, make money, all sorts of things, but they do not have to pay to sign up. Our advertisers work with what information is public and what is private. The information that a user leaves as public generates more exposure for an advertiser and more profits for us. That's why we encourage our users to leave their settings on public and that's why it's set as the default. It's the user who has to take responsibility for his activity on *Real*. *Real* has always catered to a more mature crowd, so we expect our users to have the wherewithal to take responsibility for their own privacy settings.

CD: There are of course children on *Real* now too...

SR: If there are problems with children, it's bad parenting...

CD: Yes, well... You mentioned advertising. Can you talk a bit about how advertising works on *Real*?

SR: Well, that was all [Harold] Brinks, he's the real genius here, he came up with it. It's what we call intuitive advertising. It takes each picture or video that's posted and public, and it drops an ad on it, or it incorporates an ad into it. It targets the user who posted it by first analyzing his *Real-ID* and then matches a particular product to that user's tastes, needs or desires.

CD: Can you give us an example?

SR: Let's say a user posts a photo. It happens to be a young trendy man, with his beautiful wife, and they're standing side by side on a beach in Miami, or wherever. Let's say also that this particular user has indicated on his *Real-ID* that he likes Radiohead, Martin Scorsese and the Beat authors. He's a cool guy. So the photo and that information would enter our intuitive ad software and out would exit a new photo of this couple, in which he might now be wearing a Vans hat and have a Converse tattoo on his chest, maybe even an air-brushed beard, while she might be drinking a Nestea. Something like that.

CD: That sounds like difficult software to engineer.

SR: Well, there are still a lot of bugs, but we've found that the bugs have actually been working to our advertisers' advantage. Sometimes a video or a photo will come out of the software with some completely bizarre or hilarious ad configuration. The fascinating thing is that it's these bizarre ads, the best ones, that have gone viral. The bugs also encouraged us to let our users tamper with their own stuff. So now on *Real,* if users don't like the generated ads, they can incorporate brands into their own personal videos or photos and post them on their Canvas as they see fit.

CD: Don't the advertisers have a problem with that?

SR: They did until I persuaded them otherwise. And this—this is another big myth, I hold their balls, they don't hold mine—meaning that they need me and not the other way around. They also recognize the old saying that there is no bad publicity. Did Andy Warhol's Coke bottles or Campbell's-soup-can paintings reduce those products' sales? Did Banksy's so-called art criticism of McDonald's or Disney do a thing to affect the success of those companies? No, not at all. Advertisers recognize this. They may need to be shown the light, but they do recognize it. If an advertiser thinks that a photo of a man shitting into a Coke can, which actually went viral, or a close-up video of a car tire backing over a Happy Meal, which also went viral, are bad publicity, then they don't know a thing about post-modern advertising.

CD: So users can manipulate the advertisements but not delete them?

SR: Yes, but look, that's not the point. Users get to use *Real* for free. They have to accept the ads and now at least they can have some fun with them.

CD: Okay, but what about those people that say this type of advertising doesn't work, that advertising based on algorithms incorrectly categorizes people, and therefore targets them with faulty advertising?

SR: [Sniggers] That's funny. I suppose you're referring to that so-called report on *Real*'s false advertising written by...what was his name?

CD: Stephen Jacobs

SR: Right. Poor, grumpy, forty-five-year-old Stephen Jacobs, who claimed he was receiving 'tween advertising, and then accused us [laughter] of mistaking him for a twelve-year-old girl.

CD: Right.

SR: Do you know what Stephen Jacobs proved with that so-called exposé? He proved what we've known for ages now, that the Internet is the best psychiatrist's couch. We learn so much about how people feel from *Real*, and he proved that our advertisers got him exactly right: he is a twelve-year-old girl; he just represses it [laughter].

CD: But why not give your users the option not to be targeted by advertisers at all?

SR: [laughter] I'm not sure how many times I have to say this, Cheryl. We provide a *free product,* for Christ's sake! Advertisers need the information from our users to target their ads, and we at *Real* need their money in order to grow and to offer bigger and better *free* services to our consumers. Without this money, do you think we could have become what we are? Do you think the Internet could be what it is these days without that? No. Governments would never have done it. They don't have the money or the creativity.

CD: Why not a pay-as-you-play option, where users could pay to opt out of advertising?

SR: We thought about that, but it just wouldn't be as profitable, and it's too elitist. *Real* is a democracy.

CD: You mentioned the government...

SR: Yes...

CD: The other side to the advertising when it comes to privacy.

SR: Right.

CD: Since all the whistle blowing and the government leaks, it's been revealed that in the past, *Real* has worked with the government to supply users' information...

SR: First, I would like to say that I think all of this talk about privacy is beating a dead horse. It's just not so damned important anymore. I have to agree with my former competitor [Mark] Zuckerberg here, and say that privacy is just no longer a social norm. People on *Real*, 87 percent of our users, do not use their privacy settings. It's just part of our contemporary reality that people—like the world, the economy, everything around them—are becoming more open. I call it the globalization of the individual. It's progressive to open yourself up to others.

CD: But what about the allegations that *Real* gave users' personal data to the government?

SR: We are subject to our nation's laws, so we do have to comply with government guidelines on privacy collection. But listen—I want to make this very clear, because it seems that you're not getting it. In the United States, there is no law that dictates what we can and can't do with the information that our users provide. The information that people provide is just facts, and there is no law against the collection and dissemination of facts. Personal facts about people are not intellectual property, and in the U.S. they are not protected under any kind of copyright law. Once those facts are out, they become public property. When I, when *Real*, *uses* those facts to generate data concerning trends in society, when we create something out of that data, it becomes private, it becomes ours. It is our secret, not yours, and that is what gets protected, used, and sold. The problem is, and it's a problem associated with individuality, people think that it is they who define a trend, when in fact, it's ten million people, all virtually identical, who do it.

CD: But don't people have the right to confidentiality?

SR: Then stay off the Internet or move to Europe. [laughter] But honestly, no, they don't have that right. Not in this country. Not by law. Not by anything. No one has the right to remain silent, to keep information about himself confidential, or even to demand the correction of inaccurate information that might be out there about him. These are not rights. You can go to court if you want, but they're not rights and you'll lose. I'll say it again, to be clear: you do not own information about yourself, and you do not have any right to demand that we or others delete information about you. Other people have a right to inform themselves about the world and about you if they want to. In most cases, you're fine, you do nothing wrong, you have nothing to hide because you're not important. But if you do cherish the right to free speech, which is protected in most constitutions around the world, then you have to accept that things might be said about you. That's the price of our freedoms. The bottom line here is that people care more about free media than they do about privacy. The market has spoken, and I don't see how talking about it further will change it. It's a dead topic.

CD: Does *Real* spy on its users for the government?

SR: We do not spy on American citizens.

CD: What about hackers?

SR: What about them? *Real* is un-hackable.

CD: That's a big claim.

SR: Just try it. I dare anyone.

CD: Well, I guess that's a good segue into my final topic. Regardless of the attempts by hackers to hack *Real*, what do you have to say to the people who resist *Real*, who criticize it for—well, for many of the things we've discussed here: its privacy issues, its challenge to socialization, its addictiveness and so on?

SR: *Real* was designed to be a perfect product because it is ever changing. It adapts like humans evolve. It can't be resisted because it adapts to that resistance. In fact, the only resistance we've had is now absorbed within it. We created the anti-*Real* group—we let it happen. It's one of our top *RealSeminars*, trending quite high, I believe. But that's beside the point. Because it is now considered to be the saviour of the global capitalist system and responsible for the Rebound, an attack against *Real* is an attack against capitalism itself. Do you honestly think the U.S., China, Russia, India and so on would let *Real* collapse? No, I don't think so. Like the banks, we're not going anywhere.

CD: Okay. So what's next for *Real*? Can you talk at all about these First Reality Lenses that we're hearing so much buzz about?

SR: I can't say much, of course, because they're a secret and a surprise, but let's just say that Smartphone companies better watch out. Apple, I'm coming for you. Google, you're finished [laughter]. But, no, honestly, these lenses will make the competition obsolete. They are both app and hardware combined. The app is the product, the product is the app, and you won't have to hold them or touch them at all; the lenses are controlled entirely with the flick of an eye. They also don't look ridiculous.

CD: Well, you heard it here. Good things keep coming from *Real*. Thank you to all our viewers, and thank you, Mr. Rothsteen.

SR: Thank you, Cheryl.

164

Addendum to the Report on Will Potenco and Julia Singer submitted by the Women Against Gender Inequality (WAGI) by Doctor Officer Elias Degair

The people of WAGI have produced a piece of real garbage here. What a waste of resources. Their analysis is so off-track—as if a drunk drove it right into a ditch—that it's hard to see how it will be of any use. They've let their political agenda—a mess of femi-socialism—taint everything! William and Julia are, according to them, "just fine" and having a good time in a normal relationship—two crazy working-class kids struggling in an unfair, "right-wing," "male-dominated" world that's stacked against them, like a song by The Boss. What a shitty mess I have to sift through now. At least the information is here. I can make my own interpretation.

Whatever the people of WAGI think, there is no social psychosis or social pathology affecting William. They are forcing their opinion. They call this social pathology a "phenomenon" but that's a complete abstraction. It removes all agency from William and places it on his upbringing, schools and institutions, when we know, from all that we have already observed, that this is William and him alone.

Regarding their argument relating to William's mother, while it might have some merits, it's misleading. The WAGI argue that the relationship between William and his mother is "not even close to what Freud described." I presume they're referring to the outdated notion that the Oedipus complex can exist only in boys in the phallic stage, between the ages of three and six. This idea is based on Freud's 1909 study, *Analysis of a Phobia in a Five-year-old Boy*. Sadly, the women of WAGI have not been properly trained or they would have known that the Oedipus complex can *also* manifest itself later in life. We are all well aware of the psychopath Ed Gein and his mother. They made a movie about him, for Christ's sake. It's popular knowledge. This later Oedipus complex is not an "uncritically examined" theory, but one thoroughly tested and based on hundreds of cases. William's relationship with his mother *is* Oedipal and we can't chuck it aside like the WAGI do. It's too important for our understanding of William's later relationships.

First was Bev. The WAGI seem to think that William's father was to blame here, or that it was William's background, coming as he does from a broken home, that had something to do with how this relationship ended. But this is wrong. Obviously what William saw in Bev was his mother, but because Bev was *not* his mother, William had to get rid of her. Don't they see? William left home; he left his mother. There was no one else in the world he missed more. She was not in Vancouver, so he picked up Bev. When she could not fill the role, he got rid of her. Case closed.

Next was Kim, who was not William's mother. She was horrible to William, this is true. But that should not steer us off track. It was not William getting "pushed [...] to his emotional limits" that led him to crack up. We have already mentioned this. It was William's emotionalism—his temper, his sadness and his aloofness—which had

166

been out of control for years, that manifested in the theatre that day with Kim, the same as it did yesterday on the sidewalk outside Eureka! when he watched that stupid bird die and lost his temper with the Syndics. This emotionalism has been an integral part of William's particular form of dementia, and it is not socially derived.

What the WAGI did hit on, however, is not to be missed. In their discussion of Kim, they talk of William's "increasing desire for solitude." How they determined this is unimportant—what is important is that they picked up on its effects even then. His past issues with women notwithstanding, what it means is that William's current delirium has much deeper roots; it goes further back than we'd previously suspected. The word "delirium" is perfectly applicable here. "Delirium" is derived from the Latin *lira*, a furrow, so that *deliro* means to move out of the furrow, to stray from the path of accepted truth and reason. William's delirium began after he broke up with Bev, meaning that the origins of William's current malady began when he chose not to accept Bev (his mother), and tried to move ahead with his life. When future scientists look back on this case, it may be this point that proves to be the key in diagnosing a whole new generation of sick people. What drove William inwards, and made him introverted long before the Scare, lies deep in his past and now very deep in his psyche.

But let's get back to the present, because the WAGI got something else right. They said that William has recently "been acting strange and erratic." This is accurate but understated. William has finally snapped. We saw him watch that crow die and it twisted something up in him. As often happens, it's an unexpected event, a sharp and sudden emotion, that jolts a person to radical forms of mad freedom. We can read where William is headed in his most recent *RealDiary* entry—just from yesterday. It's not pretty.

Today, like I was punched right in the face, Tom's words cracked open certain ideas that rested at the very heart of my most basic assumptions. And now, I don't know if I can ever again feel cheerful about my work, or Eureka!, or any of it.

Eureka! and presumably *Real* and Blabber too, they call people data and they treat people like things. Me, what I do is acquire and manage data, which are people. What does that make me? It makes me delusional. I'm not like I thought, like a forklift driver moving boxes of information around an open grid. I am like a guard in a Nazi concentration camp. I am doing evil, herding people into cells.

Me, Tom, Stu, the guy with the dreadlocks, the girl with the green-framed glasses—all of us—we go to work every day and push and prod, shove and label and organize people without their knowing. This can't be right—yet we all do it, and we take money for it. My guilt has never weighed as heavily as it does now.

Tom says these people we herd around are idiots. He thinks most people are idiots and says he doesn't care about them. But he's wrong. They're not idiots, they're just people—trusting people who don't know what's going on. And why should they? They're not told that once they give us their data, we manipulate their personal lives. They think privacy is protecting them. Their personal information is Play-Doh in the hands of us grown children.

I can't give in to the idea that they're dumb idiots. They're people and they deserve my compassion.

When I look down at my hands typing, I see what they're doing, and what they're capable of doing. I can move the mouse here, there, pick up someone and drop them there. These actions are utterly impersonal, removed from the material universe. They're as remote to the people—to my victims—as distant stars in the deepest reaches of space. Stars explode and reform without any witness but themselves. The stars in the night sky are so cosmically unaware of the many eyes on them each night. Out my window now, I see the stars, I stare at them. The darkness magnifies them for me alone. I see them and I see my hands as I type, and I realize how a person comes to think they could play god.

But that's enough. Night is taking over the city and I can't think

168

any more of the mistakes I've made. Tom hates the people, but I forgive them, and I have to forgive myself. For now, at least, I can do that. I stare into the dark sky and watch as the night pours over the city like a cauldron of black oil, filling every street, alley and bedroom. I watch and wait as it comes to me—comes to sweep me into a dream and remove me from my thoughts, my guilt, myself. Tomorrow everything will be fine.

So many negative thoughts and such delusion require intervention. A frightening disconnect from reality has occurred in William's mind. He speaks here of cauldrons, god, his hands and the cosmos, as if he'd discovered he was a superman and had the power to fly to the sun.

Ship of Fools
by Thomas Vickers

I can hardly believe he texted me. I never thought he'd actually want to come. Some people find me a little abrasive or offensive at times. The thing is, you have to test people, force them into situations where they say what they actually think. Will has been honest with me the entire time. It's not often I meet people like that. I reply to Will's text, saying I'll meet him downtown at the Vancouver Steam Clock at 8:00 p.m. that evening.

My plan to meet at the Steam Clock, a semi-crowded tourist attraction, is tactical. We won't be the only two people for the cameras and Syndics to watch. I figure there will be at least a couple dozen or so tourists milling around and snapping pictures of the Clock to provide a distraction as we sneak off. Where we're going is a small inlet, almost a cove, on the coast north of Gastown. It's still off-limits. The whole coast is blocked by fences that were put up during the Scare to cut off the coast from people who might have wanted to illegally paddle away or hop a train or boat or something—pretty stupid if you ask me. Anyway, if Will and I want to get out, we're going to have to slip past the fence and cross an old train yard before making our way down to the small rocky inlet where I've arranged to meet my friends.

Will is at the Steam Clock before me. Our punctuality game has taken on ridiculous proportions: he's thirty minutes early—me, twenty-five. But it's fine. There's this Edmonton-themed bar around there called the Black Frog. It's decorated up in the good ol' Eskimo green and yellow and it reminds me of growing up in Alberta and watching CFL games with Dad. I often went to the Black Frog when I lived in Vancouver, because they serve cheap beer and this cheap piss Yugoslavian firewater called Slivovitz that gets you real drunk. So to pass the time while we wait, I invite Will for a beer and a shot. The place is dead empty.

"I don't drink, so I won't have the beer," he says when we sit down. He does take the shot though, and sips on that. "That's tasty," he says.

"Will, that might be the first time I've ever heard someone say 'tasty' about Slivovitz," I laugh.

Will says nothing, but smiles.

"You know," I continue, "I brought Jen from work here a couple nights ago."

"Really? How was that?"

"Good. I fucked her afterwards."

He opens his eyes wide and starts glancing back and forth, grinning, and crinkles up his brow. Before he says anything, I interrupt:

"I'm just kidding, Will. I just wanted to see how you'd react. I didn't fuck her, she's a lesbian. You should talk to her and hang out with her sometime. She thinks you're interesting, in a kind of weird way, but..."

"Weird? She said that? I've only ever spoken to her once or twice."

"She said that, Will. You really need to get out more, man."

Silence.

"Anyway," I say, taking a drink of beer, "I guess you're not meeting your girlfriend tonight since you're here?"

"Yeah, that wasn't a problem. I mean, I don't have to ask her or anything, she'll just understand. We have a pretty loose relationship."

"That's good. What's her name, anyway?"

"Umm," he scratches his head. "Well, she hasn't exactly told me her name…"

"Really? Why not?"

"She's quite secretive, I guess. I don't press her."

I'm very confused. "Will," I say, "that sounds a bit strange. Isn't it strange to you? I mean, what does your girlfriend do? Is she a spy or something?" I grin.

His eyes dart around and he shifts on his stool like she *is* a spy, but it's obvious that he's just uncomfortable so I ease off.

"Sorry, I won't push you. If you don't want to say, you don't want to say."

"It's just complicated is all. She's not a spy. More of a working girl."

"Okay," I pause. "Hmm." I scratch my head. Now *I'm* uncomfortable; we're both uncomfortable. "Anyway," I change the subject, "as far as tonight goes." I lean in close to him and lower my voice—the bar isn't crowded, but I get paranoid in Vancouver. "We have to be a bit careful," I whisper, "because the place we're going and what we're doing aren't exactly legal around here anymore. I guess drinking outside was never legal, but… I mean it's nothing terrible, but if the Syndics show up, we might have to run for it, and if we get caught, well…"

It's hard to read Will's reaction to this. He opens his eyes wide again and I can see that he's excited. I think it's excitement. He is smiling, but who knows what the fuck that means. All he says is,

172

"Sounds fine," and then slams back the rest of his shot. "That's warm," he coughs.

I slam mine back too and finish my beer in a few gulps. It's getting dark outside when we step out the door. The sun is about to set. Dusk is the best time for sneaking around—the hazy sunlight confuses the cameras, blurs their vision. At dusk people can't see as well. It's a proven fact.

We leave the Black Frog and head north towards the ocean. The distance to the bottom of the street is short, maybe twenty yards or so, and not too wide. There are no sidewalks and no parked cars. On both sides of the street are old, red-brick factory-like buildings a few stories high. At the end is the fence that blocks our way. It's an eight-foot high galvanized wall, a towering obstacle that runs the width of the street. But there's a narrow gap in the right corner, and if you're skinny enough, like Will and me, you can just slide through. We get to the spot. I give one last glance over my shoulder, then I gesture to Will and we quickly slip through the gap and slide around the corner of the building, where we pause. My heart is beating fast. In front of us is an old train yard, with twenty or so sets of unused train tracks. We'll have to scurry across the tracks to get down to the ocean. It smells and tastes of steel and old used oil, masking the smell and salty taste of the ocean. There are no railway cars left to hide behind, just an open space of empty tracks; if any Syndics come around on patrol, they'll see us for sure. When we cross, we have move fast.

"Stay low, Will. You ready?"

"Yes," he says.

We crouch and move quickly, hopping and skipping across the tracks, careful not to trip up and fall. That would suck and probably hurt. On the other side of the tracks is the now disused Waterfront Road. It wasn't used much when it was open, but now it's totally

173

empty. We make it onto the road, turn northeast to the inlet, and slow down to a walk. It's quiet; just the sound of the breeze, a few gulls and the faint noise of waves lapping at the shore. The fishy, salty smell of the ocean is in my nose now and it's strong. Across Vancouver Harbour I see the lights of the north shore. Other than those lights and the reflection of the emerging stars on the ocean, it's oily black and we're safe.

"Why did you and your friends want to meet way out here?" asks Will.

"You mean why not just got to a bar or something?"

"Yeah, or the beach or a park?"

"Well, where we're going is hidden and it's a pretty nice spot to hang out, and my friends and I all know it, so it's like a meeting point. It *was* a park, or connected to a park, until things went to shit around here …."

"Did you ever like Vancouver?"

"Not really. You?"

"I did. I mean, I do. I don't know. When I got here it was different, and I made some good friends living on campus and it felt like an adventure to explore a new city—a big city. All I knew of big cities was Toronto. But then, after my friends left … yeah … I didn't go out that much …. And then—I don't really know how to describe it. I just sort of spiralled into *Real.*"

"You've got to get off that, man."

Will was silent.

"Anyway …" I trail off and stare out towards the ocean.

"I've never been down here before," Will breaks in. "It's nice. It's quiet and peaceful."

"For sure it is."

We walk quietly side by side for a few minutes.

"So Will," I say, "the people we're meeting, my friends…"

"What are their names?"

"They both live up north. Neither are big fans of the city. Eugene is one. He's a doctor who works in Bella Coola, which I guess it isn't 'north' north, but pretty far north. You ever heard of it?"

"No."

"Well, it's up the coast. Native town, mostly. Eugene's pretty grumpy a lot of the time ..."

"What's he doing in Vancouver?"

"I don't actually know. Maybe he's here for some doctor conference, or just down to have drinks. It's hard to say. Anyway, the other guy is Erik. I think I told you this. I live with him when I'm not here. He's an artist—painter, sculptor—a musician, a documentary filmmaker, a farmer, a mechanic … a garbage man. He can do most things, actually. His farm's in Rolla, north of Dawson Creek. You heard of it? It's real far north and inland, close to Alberta."

"I've never heard of Rolla. Dawson Creek I know. What's he doing down here?"

"I don't know that either. I just got an email that they'd be here. He and Eugene go way back."

"And how do you know them?"

"We met … I guess it was around twelve years ago, when we were all tree planting."

"In B.C.?"

"Nope, in Manitoba, near Thompson."

"They plant trees in Manitoba?"

"Ha. Yeah, a few here and there."

We're coming up on the place. I can see the glow of the illegal fire my pals have made. The light from the fire radiates orange and warm out of the inlet to the sea. As we approach, I hear Eugene's nasally voice. A few trees and a wall of boulders block the road, so we go around and walk down a narrow path to the inlet. It's hidden—just the glow from the fire and the sound of voices, if anything, could give us away. As we approach, it begins to feel warm and safe.

I see Gene first. He's sitting on a big driftwood log smoking a cigarette. A lot of logs wash up on the shore or drift in the water and crash against the breakers. Gene has a beer in his hand. Scattered around him are many crushed empty beer cans. Honestly, seeing him sitting there, to me he looks like a clothed Neanderthal, or a drunk homeless guy. He's a bit fat and he's slumped over. His hair and beard are long, unkempt, greasy and scraggly, and he's dressed in dirty, threadbare clothes and work boots. The light from the fire hits his prematurely aged face, putting into relief every deep crease and wrinkle, giving him the mask of a sixty-year-old man when he's only thirty-eight. It looks like he's stepped out of one of Breugel's medieval drunken-festival scenes.

Standing with his back to us a few paces behind him, just out of the glow of the fire, is Erik. He's pissing in the ocean, but when he hears us approach he turns his head. He's wearing a jean jacket and work pants. His hair is cropped short, and he has a long beard, slightly better groomed than Gene's. A cigarette is hanging from his mouth, but as Will and I get to the fire, he still manages an enthusiastic, "Hey pal," without letting it drop.

I don't know what Will is thinking. He's standing slightly behind me. He doesn't seem hesitant, but I can't imagine he's met many people like this. No one has. When I turn to look at him, he's staring down at the fire, smiling. He looks happy. Glancing up at me, he says, "I haven't been around a fire since I was a little kid. My dad would take my mom and me camping sometimes ..."

"Tom," interrupts Gene, slurring and pointing a finger at Will, "who's this guy?"

"This is Will, Gene. I work with him. He's one of the better guys, so be nice."

"Will, huh? Some office guy—city guy?" he says accusingly. "You aren't gonna rat us out, are you Will?"

"The drones will see the fire soon enough," says Will with a smile. "I won't have to rat on you."

"Pfft. Fuck the fucking drones! Here, come sit next to me Will," says Gene as he opens a beer.

Will sits down. Erik's finished pissing and we start to talk.

"Drive down go all right?" I ask.

"Yeah, yeah." He hands me a cigarette and the bottle of whiskey he's holding.

"And him?" I ask, gesturing toward Gene.

"He's fine. Been drinking all the way down, since I picked him up in Bella Coola, twenty, twenty-five beers already, I don't know."

"You?"

"No, I don't drink and drive any more. I just started into this whiskey when we got here. What about you? How's it going here?"

"Fine I guess. City sucks. Job is bullshit to be sure. But I have a lot of time to myself, reading lots."

"What's with this guy?" Erik gestures to Will.

I look over. "He's good, I like him. He's a bit sensitive though, so go easy on him. He watches a lot of films."

"Films. Okay, okay."

"Where're you guys staying?" I ask.

"I don't know. The doctors put Gene up at some hotel. We'll find it when we leave. It's downtown somewhere."

"Not bad," I say. "Hey Gene," I call over, "the doctors put you up in some fancy hotel, hey—looking out for their own, hey?"

He's squinting and shaking his head. "Fuck you man, fuck you, I didn't ask for that." Then he turns back to Will.

"I'm just kidding, pal. Relax," I say.

Erik and I are standing next to the fire. We sit down on a log opposite Gene and Will. The fire is warm and glows off all of our faces. It battles with the dark night. The flames aren't big, but the red-hot coals are bright and fluorescent.

"Pass me one of those beers behind you, Gene. Will, do you want a beer or some whiskey?" I say. "Gene, did you bring some dope?"

"Yeah, I did." Gene always has dope. He hands me a beer and a bag of dope that he pulls out of an inside pocket in his ratty, soot-stained yellow windbreaker.

"I think I'll try some of the whiskey," says Will.

Erik passes me the bottle and I take a long pull before passing it to Will.

"It's not that good," says Erik

Will takes a big swig, coughs a bit, wipes his mouth and passes the bottle back to Erik.

"It's smoky."

"So you like movies, Will? Tom says you like movies," Erik says as he receives the bottle.

"I watch a lot of movies, yes. I don't go out much …"

"What do you think of the movies nowadays?"

"There're some good ones. I don't know. I prefer the older ones. I don't watch so many foreign films, or, you know, art films. I guess it depends what you like. A lot is bad. I mean these days there're a lot of remakes, reboots, reduxes and things like that. It's hard to say …"

Eager to talk, Erik cuts in. "I know" he says, "it's really something, right? I was trying to talk to Gene about this on the way down, but he hasn't seen a film since, I don't know, 1987 is it, Gene? *Back to the*

Future Part II, was it?"

"Ah, fuck off," says Gene.

"Ha. So what do you think of all these remakes, then?"

"I don't know. I watch a lot of that stuff and some is really entertaining. It just depends on the day of the week for me. If I want to laugh, I'll watch a comedy. If it has one or two good jokes, it's fine. If I want to relax I watch something else. It's entertainment. What are you getting at though?"

"What am I getting at!? Originality, man!" Erik smiles and leans in to the conversation with all his energy. "Entertainment is one thing, sure, but as far as creativity goes, it's like *No Exit II* these days in Hollywood."

"I don't follow you," says Will. "I understand what you mean about no originality. But *No Exit II*?" He shakes his head. "What's that?"

"*No Exit. Huis Clos*. It's a play by Jean-Paul Sartre, you know him?"

Will said nothing.

"No? Well it's not important. He's a bit of a grease ball anyway. But *No Exit* was a play he wrote sometime in the 1940s. A man and two women—strangers—are left in a room together, a room they can't leave. They don't get along and end up bickering and arguing. Slowly, over the course of the play, they realize that they're actually dead and in hell, and that their punishment is eternity spent together in the same room bickering and arguing. Sartre's joke, his point, is that hell is other people. But that's his play; it's not really my point, because when you read the play now, Sartre comes off like some kind of a pie-eyed optimist."

Erik takes another big pull of whiskey and then passes the bottle to Will. Will takes a drink and leans in closer to the fire, warming his hands and listening closely. Gene's head has dropped. He might be sleeping or maybe just not paying attention. I've finished rolling a joint and lit it.

"So, *No Exit II*," Erik continues, "that's my point, that's the real horror show. Just try to imagine that room in hell and those three people fifty or so years down the road. Three undead people that hate each other. They would have come to blows, ripped off ears and noses, gouged out eyes, bit off fingers, clawed up each other's faces. They would have mutilated and cannibalized each other—a real fucking blood bath. That's Hollywood these days, cannibalizing itself over and over again. Nothing is getting reinvented, rebooted, or re-imagined. These are just new words for copying. It might look different, but that's only the technology. Hollywood, our so-called culture, is stuck in a loop. We're like a starving snake eating its own tail." Erik is addressing Will, but he looks at me too.

"I understand," says Will.

I nod in agreement. "I don't watch so many new films," I say.

"But it's not just films," continues Erik, getting pretty worked up now "and that's the bigger point. It's art altogether. I'm not even sure if I agree with myself here, but looking back at it, there seems to be this sort of loop in art since, say, the abstract impressionists, since Pollock. Nowadays, artists try to imitate not Pollock's art, but his experience, his 'moment'—his original discovery, you know, when he accidently dripped the paint onto the canvas? They want that moment, because that's the myth behind great art and artists. So an artist will paint and paint, trying to have an accident—a moment of genius—like Pollock supposedly did, where he discovers the next big thing in art …"

"That was a good movie, by the way. *Pollock*. Ed Harris directed and starred in it." Will cuts in.

"I know! It was fucking great!" says Erik. "Totally perpetuates the myth I'm talking about!"

"It does," says Will. "I get it."

"The problem," continues Erik, "is that artists never know if they've had that Pollock moment. Legends are made after you're dead. Few artists ever get mythologized in their lifetimes. They may get recognized if they 'make it'—Pollock was covered in *Life* magazine in '49—but mostly only after they're dead. In the meantime they produce a lot of mediocrity, repeating an endless cycle *ad absurdum*. This is art. This is Hollywood. This, Tom, is also your political economy."

"Well, not really, but you're on a roll," I say.

"I get that about art and Hollywood," says Will. "But what about other kinds of art? Innovation art. Technological or innovative art like Rothsteen and *Real*, for example, or like Jobs…"

"Rothsteen!?" exclaims Erik. "You've read the 'Secret History,' right? The only thing artistic about him is artifice. He's a charlatan, an imposter. He's like a character out of Huckleberry Finn—he's Ephraim Gursky. You can't call what he's done art. There's something happening today where we want to call art anything that anyone does. I bake a cake and now I'm a fucking baking artist. I mean, whatever … but look, Rothsteen is no artist. People try to compare him to Edison. They want to say Edison was some great artist. If anyone called Edison an artist when he was alive—to his face—he would've punched them out. Anyway, a mass-produced object is not art. Not to me."

"But what about Warhol?" says Will.

"Images and copies of mass production. And frankly, garbage."

"What about R. Mutt?" I say.

"That was a fountain." Erik smiles. "Anyway, it's all a bit confusing. Is there any of that joint left?"

"Here," I say. He takes a few puffs and passes it back. "Gene," I say. "Do you want some?"

"Ah, let him close his eyes for a while," says Erik, lighting up a cigarette. He takes a drag. "The artifice of the man or the woman creating the art has to be expressed in the object and not in the person." He takes another pull, thinking. "That was Duchamp/R. Mutt's *Fountain*. It was pure artifice. Ugh, I don't know. I guess it's not such a good explanation." He shrugs.

"That's fine." says Will. "I get you about the films, anyway."

"Tom," says Erik changing the subject, "what have you been doing here, besides the job?"

"Mostly just reading and lying around," I say. "I work every day for four hours. I'm trying to save as much as I can, so I won't have to come back for a while."

"Read anything good?"

"A lot. Last thing I read was *Neuromancer*."

"Pass that whiskey, would you?" says Erik to Will. "And? What about *Neuromancer*?"

"It's a good Vancouver book—Vancouver author anyway. And, talk about moments of genius, it's been almost thirty years since Gibson wrote it, which is crazy. Thirty years of 'cyberspace,' a word he coined..."

"And how many people have pillaged his work?" says Erik.

"Shit-tons, it seems. Anyway, I started to read it because I was told it has one of the best opening lines of modern or postmodern literature."

"Can you remember it?" asks Will.

"Of course I can. It's: 'The sky above the port was the colour of television, tuned to a dead channel.' I guess it sounds a bit dated when I say it, what with monitors, HD and all. Anyway, since reading it, I've been thinking a lot about dystopia. Have you read it, Will? Erik?"

"No time to read, pal," says Erik.

"No. I don't have much time to read, either," says Will. "I know the book though. I know of cyberpunk and all that. It's like Ridley Scott's *Bladerunner*, or Terry Gilliam's *Brazil*. It's the same sort of thing, right?"

"Exactly. So you have these dystopias, and they're called that because the societies they depict show a kind of shitty future, not where humans are all dead like in post-apocalyptic films, but where we're all just miserable and suffering. These dystopias—especially in *Bladerunner* and *Brazil* and *Neuromancer*—they deal with the anxieties we feel about machines and computers and the death of man as a so-called independent, unpolluted being. Or fears that technology will take over completely, which it has by the way, we just haven't admitted it. *The Matrix* is another version of this. *Tron, Terminator*—there are tons. They're all frightening, of course, but I'm not sure if they're honest .... They're afraid to take the next leap, they don't express the same kind of fear that say, *1984* does. The thing about *1984* is that Orwell's not depicting a dystopia. He knows what we're in for if we keep pushing and calls it what it is—it's our utopia.

"That's the *real* fear. In *1984,* the questions and anxieties about computers and all that couldn't even be asked—in fact, all questions and anxieties— they were either forgotten or just erased. In *1984,* it's as if everyone is just a skin-job, an unfeeling drone like Rutger Hauer's character in *Bladerunner*. In *1984,* at the end, we're left with Winston playing chess, watching people on TV being denounced, and drinking his gin, with no more questions left. He's the perfect citizen.

"Today we have *Real*, and so many people buy into it—Will I'm not attacking you personally here."

"It's okay."

"But so many young people on *Real*, they don't even care or question things like privacy. They don't recognize the same boundary between their private and public lives that we or our parents or our grandparents did. These questions, these problems, are vanishing; they're being systematically erased from our collective memory. And it's the same with these dystopias—*Bladerunner* and such—they're born from twentieth-century anxieties, but eventually, like in *1984*, those questions will cease to exist. We'll all have computer implants, *Real*'s First Realty Lenses, and slowly merge with machines, with computers. The alienation that Deckard, the Harrison Ford character in *Bladerunner*, feels, won't be possible. It'll be out of the realm of future thought. The future for Deckard is Winston Smith. When the questions are gone, we're in our utopia."

"What does that mean for us then?" Will has the whiskey bottle back and is taking a slug.

"It means the end of opposition. So it's dialectics, right, opposing questions, but in this dialectic, we lose. It's like Vancouver, which wants to be a utopia. They've eliminated poverty. How? They eliminate the poor. They've eliminated hunger. How? They eliminate the hungry. Sydney Rothsteen eliminates the economic crisis. How? He invents a new type of resource—his own damned money. When this stuff happens, it kills opposition. It's a new synthesis, but it's the wrong one. Today, the anxiety over privacy is being eliminated by just ignoring it —acting like it never even existed in the first place—"

"Buddy," says Gene, abruptly cutting me off.

"Gene. You're up!" I say, "Feeling better, duder?"

"Never better, never better," he says, nodding his head, "but listen, you have no idea what you're talking about. It's way worse. I mean, fuck your stupid dystopias and movies. You guys, that's all you ever talk about. The real problem is that no matter how terrible it gets, they don't even *let* you die anymore. All that computer-man shit is because we want to live forever. But the world is garbage. It's a fucking garbage heap and they're forcing you to sit in it for as long as they can. You have no choice in the matter unless you kill yourself."

"Doctors, you mean?"

"Medicine. That's the point of all this machine-human shit. It's not about dystopia anxiety or whatever, it's about medicine keeping us going. It keeps us around, just to stomp on our faces for longer and longer. Medecine is the perpetuation of suffering. People today die helpless in their hospital bed with needles and tubes coming out of them, while their poor relatives watch. To die a clean death—no tubes, no needles—to just die, that's a distant memory."

I look across to see how Will is. He's still smiling, still having fun. He's got the bottle of whiskey back up to his lips. The fire has died down. Gene, who seems happy with his point and is again fully cognizant of us and of his surroundings, stands up. After pumping his arms a bit and stamping his feet to get the circulation back, he scrounges around behind the logs looking for a full beer and some small wood to charge the fire. I walk toward the ocean for a piss. The sound of the waves on the shore soothe and help me start the flow. I look over the water towards North Vancouver and I imagine that I'm on a boat floating in the sea, unmoored. Drifting away from shore, I look back and lament the sad condition of a city and people in breathtaking decline. I imagine floating away for good. Was it ever better here? Will it get better? Probably not. I'm far from shore now. I've made my escape and I'm free, so why turn back? What's the goddamned point?

A sharp crackle from the fire brings me back from the watery abyss. I look over my shoulder and see Gene stoking the flames. I finish pissing, zip up and walk back. The flames grow. The coals crack and cinders and sparks shoot high in the air, lighting up the inlet. The boulder wall reflects the firelight like a mirror, and like a brightening bulb in a pitch-black room, that alcove by the sea glows like a beacon in the night. We, too, glow as we sit by the fire, but no one seems to care that the drones can't miss the light, could soon signal the Syndics to viciously interrupt our night.

Will and Gene are talking. I sit back down next to Erik, who is drinking whiskey and smoking a cigarette.

"Your buddy there, he seems like he's holding his own," Erik says to me.

"Not bad, huh? Hey, Will," I say. "What are you guys talking about?"

"I wanted to know," says Will, "why Eugene's a doctor when he seems to think so poorly of medicine." Will's eyes move from mine to Erik's, then back to Gene's.

"I'm not a doctor, Will. I'm a phone book between a baseball bat and human flesh. I soften the blow. In this place, in happy, liberal Canada, there are those who suffer—the Indians, the poor—and those who inflict suffering—the rest of us. I may be able to stop the skin from being split open and the blood from pouring out, but I'll never prevent the wound from being inflicted."

"That's so sad." asks Will.

"Sad. It's fucking tragic. Do you know how many times I've had to listen to our so-called experts—doctors, learned members of the government, fucking celebrity Vancouver Doctor Chief Stacy Starr—try to justify inflicting suffering? How many times I've had to listen to those fucking people tell me that they can't help Indians because they need to save money? They build their drones and Indians get cholera and TB, fucking TB. The pathetic rich of Vancouver need the expensive equipment, so fuck the Indians. That's the logic."

"I don't understand," says Will. "Why don't people like me know about this? Why doesn't someone say something? Why not? I mean, you have to tell people. Use *Real*, or Blabber, whatever it takes…"

"Blabber!?" Gene cuts him off. "Fucking Blabber!? They might as well say: 'Let them eat Blabber!' It's fucking running water they need, not fucking Blabber! Tom," Gene pauses and looks at me, "who the fuck *is* this guy!?"

"Gene, calm down." I say. "He's just trying to talk to you."

"Fuck man, you need to know the basics…" Gene says, shaking his head.

Will drops his head. He's looking at the ground between his feet.

"Will," I say, "Do you want another sip of whiskey?"

Without lifting his head he shakes it no.

"It's okay," I say. "Gene's a fucking asshole sometimes."

"It's fine," Will says, raising his head. "I'm just confused and my head hurts. I don't drink often."

"*I don't drink often.*"

"I don't."

"*I don't.*"

"Who said that?" I ask.

"*Who said that?*" Laughter.

"It's coming from behind the rocks," Erik says.

"*It's coming from behind the rocks.*" More laughter.

Will is up and off his log long before the word "*Run!*" comes screaming from my mouth. Like a deer over a fence, he's over the boulder wall and gone in the direction of the tracks. I glance at Erik. Things have turned slow motion. He shrugs and throws back the last of the whiskey before getting to his feet and arming himself with the bottle.

"Fuck it," I say, and stand and turn and begin to clamber up and over the boulders.

"*Run all you want,*" I hear. "*We know who you are, Thomas Vickers.*"

I reach the top of the wall and turn to look back. Erik is moving slowly. He's backing toward the ocean. His knees are bent and he's braced and waiting. His eyes are wide. The whiskey bottle is in his right hand. He's holding it by the neck like a club, staring down the approaching Syndics, watching to see which of them will make the first move. Gene, however, is still sitting. His left elbow is resting on his knee and he's stroking his beard. I make eye contact with him and he smiles at me. Just before they drop out of sight I see one of the Syndics lunge at Erik, then the shit storm. But I'm over the rocks and they're gone and I'm running as fast as I can toward the train tracks with sweat running down my face. It's pitch black and I can't see Will anywhere.

Observations

by Doctor Officer Elias Degair

I

Well, well, William had a night. Out with the boys, indeed: Tom and his vagabond friends and William the loner—a most motley of crews. It was a fortuitous moment for us, though.

Let's review: William left home last evening to meet Thomas just after 7:00 p.m. Our technicians entered his room at precisely 8:00 p.m. They installed the video and audio equipment and were out by 8:30, just as William and Thomas were recorded leaving the Black Frog. Thomas, who is obviously well versed in subversive deviancy, led William north to the end of Cambie Street where our cameras lost them entering a restricted zone.

Our Syndics had a bit of a hard time tracking them after that, but with the aid of the health and safety drones, they had William, Thomas, Erik and Eugene pinpointed by 9:10 p.m. After that, it wasn't hard for our men to sneak up on the fools, drunk and high as they were. We had the perimeter secured and were recording by 9:30. After listening in on their drivel for over an hour, I ordered the men to make contact at 10:30. On their Smartphones, our Syndics recorded William fleeing the scene, quite nimbly I might add, and our cameras at the

189

Steam Clock have him again at 10:45 p.m. heading in the direction of Harmony. It should be added that a clear stagger was detected in his walk, which indicates an illegal level of public drunkenness.

We could have intervened at this point—public drunkenness is no laughing matter. We don't tolerate that kind of behaviour here. Our case against William is robust enough now that we could have used the public drunkenness to bring him in. But it wouldn't have been enough. He's very lucky that it's me in control of his case; some of my colleagues would have done differently and hauled him in, but I reasoned with them to leave him be for now. Taking him in then would have been a mistake—like showing the rat the way out of the maze before the experiment is over. For the sake of science, I argued, William must be left to think all is well, that he is okay and that everything is normal. We gain much more insight into his condition if he continues to believe he's normal and remains on his own to function in his so-called average life.

Our cameras recorded him entering his room at 11:03 p.m. He didn't immediately turn on the light. Seconds after entering his room, we saw him stagger, recover. Then he saw something on the floor, some nameless terror that triggered a sudden frightened gesture, causing him to stumble and trip. As he fell, his hands grasped for support and he clung to the only thing he could to slow his fall, the curtains, which ripped from their rod as he fell to the ground in a thundering racket. The room lit up like a struck match as the light from the Chinese import/export across the street poured in through the uncovered window. William lay on the ground bathed in neon glare, motionless and partially covered by the fallen curtains, for more than an hour. It wasn't until after midnight that he got to his knees and crawled into bed. The fluorescent light shone through the window directly on his head all night.

His eyePhone's 1920s jazz app goes off at 6:00 a.m., playing Paul Whitman's 1922 classic melancholy hit "Three O'Clock in the Morning," but William barely stirs. The song ends, and the voice of a 1920s sports reporter drones in with baseball scores from 'last night's' games, but he still does not move. For twenty minutes he lays in bed. It's not clear from the video footage if, when he finally sits up, he is in his right mind.

What I see is a confused man, someone who does not know if he is awake or dreaming. He rubs his eyes and blinks rapidly; he wiggles and clinches his toes; he smells his armpits; we see his mouth move, contorting his lips, as if tasting his own morning breath. All of this is a way of trying to convince himself that he is indeed awake and not dreaming.

Once convinced he's in his right mind, awake and cognizant, William slides his legs off the bed and looks to the ground where the curtains lie in a heap. The mass of fabric elicits another look of confusion, as if he doesn't remember tearing them off the rod. I see and hear him let out a long sigh as the memory filters back into his mind. But there's something more—something like remorse or maybe depression appears on his face, a natural sensation after destroying his room, associating with lawbreakers, sneaking into restricted areas and breaking the law. Yes, it would be natural for him to be remorseful. But then, something strange. On his dry lips, a grin forms and then a smile, William breaks out in hysterical laughter. He kicks the heap of curtains, then lifts and bundles it in his arms. Red-faced and laughing, he does a little pirouette in place, then tosses the curtains into the corner. When he glances down, he pauses and stops laughing. The smile leaves his face and his eyes screw up and fix on something on the ground where the curtains had been. A look of disgust crosses his face. What is it he sees? When he bends down to pick it up, we can see it quite clearly, held by a leg between his thumb and index finger—the dead corpse of a glistening, rust-colored, two-inch long cockroach.

Is this the unknown terror from the night before that shocked him into his fit of destruction? Perhaps—or perhaps it was a fit of rage, another symptom of his disordered mind. It hardly matters at this point. William stares at the cockroach, twirls the rotten thing by the leg between his fingers. He drops it into his palm and pokes it, examines it, and then, hardly thinking it seems, he tosses it the four or five feet into the sink, where it lodges in the strainer.

William sits at his desk: there is work waiting. RWM has orders that need to be processed. Messages are waiting. In the corner of his *Real-ID* page the light is flashing: "Message from Mike George," "Message from Ryan Jeffreys."

(6:10 AM) Mike George: what's up will?

(6:15 AM) Ryan Jeffreys: Where are you man? We have lots to do this morning.

(6:23 AM) Mike George: will?

(6:24 AM) Ryan Jeffreys: Idiot.

William reads and ignores these messages. For the first time since we've known him, he changes his routine and neglects his work, instead navigating directly to his diary, where he begins to write:

What happened!? My head hurts. Did those Syndics see me? What about Tom and Erik and Eugene? I have to talk to Tom. Did the Syndics get him? Was I a coward to run away like that? It was so natural to run, as if it was all I could do. I feel no guilt about it. I feel no guilt about any of it. The opposite, in fact. Welling up inside me is not guilt but profound happiness. It's a joke. It's a funny joke. There, last night, was a real experience with actual people. I've never done a thing quite like that. Adrenaline! I have never come home in such a state. *Such* a state!

He pauses. Some physical change occurs in him, I can see it in his face. He leans back in his chair. It might be he's finally feeling guilty —it should be. It should be guilt that's rising up in his stomach, twisting and turning it, amplifying the hangover nausea. I've never known anyone to vomit from happiness. It must be guilt that he feels, guilt that makes him suddenly stand and rush to the counter, brace himself over the sink and violently retch—retch into the sink all over the dead cockroach. Disgusting. When he finishes, he turns on the faucet and the water dilutes the stinking, bile-rich sick, as William uses his fingers to stuff the bits down the drain. With his hands, he wipes clean the sink, and then, with great care, he rinses off the cockroach and places it on the counter. He splashes cold water on his face puts a cup of water to his mouth—swish, spit and drink, rinsing out the taste of puke. He returns to his desk and continues writing.

What was that dream!? Like rain running down a window, little men dressed all in black rappelled down the building in front of my eyes. Their black boots kicked off the glass and they stopped to look in, then rappelled down again, hundreds of them merging together in never-ending streams of black...It's fine, I feel fine though, all is normal and I feel great. Everything *is* fine.

A new day. I want to do it all again! I *have* to do it again. I need to meet more people. They're out there. I need more experiences. Friends—friendship—drinks—conversation about real things. The world. The world! What have I let myself become? I was not aware of it. I was lost in a bad movie written by a terrible screenwriter, but now I'm awake. I'm conscious of life and all its possibilities.

He stops writing, as if exhausted from running a marathon, falls from his chair and collapses into bed.

What can we make of it, though? These are surely the ramblings of a true hypomaniac. The way he shifts from topic to topic, sentence to sentence, without finishing an idea—indications of a man no longer

193

capable of linear, reasoned thought. Then there is the dream, little men in black rappelling down a building—are they coming to get you, William? Is this his repressed guilt haunting him? A man who surmises that he has committed a crime in his sleep is immediately guilty of something. He must feel, deep down, his guilt.

And there's the retching. A schizophrenic will run about in the freezing cold, splash in freezing water or roll in snow, all without recognizing the effects of the cold on his skin. William is not schizophrenic. We must be careful not to look for symptoms where there are none. However, that he did not acknowledge the retching, did not sit or lie down afterwards but returned immediately to writing in his diary—this is pretty much the same thing. William is like a schizophrenic in subjecting his body to vicious tortures and feeling as if nothing has occurred. And then, of course, there is the act of preserving the corpse of a cockroach—macabre morbidity.

So he's collapsed into bed and neglected his work. He's neglected his friends. He's even neglected masturbating and his "What's a dickfer?" *RealSeminar*. He sleeps three more hours. When his eyes open again, it's not happiness they express, but fear. Waking after 9:00 a.m., he's late for work. Clearly confused, he darts here and there in his room, trying to get dressed, brush his teeth, put on his shoes and wash his face all at once. Finally, he sits down in a heap at his desk. He could not possibly be thinking that it is still okay, that it is all fine. It's not fine for William any more. He's late for work, and he can't fight what his habits, his nature, are telling him. He has never been late. He's the one who's always early. Over days, months, years, he's given himself that duty, that responsibility. It's become an instinct that has now failed. He's failed and guilt seeps in, penetrates his consciousness and it forces him to his feet. He gets his shoes on in a rush, grabs his coat and heads out the door.

With his head down in shame, he walks briskly to work and arrives at 9:45 a.m. Two squirts of sanitizer into his hands and into the elevator where, panting, he takes deep breaths as if to calm himself. He looks up at the camera, emotionless. No snide smile or contemptuous looks this time. The questions that are running through his head: What will he tell Stu? How will he get out of this one? He expects to see Tom, and I bet it's a comforting thought, that he'll see a familiar face, his partner in crime, and have someone to commiserate with.

The doors open on the tenth floor, William steps out and begins to walk down the hall to Data Management. What happens next, though, he didn't expect. I didn't expect it either. On the screen, I see walking towards William, Brian Fogel, CEO and founder of Eureka!, and he's flanked on either side by co-owners Dana Burrows and Frank Belfour. Dr. Fogel is looking regal, dressed in a fine black, tailored suit with patent leather shoes and designer glasses. He is tall and handsome with broad shoulders. The hallway is not wide enough for the three men to walk abreast. Dana and short, squat Frank, must walk behind, to the right and left of Dr. Fogel.

But for William! What will he do? He can't conceal himself, blend in with the background garbage as he normally does, and there is no nook, no broom closet for him to hide in. Oh, William. Everything is not fine. *Of all days*, he must be thinking. He can't keep his head down and try to squeeze by—nobody squeezes by Dr. Fogel. And anyway, he must stink of whiskey and vomit. Maybe Fogel will ignore him.

The two forces collide.

"William, is it?" asks Dr. Fogel, with a pleasant look on his face.

William raises his head and opens his mouth, but nothing comes out. His lips quiver slightly.

"William," continues Dr. Fogel, "we've heard good things about you up in the big office…"

He knows William. He knows his name, and even thinks he's done "good things."

From humiliation, William's face turns a shade of crimson I've not seen in years. It's the deep shade of pink one only sees in a man's face who is about to die from strangulation.

Dana, smirking in the background, opens his narrow lips and says, "William is late, Brian."

"Oh, is he? Well, that happens." Dr. Fogel smiles.

That should put William at ease. But he's started to sweat. I can see it forming in drops on his forehead. His mouth opens once more. English-sounding words come out, but it's all a jumble.

"Uh, uh, uh, hello sir, thank you sir, thank you, have a nice day sir, thank you...I'm fine, I'm alright. Good. You too. Great."

As this mess of words passes through William's lips, he deftly maneuvers himself around the group of three, choosing the side furthest away from Dana, where little fat Frank is standing. He keeps tight to the wall, mumbles as he moves, and is able to slip around. He keeps on going without looking back, almost running. Behind him Dana is laughing, Dr. Fogel is smiling, and Frank is looking confused.

For a moment, as he rounds the corner at the end of the hall, we lose him, only to pick him up again as he enters Data Management. The room is half full. Stu is at his desk. Tom is not there. William passes Stu without saying a word. Still flustered, he turns on his computer and logs in.

What will he tell Stu? he must be thinking. What excuse would Stu be sympathetic to and how should William present it? Maybe he should walk over to Stu and say hello. That would be the right thing to do, but he's missed that window. Getting up and going over now, everyone would stare at him—that would be a huge, guilt-laden blunder.

What would Thomas do? I wonder if William is asking himself that question. Is Thomas a role model for him now? It seems unlikely. And even if William were thinking like that, it would be impossible for him to follow through. That dirt-bag Thomas is extroverted, he would stand up and announce to the whole room that he was hung over. He would crack a joke, be forgiven and that would be that. William could never do that. No. What he does is log in to Speaka and waits. Saying nothing at all, he simply gets to work. It's finally Stu who types first:

Stuman: Will, you ok? Not like you to be late.

William's answer surprises even me. He doesn't lie, but tells the simple truth, and even adds a touch of humour.

William01: I'm sorry Stu. I had one too many last night, haha.

Stuman: Well, let's try not to let it happen again, okay?

William01: I'll stay late today to make it up.

William rubs his chin, scratches the bit of stubble on his face and leans back in his chair. Something is going through his head. We don't know what, but from what he does next, we can infer that what Stu said has angered him. That, and perhaps hearing Dana laugh at him, angers him so that he begins to act out in a way that we'd never have thought of: he emulates that scumbag Thomas. He resents his superiors being mean to him—*after all I've done for them*, he probably thought —and like all disgruntled employees, he takes it out on his job.

He leans into his computer and begins sorting. He sets up twelve new institutions, none of which pass Eureka!'s research-based code of standards, all of which are progressive "leftist" organizations. At the same time he denies access to six companies with clearly indicated research divisions committed to the furthering of academic knowledge: one pharmaceutical, two government-sponsored think-tanks, one oil-exploration firm, and two mining companies.

At 11:45 he takes a short break to write to his mother on *Real*.

(11:45 AM) William Potenco: Hi Mom. I hope you're having a good day. I had such a great night last night with some new friends. I've had a bit of a hard start this morning, but I think I'm fine now. I think I'm getting better. I just wanted to say hello, and tell you that I miss you.

(11:53 AM) Margaret Potenco (MOM): We miss you too Willy. I'm just leaving for work, but we can talk about your day later. Love mom.

At 12:35 he takes his lunch break and sends a text to Thomas:

You must have got away. Feeling too sick today? Call me. This is Will.

Then he responds to Ryan and Mike on *Real*.

(12:45 PM) William Potenco: Sorry guys. I had a late night last night. I'll get to the work later today when I get home.

(12:47 PM) Mike George: its [sic] fine will. we got two of the other guys to do it. there was just so much to do. did you have fun last night?

(12:49 PM) William Potenco: I did. Thanks Mike. I was out with a friend from work, Tom. It kind of reminded me of the early days when you were here. I'm glad you got the work done. Sorry again.

(12:50 PM) Ryan Jeffreys: Its [sic] not fine Mike. Will, you better not do that again. I told you not to hang out with that loser. If you can;t [sic] do your work, we can find someone who can.

(12:51 PM) William Potenco: You don't have to be a jerk, Ryan. I saw that you called me an idiot earlier. Why did you do that? What's your problem recently? You've been so mean. I helped start the company and you just shouldn't just talk to your friends that way. And don't talk about Tom like that. You don't even know him. What's happened to you?

(12:54 PM) Ryan Jeffreys: You better be careful Will. I'll fucking fire you. That guy Tom is an asshole.

(12:55 PM) William Potenco: You're being a real bastard.

(12:56 PM) Mike George: guys, guys. don't let this get out of hand. it's fine will, it's fine ryan. it'll be fine.

(12:57 PM) William Potenco: Whatever. I have to get back to work. Bye Mike.

The rest of the day, William hardly does a thing. Stu gives him a task that requires looking over a spreadsheet of keywords and deciding on the feasibility of introducing these particular keywords into Eureka!'s database. He has to type a "yes" or "no" beside the word, based on a simple set of guidelines. It's hard to say if he cares about this task. Our facial recognition software calculates a 78 percent chance of his having listless, distanced feelings about the work. From my own observations, and from reading portions of the spreadsheet, it seems likely that he didn't give a damn about it, and that he just typed in "yes" and "no" at random.

This distraction of the mind, however, is expected. William's blind surrender to his passions, his pathetic emotional attachment to his so-called friend Thomas who has not yet texted him back, the sorry crumbling of his much better friendship with Ryan, the shock of running unprepared into Dr. Fogel (not to mention the chemical imbalance brought on by the alcohol in his system) have all made it impossible for him—already with a weak mind—to moderate his feelings or to focus on the task at hand. In short, William is spiralling into the abyss of mental failure.

But we're willing to let him continue on his way, to see how far and in what direction his particular mania will take him. At the moment, William is still alone. In thought as well as action, he's no real threat to good, healthy citizens. We must be careful though. We need to keep him isolated as long as we can—we can't afford to let up. If he starts making conversation or chatting to people, his disposition has the potential to become highly contagious.

William did stay late at work as he had promised. He didn't do anything, but he sat there until 7:00 p.m. When he got home, he didn't eat, but went straight to his room and tried, as we feared, to reach out to Julia. However, a small light on her photo at www.thegirlnextdoor .com indicated that she was unavailable. Disheartened and clearly melancholic, William fell into bed and was soon fast asleep.

II

Intervention, cure, diagnosis, treatment, prescription, medication—these words have varied in meaning and practice across the ages, and come in forms that were sometimes conflicting, sometimes similar. Throughout history, those like William—those sick in the head—have been cared for in different ways. In the middle ages, they were seen as freaks—carnival-like entertainment for the masses, to be paraded through villages for coins and food scraps. Later, the mentally deranged were cast to the margins of society. Forced into exile, they lived solitary, lonely lives as wanderers, witches and beggars. Later still, they were confined in the great madhouses and prisons of Europe, where they mixed with, and were treated like, criminals. Only within the last two centuries have the head-sick and mentally screwed up been aided in their recovery by us dedicated and sincere men of science.

At first, the care was brutal, but it did work, and men and women who were once sick returned to society to again take part in the grand project called human progress. Symptoms of modern mental disease have called for different courses of action, from inclusion to banishment to confinement and chains—from forced labor to understanding to electroshock and lobotomy—from lithium and Prozac, to a good night's sleep. But in all cases, our motive to cure, we men of science, has been love. We doctors love the mad; we just hate their madness.

William's eyePhone did not go off the next morning at 6:00 a.m. as it normally does. He didn't even set it. Instead, he was awoken by a knock at the door at 7:20. Rubbing his eyes after a restless night's sleep under the beam of light from the Chinese import/export shop, he got to his feet to answer the door. But whoever it was had gone, leaving a letter slid under the crack at his feet. He examined it, then opened it. It was two pages long:

Public Health Agency of Canada
Agence de la santé publique du Canada

134 Hobart Road
A.I. 75951H
Ottawa, Ontario H4D 3G8

May xx, 201-

TO BE OPENED BY ADDRESSEE ONLY

William Potenco
1 West Pender, Suite 8A
Vancouver, BC V6B 1R3

Dear WILLIAM POTENCO:

I am writing to inform you that an external portable hard drive that contained some of your personal information was misplaced by an employee. The device contained the following types of information: Social Insurance Number (SIN), surname, first name, mailing address, birthdate, health insurance number, and credit history.

While there is no evidence at this time that the information has been accessed or used for fraudulent purposes, specific measures have been undertaken to safeguard the protection of your personal information. We will monitor your public health record to ensure that no changes are made without your authorization.

The Public Health Agency of Canada has announced a series of measures that the agency is taking to address this incident, available at: www.publichealth.ca/privacy/spotlighton/index.shtml

The protection and security of personal information is a priority for the Government of Canada. Attached is additional information about steps that you can take to safeguard your personal information.

Sincerely,

René Lépine, Director General
Privacy Protection Unit
Public Health Agency of Canada

Without reading the second page, William mumbled something about bureaucratic dickheads and tossed the letter onto his desk. He sat at his computer where his first impulse was to try Julia once again. She was still unavailable. He next went to his Canvas to compose. He drew three little men dressed all in black, wearing oversize combat boots, rappelling down the side of a building. He drew a dark rain cloud, and clicked the animate button to make the men and the rain fall at the same pace. He added a recording of "William, It Was Really Nothing," by the Smiths and posted it.

Strangely optimistic—or not? It's hard to discern, but one thing is clear: William is having recurring dreams of little men dressed in black.

With "William, It Was Really Nothing" playing in the background, he stared at his computer screen. The first to notice his composition and write was his good friend Ryan.

(7:47 AM) Ryan Jeffreys: Hey Asshole!

(7:48 AM) William Potenco: Ryan, I know you're pissed, but I don't care. I can't do the work. I need a break. You can fire me, replace me, do what you want.

Next was Mike George:

(7:53 AM) Mike George: hey will. you okay? i like your drawing.

(7:55 AM) William Potenco: Hey, Mike. Thanks. I'm fine. I just told Ryan that I need a break. I'm having a bit of a hard time and I need some time off. You guys can fire me or whatever.

(7:58 AM) Mike George: don't worry. you aren't fired. i'll talk to ryan. whats [sic] the problem, anyway? can I help?

(8:02 AM) William Potenco: I don't know Mike. I just need to get out. I need to meet people. I need to break this routine.

We can't let him meet new people. It alarms us, his urge to do so. Think of the harm he could do. After seeing these desires on screen, some wanted to bring him in again immediately. The letter had not worked—he discarded it, they said. He did not read the second page, they said. But in the end, cooler heads prevailed. I told them my form of treatment is a process. I said it takes time. We have to rely on what we know, and what we know is that William can't make friends. It's not easy for him. Despite his desire to meet people, he's far too introverted. His attempts at social interaction, whatever form they may take, will fail. I'll make sure of it, I said.

William stared at his screen for another ten minutes, concentrating, and then he masturbated. His loncliness and perversion guided him to two of his favourite sites: www.girlsxxxvideos.com and www.triplex. com, where he searched for "Asian" and "big tits." He found what he was looking for, I watched him watch a couple of porn videos and he ejaculated into a wad of tissues.

Afterward, he showered and dressed as usual. He packed his things and got his raincoat—it was raining, after all. The one thing he hadn't done was make a coffee. William always makes coffee—it's an integral part of each morning. I thought I had him figured out and here breaks his routine again. It's fortunate that I have the power of foresight and predicted weeks ago what he would do next. I had no idea it would happen like this, but I guessed he might try something radical and so I took appropriate measures.

On normal days, William grabs a piece of fruit from Harmony's cafeteria and hits the road. It's the same pattern every day. But today is not normal. William's world is unravelling and this morning he's filled with an unhealthy courage that I can only guess has been brought on by his sickness. He has not made a coffee so he can ask for one from the pretty young woman. This was his ploy. He walks into the cafeteria, and with a reduced libido and lots of confidence, he charges straight to the pretty young woman who and strikes up a conversation.

"Hi. What's your name?" William says.

"Heidi."

"Hi Heidi. My name's Will."

There's no one else in the cafeteria, so he doesn't have to hurry. Our microphones, nonetheless, pick up anxiety in his voice.

"What can I get for you, Will?" she asks, eyes wide. She is very cute.

"Oh, nothing today. Or wait. Maybe a coffee. Yes. A coffee."

Heidi pours William a coffee from the machine.

"Say, have you worked here long?" William asks, knowing full well how long she's worked there.

I don't want to judge. I hate to judge, but watching William, frankly, it's like watching a children's recital as they try to play Mozart. You just know they'll never get it, and it's excruciating to experience, but you have to sit through it and act hopeful nonetheless.

"About six months. I have a *RealJob* too," she replies. She's doing great.

This makes William smile. "Really!? Me too," he says.

"I sell nail polish in the role-playing sector."

William scratches his head. He wasn't expecting that.

"You sell fictional nail polish? Does that earn you anything?" He looks confused.

Heidi hands William his coffee and grabs a piece of her hair and begins to examine it. "Not much," she says. "But it's super-fun."

"I see you have the newest eyePhone there." William is trying a different subject. "I have the same one. How do you like it?"

"It's amazing," she says, with a big beautiful smile. "Have you seen this!?"

She picks up the eyePhone and shoves the screen into his face. William looks at it, looks at her and then looks back to the eyePhone. "All I see is my own face," he says.

"It's the newest mirror app. It's called the vanity app. Isn't it great!? Look!" She turns the phone to look at it herself, then thrusts it back in William's face. "Look at the detail! This app is so cool. It helps you with putting makeup on and putting your earrings in and all sorts of stuff."

Heidi's doing wonderfully.

"Wow," William says, without enthusiasm.

"I also think the camera is just amazing," she says.

"It's a great camera," says William with more animation. "They really upgraded it. It has burst shooting, up to fifteen frames per second, autofocus, automatic exposure adjustment. Unfortunately they didn't upgrade the megapixels, but eleven is still really good for…"

Heidi acts confused. She shrugs her shoulders and pouts.

"It takes great photos of my cat." She shows William a photo of her cat and then turns the phone to look at it. "He's *sooo* cute, isn't he?"

William watches as she goes back to her vanity app, begins to pull faces, pucker her lips, straighten her hair and smooth her skin.

What's going through his head? Is he angry? Does he want to smash her phone, maybe smash her? Not what he expected, is Heidi? Not quite up to par. What will he do now? Who will be his next target, the object of his next attempt at social interaction? Who else does he see in his daily routine? Heidi was covered, so who could it possibly be next? William doesn't know anyone else. He has no friends. Tom perhaps, but where is Tom? He still hasn't returned William's texts.

William tells Heidi it's been nice meeting her, but he has to get to work. With his coffee he takes an apple. As he leaves, Heidi is still staring at her eyePhone.

On his way out of Harmony, William asks at Reception about the letter from the government. The dolt that's working says he has no idea what William is talking about, but that doesn't seem to bother William and he doesn't press further.

When he gets to work, he's not early—just right on time, 9:00 a.m. He lets himself in—he's still earlier than everyone else—and goes to his desk. There's no sign of Tom. He logs in and stares at the screen. He picks at his eyebrows and rubs the bit of stubble on his face, but he does not work. Stu arrives at 9:20, waves to William from across the room, but says nothing. William waits what he thinks is an appropriate amount of time for Stu to get logged in and then via Speaka, he writes:

William01: Hey Stu. Have you heard from Tom?

Stuman: I haven't.

William01: Okay. I'm working on sorting. Is that okay?

Stuman: Great.

At 9:46, William walks to the front office. The three office assistants: Deirdre, Stef and Maggie, stop what they're doing and scrutinize him. He must feel embarrassed.

In her singsong, Deirdre says, "William, what can we do for you?"

and smiles.

"Deirdre, umm, I'm just wondering, Deirdre, if you've heard from Tom. He hasn't been here for the past two days. And..." He's speaking rapidly.

"Stef, have you heard from Tom?" Deirdre turns back to William. "Stef's in charge of human resources."

"No. Wait—I don't know," says Stef. "Do you know his number? I got a strange text on my phone, but I don't know how he could have got my personal number. All it said was 'sick.'"

"Can I see the number?" William is frantic.

Stef hands him her phone.

"That's his number, Stef, that's him." William hands it back.

"So then, I guess he's sick," says Stef, matter-of-factly. "Oh, and if you talk to him, tell him that's not how we do things around here. We don't send excuses to personal phones."

"But you don't understand, Stef," William blurts. "Tom's not like you, he's not like me, Stef. He has no computer or Smartphone. I mean, did you check the old mail, the "mail" mail, Stef? Did you?"

Maggie restrains a laugh and Deirdre smiles. "William, that's absurd," she says, shaking her head.

"But what if he's really sick, Deirdre?" He turns his head. "Maggie? I haven't heard from him in two days."

"What do you want us to do, Will?" says Stef. "He's not our responsibility."

William stands motionless. The three women go back to work, fingers clacking on keyboards, ignoring him. He looks at each one in turn, but they don't respond to his silent gaze, so finally he turns and walks out. They shake their heads and laugh at him behind his back, but he doesn't seem to notice or care. When he gets to the foyer, the elevator doors open and the girl with the green-framed glasses steps out.

William turns to her. His desperation obviously overcomes his shyness and he says, "Jen. It's Jen, right?"

"It is, Will. How are…"

William cuts her off. "Jen, you know Tom, right, Jen?" He's talking very rapidly now, and there's sweat accumulating on his forehead. He is clearly distraught.

"Yes. Why? What's wrong?" She can hear the hysteria in his voice. Her face shows concern.

"Jen," William leans in to whisper, "I haven't seen Tom in two days. The last time was when we were doing some bad things and the Syndics showed up. I ran away, but I haven't seen him, Jen. I'm getting scared, Jen."

She places her hand on William's shoulder to comfort him. "William, what did you do?" she asks.

"Nothing terrible, Jen. Smoking and drinking outside in a restricted area. That's all."

She sighs. "Don't worry then. I haven't heard from him either, but you know him. He probably lost his phone. He doesn't have a computer. He may have just up and left. Give it a couple days. Come on," she says, coaxing William to follow, "work will take your mind off it."

"Maybe you're right, Jen. Maybe. But he wrote a message to Stef, Jen. It was one word. All it said was 'sick.' You know it's bad to be sick here, Jen. You know what can happen. You know…"

"Will, you need to calm down. If that's the case, then maybe he left. Maybe he just got out. What's the worst that can have happened?"

"I … I don't know. I just don't know. That's the problem."

"Come on, Will. Come with me, let's go and sit down," she says.

She walks next to him back to Data Management where William

goes back to his desk. He sits and a few minutes later, gets back to work.

Sporadic is how I would characterize his working behaviour the rest of the day. He would get down to it, but only in spurts, work hard for twenty minutes, then stare out the window at the rain for twenty minutes. He spends lunch sitting alone (nothing new), staring at his eyePhone, waiting perhaps for that text from Tom, doing nothing— staring, contemplating, watching the phone as if it might hold the solution to all of his problems.

Late in the afternoon, the employees of Eureka! receive their weekly newsletter. William habitually scans and then deletes them. On this occasion, though, he spends more time than usual reading it. The newsletter indicates that that night is the "Eurekites" third night of their *Star Wars* retrospective, and *Return of the Jedi* (remastered), would be shown. William, who has never gone to a Eureka! movie night for the obvious reason of his emotionalism, is nonetheless thinking hard; he reads the newsletter over and over, working out the mathematics of attending. He even checks his *RealDate Book*. His date book has never had anything in it, but he writes in for Friday: "movie night" and closes it.

At precisely 6:00 p.m., he leaves work with a "see ya later tonight" to Stu on the way out. The retrospective would begin at 8:00 p.m., giving him two hours to go home and eat before returning to work.

On his way home he only stops once, on the corner of Abbott and West Pender, where he pauses to read some of the new city posters. I'm not one to brag, but these particular posters are some of my best work—the poetics of the continuing war against illness and bad behaviour in the city. One of them, one that William surely reads, proclaims: "Vancouver helps those who help themselves," and depicts a young couple; the wife is pregnant and they are at the doctor's office getting help. As a statement, this particular slogan offers comforting assurance to our citizens: as long as they are there for the city, it will always be there for them. It says that when you love and trust Vancouver, it will love you back.

The other one that William reads while I watch says: "Be nice. This is Vancouver." That one isn't so impressive, I'll admit. Still, it does have a nice ring to it. I actually submitted a variation of it ("Be Nice. This is British Columbia") to the provincial competition for a new license plate motto, but unfortunately it was rejected. With a quick adjustment though, it became what it is, and is now posted all over the city. The picture under the slogan is of a smiling social worker covering a poor, just-arrived immigrant from the Philippines with a blanket—a nice Vancouverite spreading the message of niceness through his deeds.

William stares at the posters and reads the words for a few minutes. Then he breaks out in hysterical knee-slapping laughter. Again he dismisses my work. He thinks it is clownish, thinks it's funny—misses the point completely and fails yet again to transcend and to achieve, through poetry, a better understanding of the people around him. One day he'll get it.

Getting back to Harmony in high spirits, William walks to the elevator, pumps two squirts of sanitizer on his hands, steps into the elevator and works his hands together while riding up to the eighth floor. In his room, he grabs his reusable plastic container on the counter next to the dead cockroach, and heads down to the cafeteria for his organic meal.

He looks around the cafeteria—empty as usual. The old Chinese man is working the line. When William approaches him, instead of keeping his head down, he makes eye contact and begins a conversation.

Another attempt at communication.

"Hello," William says, smiling.

The old man does not reply.

"What's on the menu tonight?" Will asks politely.

"Tonight is free-range turkey, with garden greens and boiled baby potatoes."

"That sounds delicious." William hands over his container. "What's your name, by the way? I'm William. I see you here every night."

"I'm Tang."

"Chinese?"

"What does that matter?"

Will says nothing.

Tang shakes his head while filling William's container with food. William looks embarrassed and fidgets with the lid of his plastic container, but he keeps up the effort.

"Wasn't it free-range turkey that started the Scare?" he asks.

"How the hell would I know? I know nothing about that. Why do you people always want to talk about the Scare? The Chinese had nothing to do with it."

Tang looks mad.

"I'm sorry, I wasn't … I wasn't trying to …"

"Here's your food," Tang interrupts, handing William his reusable plastic container full of food. "Now get out of here, you're holding up the line."

William looks to his right; there is no one else in line. When he looks back, Tang has disappeared into the kitchen.

It didn't go so well for William. It's apparently not as easy for him to talk to people in real life as it is on *Real*. Or maybe it's him? William must be thinking that by now: that there are only two people in his daily routine outside of work—the pretty young woman and the

Chinese guy—and he couldn't communicate with either of them. He must be thinking by now that he has a problem. It must be sinking in that in a world where communication has never been easier, that to be unable to talk to people, real people, signifies a real problem. He must be realizing that this problem is him—that it's a deep malady going to the very core of his being.

Back in his room, he's feeling rejected. His computer is on, but he just stares at his *Real-ID*, at the photo of himself, while he eats. When 7:30 arrives, he puts on his coat and goes out into the rain to walk back to Eureka! for *Return of the Jedi*.

William is doing this to socialize. In spite of one of his greatest fears—breaking down and crying in public—he's going out to attempt to make friends. He had a real fun time with Thomas and the boys and he thinks he can recapture that. He's trying to recreate the feelings of inclusion and camaraderie he felt that night. He should realize it's impossible—movie night will never live up to his expectations. He knows who'll be there watching the film: some of the programmers he hates, maybe Deirdre and Stef who don't even like him and think he's a weirdo, and Stu. He thinks maybe Stu will be his friend. Stu is part of his *RealSeminar*; he's a pretty cool guy, and now William wants to make him a real-life pal. That's what William is thinking about on the way to work.

The film is being shown in the cafeteria. William arrives ten minutes early. Deirdre's there, setting up the digital projector, and even smiles at him when he enters. There are four other people in the room, all men, all programmers William doesn't know. About five minutes before 8:00, Stu arrives and sits next to him.

"Will! I never thought I'd see you here."

"I thought I would try it out," he says, smiling.

Then Deirdre presses play, turns off the lights and sits next to Stu on the other side. It's not necessary to describe the film. It plays and they watch. William, in spite of his fears, does not cry, though it must be agonizing for him to have to watch Yoda die, to experience the rekindling of the father-son relationship between Luke and Vader, one that William has yet to achieve with his own father. It must be truly hard for William. How he did it is a mystery, and I have to applaud him for his fortitude. He doesn't shed one tear.

When the film ends, Deirdre turns on the lights. The four programmers talk among themselves. Stu says to William, "It's been a while since I've seen that one. I think the remastered version actually adds quite a bit."

"Really? I mean, it looked a bit more fancy, but I don't think anything was really added. The story's still the story."

"Yeah, sure."

"It's been a long time since I've seen it too. I remember it differently, though. Maybe it's the three newer films that are the problem. This time watching the characters' emotions, they seem so unbelievable. Luke's unwavering forgiveness and Vader's capacity for good—they don't make sense. Assholes grow up to be fathers, and Vader's an asshole. That's the impression we get from all the movies leading up to this one—that he's a cold-hearted bastard—he is a bastard. It's hard to see how it's all supposed to fit together. It just didn't convince me this time, and it seems really sloppy—the six films together, the new ones and the old ones. Lucas messed up somewhere. The emotional arcs just don't work. I didn't feel a thing." William smiles confidently.

"It's an action movie, Will."

"Yeah, but that shouldn't matter."

"Okay, man, whatever." Stu rolls his eyes. "You take this movie stuff too seriously, dude."

"I'm ready," interrupts Deirdre, "you ready?" She's addressing Stu.

Stu turns to her. "Yep, let's go," he says. He turns back to Will. "We're getting out of here, Will. You have a good weekend. See you Monday."

"… sure. See you Monday."

Deirdre and Stu leave and William sits down. A few moments later one of the programmers says, "Hey pal, you got to leave. We need to lock up."

William walks out. He takes the elevator down and exits the building, walks back to Harmony in the rain with his head lowered, and goes directly to bed.

III

William should really fix the curtains in his room. It's unhealthy for a man to sleep like that with a light shining in his face all night. He tosses and turns and thrashes in his sleep in a clear state of agitation. What that light is doing to him is more than he can possibly know.

On Saturday morning he wakes early: 6:00 a.m. His first instinct is to sit at his desk and wake up his computer. His first destination is www.thegirlnextdoor.com. This time Julia is available.

jewels: Willy!

Will-i-am84: I'm glad you're there. You look beautiful, you. I've been trying to reach you for the past couple of days. I really needed to talk, a lot has been going on. I wish I could call you by your name. How are you?

jewels: Oh, Willy, you're so sweet. I'm great! I just got off work. I'm a bit tipsy. Do you want me to undress? [She smiles coyly].

Will-i-am84: No, no, not at all, not today. Please just listen. I … my friend Tom, he's vanished. I've been trying to meet people, but no one wants to talk to me. I can't work, I've been having this strange recurring dream about little men in black rappelling down the window like rainfall. There was a dead cockroach in my room. I threw up in my sink. I had some friends, then lost them. Tom is gone! No one wants to talk to me.

jewels: Will, are you going crazy?

Will-i-am84: I'm not kidding. I feel alone. I'm so lonely. No one will talk to me. No one. This is not a joke. I just can't seem to talk to anyone. Don't you understand?

jewels: Jesus, Will. [Her face changes to one of concern]. Tell me what happened? It can't be all that bad, can it?

Will-i-am84: I went out with Tom and two of his friends on Wednesday. We drank outside and the Syndics showed up. I ran away. Tom didn't show up to work the last two days. I can't get in touch with him. I wanted to meet new people. I wanted to try and make friends, but no one wants to, no one wants to talk to me. I can't talk to them. I don't know what's wrong. My room is trashed. I tore off the curtains. I'm having this dream …

jewels: Try and calm down, Will. I'll start to worry about you. [She smiles with genuine affection].

Will-i-am84: I want you to see me. I want to know your name. You're the closest thing I have to a friend right now. I just want one real connection in my life.

Although Julia cannot possibly hear or see William, he begins now to simultaneously speak aloud and type what he is saying.

jewels: Oh, Will.

Will-i-am84: *Please.*

jewels: It's Julia. My name's Julia, okay? But stop exaggerating Will, please. We are friends. We're more than friends. But as far as me seeing you. I can't do that. That's just impossible.

Will-i-am84: At least I can see you, Julia.

jewels: I'll turn on my mic too, okay? Then you can hear me too. [She does].

"Is that better? Can you hear me, now?" she asks.

Will-i-am84: I can [he smiles as big as I have ever seen him do]. You sound like I thought you would.

"Oh, shut up, Will. Now listen to me. I'm sorry you're having a hard time. But you'll get over it, and you'll get back on track. Your friend did not vanish, and you are not alone. Do you hear me?"

Will-i-am84: I do. I'm sorry. No one ever died of loneliness, I know. I know I sound crazy. I'm just, I don't know, something isn't right, Julia.

"It'll be fine, Will. And you'd better not die, you bum. You're one of my best clients."

Will-i-am84: Wow, thanks.

"Don't be sarcastic, and try not to take it all too far, Will. Okay?" She smiles. Her eyes are wide and encouraging.

Will-i-am84: It's so hard sometimes.

"It is for us all, Will, but it will get better. I promise it will."

Will-i-am84: Okay. Well, I better go then.

"You still got time Will. You don't have to leave."

Will-i-am84: I know. I'm feeling tired though. I'm happier just to have heard the sound of your voice.

"Shut up, Will. You're too sweet and far too sensitive for your own good. I'll see you again soon, right?"

Will-i-am84: You will. Have a good weekend.

He closes the window and Julia's gone. Her words help him to forget his recent social failures, to forget about Tom, Ryan and his inability to make new friends. Her soft, affectionate look and soothing voice have put him at ease. So much so that he goes back to bed and falls soundly asleep for three hours.

When he awakes, it's as though he's back to normal and he begins his weekend routine. He goes online and orders two large pizzas. These are the same two large pizzas—one with pepperoni and cheese, one with bacon and mushrooms, always from the same place, Goldie's Pizza on West Pender—that he's been ordering every weekend for the past several months. One of the pizza's he'll eat today, Saturday; the other he'll save in his fridge for tomorrow. For the next two days, William won't leave his room unless he absolutely must. He'll stay inside and he'll chain-watch movies, television series and *RealVideo* clips in an ascetic display of behaviour characteristic of a paranoid recluse. It's an unhealthy and frankly ridiculous way to spend one's time.

The problem, too, is that it's a relapse. Julia seems to have had too strong an effect on him. Naïvely, he thinks that he's back to normal and that by reverting to his run-of-the-mill schedule, he'll feel better.

For us, it means that we'll have to step up our timetable. William must be made to feel totally isolated. For my treatment to be effective, he must, when we do call him in, be entirely alone in the world. He must feel so alone and so broken that he actually wants to come and see us. He must believe, with a little coaxing of course, that it was his free will that brought him to us. It will be as though we, and no one else, are his last and only true friends. Our hands—soft, warm and gentle—will be the only ones open to him. "Vancouver helps those who help themselves." William must remember the poetry. He must transcend himself to be saved.

The pizzas arrive and William watches, in order, Sergio Leone's western, "man with no name," trilogy: *A Fistful of Dollars*, *For a Few Dollars More*, and *The Good, the Bad and the Ugly*, with Clint Eastwood.

This must be William's way of examining the theme of friendship.

He watches the films, and he tries to identify with the Eastwood character, the man with no name, the perpetual loner and outcast who, in spite of his troubled and isolated nature, is able to experience the joys of friendship with the most unlikely people in the most unlikely of places. It's hard to know what affects him most, or what he wants to get out of these films. He does not cry once, meaning that somehow he's managing to control his emotionalism, or that watching the films is, in fact, a positive emotional experience for him—a catharsis, a way to gain back some of the courage that was so recently stripped from him in his failed attempts to make friends. Like the Eastwood character that William identifies with, he may think that suffering is just one part of the process, a necessary step before finally experiencing the true feelings and connection of real friendship.

After watching the westerns, William continues his personal exploration of friendship by watching two episodes of the 2001 World War II-themed HBO miniseries *Band of Brothers*. I've seen this series before. The episodes he chooses to watch are two of the most gut-wrenching: "Bastogne" and "The Breaking Point."

William has seen it before too, and he knows exactly what he wants when he picks these episodes. He hunts for them specifically in *Real*'s database because, of the ten in the series, these two episodes focus intensely on the theme of friendship. Friendship comes literally under fire, as the band of brothers in "Easy Company" are bombed to bloody bits by German artillery. William tries to watch to learn how friendship can endure, even in the toughest, most horrific situation. Perhaps he was watching because of his failing friendship with Ryan. He watches best friends Guarnere and Toye in *Band of Brothers* get their legs blown off by German artillery. There they are, strewn on the snowy battlefield, legs blown apart into ribbons, yet they manage, stoically, to crack a friendly joke or two as their wounded, legless bodies are carried off the battlefield. Is William's friendship with Ryan that strong? The values of "the Greatest Generation" are only a myth, William.

He could hardly stand watching friends see friends die in *Band of Brothers*. He weeps (I cried, too, when I watched these episodes, William)—for almost two straight hours. As the episodes play, tears pour down William's face. Eventually, around 11:00 p.m., after this forced emotional pain, William manages to doze off. Again, all night long the bright light from across the street pours in the window, and shines on his head. He tosses and turns as he sleeps.

When he wakes up Sunday morning, it's 8:00 a.m. Again, instinctively, he wakes up his computer and goes to his *Real-ID* page. The first thing he notices is Ryan's *RealAnnouncement*—a priority post sent from Ryan's Canvas to all his contacts. Flashing in the middle of William's screen in bold, fluorescent letters reminiscent of the title sequence from a 1980s computer game, blinks the words PHOENIX IMPORT, under which is a crudely rendered drawing of a fluorescent orange phoenix bursting forth, wings spread, from a pool of lava.

William cringes at Ryan's childish effort at animation, but keeps reading. The announcement goes on in smaller, fluorescent print to say that Phoenix Imports is the brainchild of two great men, Mike George and Ryan Jeffreys. It proclaims that RWM Solutions has outlived its usefulness and grown redundant, and that to inaugurate the reimagining of the grand "new and better two-man business venture," friends will receive discounts on cell phone batteries and eyePhone covers.

There is no way of knowing how many times William reads these words, or how long it takes before the message sinks in. No doubt it is denial that first surfaces, then perhaps it is betrayal that keeps his eyes fixed on the screen. Finally, deep loathing sets in and locks his gaze to the image in hatred.

Ryan is available on *Real* and so is Mike, but William just stares. Something keeps him from confronting them immediately. He gazes intently at Ryan's rendition, his interpretation of what he thought was going on. In all its crudeness, the phoenix rising from the lava is Ryan rising from the ashes of his friendship with William. He is the success and William is the redundancy. William does not know how to react to this. He does not know how one can even begin a dialogue with a person who has committed such treachery. To be stabbed in the back by your best friend and then turn around and say to him "don't worry about it." It's a situation most of us will never have to confront. But poor William, he is forced to sit there and think about it. After an hour, he decides to write something. He addresses Mike and Ryan together.

(9:18 AM) William Potenco: So that's it then? RWM is just RM now?

(9:20 AM) Ryan Jeffreys: No. It's Phoenix Imports, and its [sic] just business Will. You didn't do shit so you had to go.

(9:21 AM) William Potenco: Just business? Three friends start a company and then two of them, after six years, turn around and kick the third one out, without even really discussing it with him at all, and that's only business?

(9:22 AM) Mike George: sorry will. he's right.

(9:23 AM) William Potenco: Mike, I know you're not really to blame here. You're just very gullible. What did Ryan tell you? That I was holding you back? That you would do better, just the two of you? Is that it?

(9:24 AM) Ryan Jeffreys: Don't talk to him like that. This was all your fault. You fucked this up. You neglected your work and you got fired. WE canned you. It wasn't Mike, it wasn't me, it was WE, a mutual decision. So stop your crying you little fag.

(9:25 AM) William Potenco: Fag? What happened to you, Ryan? What the hell's wrong with you? Your picture, it's not even you. Who are you? Do you even remember that we're friends?

(9:26 AM) Ryan Jeffreys: I grew up, you didn't. That is me, William. Have you forgot what your friends look like? I've grown up. It's you that needs help, you fucking mental retard.

(9:28 AM) William Potenco: That is not you. You have not grown up. Unless growing up is becoming an asshole and a traitor. I don't even feel like I know you anymore. I can't recognize you. We've been best friends for over ten years. How can you do that? Mike, why are you not saying anything?

(9:29 AM) Ryan Jeffreys: Like I already said. It wasn't me. It wasn't Mike. It was you. You started to hang out with that guy, the loser, Thomas, and you fucked up. You have to take responsibility for your actions, William. So, you're fired. That's it. End of story. And William, I took that picture yesterday. Have you completely forgoten [sic] what I look like? You're sick, man. You need help.

(9:31 AM) William Potenco: Mike? You have nothing to say…

(9:34 AM) Mike George: he's right. i already said it. i'm sorry.

(9:35 AM) William Potenco: God, you're a moron, you fucking lackey. Do you have any independent thoughts at all? And Ryan, I really don't know what to say. You're just such a piece of garbage. I want my investment back.

(9:36 AM) Ryan Jeffreys: haha. Take it more personally, why don't you? Go cry to your mom, like you always do. You mad bro? hahaha. You get nothing back.

How infuriating for William. He's never been one to hide his emotions, and at this moment it's no different. It's quite clear, from the way he slams down the mouse on the desk, how hard his fingers come down on the keys, the shade of crimson his face goes and the tears welling up in his bulging eyes, that if Ryan were in the room, William would have strangled him. Finally the inevitable explosion and these glorious last words:

(9:42 AM) William Potenco: FUCK YOU! FUCK YOU BOTH!

Then William initiates the *coup de grâce* and removes Ryan and Mike from his list of *Real* contacts. He spends the next two hours systematically removing all traces of Ryan, Mike and RWM Solutions from his computer by deleting files, folders, photos and contact details and erasing anything else that reminds him of his two best friends. When he finally calms down he might realize that it was his fault. He had neglected his work. Whether Ryan should have been so vicious is another question. Mike being bovine and unresponsive is characteristic of the simple-minded, but that's not the problem. The real problem is and always has been William and now he's beginning to understand.

Utterly alone and confined to his room, William is friendless. It must be a terrible emotional trauma he's going through. I can see it. I can see how he's running his hand through his sweaty hair. How he's breathing deeply and erratically. Holding his head in his shaky hands with so much force. It's taking it's toll. He needs to rest. He collapses into his bed and lies awake until evening. At 8:30 p.m., he goes to his computer and opens his *RealDiary*.

The feeling, if it is a feeling, for it may be the lack of all feeling that I'm experiencing, is one of lonely exile. It's like banishment from the real world and from the *Real* world. I'm so sad. I feel hungry, but I can't eat. I'm empty inside. Any why? What did I do? Tom is gone, and Ryan and Mike. And what's left? Eureka!? The job I've discovered is nothing more than cattle prodding. My family? A father I hate and a mother who could never understand what I'm going through. A girl? Beautiful Julia who I might love, but who will never love me back. What is this if not prison? Is this my sentence, my punishment for being me? Permanent loneliness is what I get, what I have to look forward to for the rest of my life? I'm my very own cell. I'm my own inescapable mobile prison; for nothing, nobody can come near me and I cannot leave it's confines.

What are my options? Do like Tom and run away north? Do like that doctor? Who do I even care about? Am I even capable of empathy for another person like he is?

We go along believing that we're free because we must; we're taught; we're conditioned to think and act as if we're free. I'm free to suffer. It may even be my choice. I don't know anymore. I must also be free to feel better, to feel happy again. Isn't that my choice too? Is there really no one to blame but myself? Honestly, am I the problem here? I just can't believe that. I didn't ask for this for Christ's sake. I was so happy just a few weeks ago—happy. It's finally stopped raining. God I hate this goddamned place and these goddamned people.

William is correct and it's good to see him realize that he's the problem, but he errs when he thinks that he'll never get better. Soon he'll be here and his treatment will be administered and all of his misplaced sentiments and blame will cease to exist. He won't want to think negative thoughts anymore. It'll be that easy. Very soon, William's Disease will have it's cure.

Treatment
by Doctor Officer Elias Degair

I

William logged out of his *Real* account. He walked to the counter and picked up the dead cockroach. He examined it and tears welled up in his eyes. The corpse of that cockroach might be all he thinks he has left—and it's dead. He gently placed it back on the counter, returned to bed and pulled the covers up to his neck. The light from the Chinese import shop had just turned on and it shone in the window onto his head, but he just lay, head illuminated, and stared at the ceiling. He stared for hours, his eyes slowly closing and snapping open only to focus again on the ceiling.

It's Monday morning, but when William's alarm app goes off at 6:00 a.m., he does not get out of bed. He lies staring at the ceiling like the night before as if nothing had changed. In the background plays the old time jazz radio program. It plays for four hours until 10:00 am, while William stares into nothingness.

What brings him back from whatever precipice he was on is a mystery. What makes him recognize that he is of this world, that it's Monday morning, and that he does have a job can only be some neurological trigger connected to William's deep sense of duty. He's

224

never missed a day of work, and until last Thursday, he'd never been late. This we know and this we count on. Our metadata predicted it and his routine demands that he go to work. He simply must go today. My treatment depends on it. After I spent so long ensuring that he would feel as low as he does on this day, he simply must get up and go to work.

Our metadata is correct—at 10:14 a.m. he wakes from his dreamlike state. But it looks like he's having trouble realizing he's awake. That feeling in his gut—the hole, the pain of loss, the emptiness in his being —these feelings are real and should convince him. Yet there is something about his expression. William has nothing left in this world except his job, it's all that's guiding him, so slowly, while he fights his loneliness and his desire to remain dreaming, he gets himself together and is on his way to work. Each of the sets of cameras along the way, each of the pairs of eyes that have followed and watched over him these past weeks, playing a role in our understanding of him, records a downcast man walking to work with his head down, hunched over with the invisible weight of lonely rejection on his shoulders. The sky above him is overcast, and there's a chance of rain.

When he arrives at the J. Griffin Building it's almost 11:00 a.m. In the doors, up to the top floor, down the hall to Data Management. He walks in as if nothing were wrong, as if nothing has changed. He passes Stu's desk, but Stu says William's name and William stops.

"Will, what are you doing here?"

"I'm sorry, Stu, I'm sorry I'm late. I promise it won't happen again."

"No, I mean, what are you doing here at all?"

"What do you mean? I work here."

"Will, you're not well." Stu shakes his heads. "Come over here next to me." William goes and stands next to Stu. "Don't you remember sending in your letter of resignation? We got the letter this morning, Will. Deirdre got it. Dana got it. I got it. It came from your *Real* account, man. We all read it. But now you're here. What's wrong with you, dude?"

It's probably best that William is exhausted for this. How he would have reacted otherwise is something I prefer not to think of. He's tired and his body and mind are capable of only so much.

"What letter, Stu?" William screws up his eyes. He's confused and he rubs them. They are very red and it looks like he may cry.

"Will, it's right here on my screen." Stu looks like he thinks William is crazy. "Look. It says right here that you're terribly sorry, but that you can no longer work here."

"…"

"Here. You cite some psychological problems, and a complete inability to work with Dana as your main reasons. Please, don't look at me. Look at the letter yourself."

William begins to read from the screen. His face loses all colour as he reads. It does read like something he would write and it did come from his *Real* account.

"I didn't write that."

"Will, we got it from your *Real* account."

William sighs, closes his eyes and drops his head back. He's thinking. Maybe he did write it. He hasn't been himself. He hasn't slept. Maybe he did write it. Maybe sometime last night he got up out of bed, went to his computer and composed a letter of resignation from his one-time dream job. He's thinking hard now.

He levels his head. "I didn't write that," he repeats.

"Will. What are we supposed to do? You've been acting strange. You show up late. You don't talk to anyone, then you send us this letter that says you're sick, that you have psychological problems, that you can't bear to work in the same room as Dana. How are we supposed to take that?"

"It's a lie! I was late once!" he blurts.

"It's a lie? Now it's a lie?" Stu sniggers and shakes his head. "Shit, Will, how could it be a lie?"

"I don't know. Someone's hacked my account. Someone's trying to ruin me. I don't know what's happening, but it's a lie. A huge lie."

"Hacked your account? *Real* is unhackable, Will, and who the hell would want to hack *your* account? You should hear yourself. You're twisted, man."

"No!" William yells and people look over. They stare at him now, but he continues in a raised voice. "And Tom! Is that a lie too, Stu? What happened to Tom, Stu? Did he resign too!?"

"Will, I don't know what you're talking about."

"What am I talking about? Don't you see what's happening!"

"Will, look, I don't have a clue what you're on about, but I think you should leave. No one's out to get you. You need help."

Dana's heard the shouts. The door to his office opens and out he walks to join in on the conversation.

"What's going on? What's *he* doing here?" He points in William's face.

"He's just leaving, Dana," says Stu.

"You quit, Will, get the hell out of here," says Dana.

"No!" William screams. "This is not right. I did not do that. You did it. I, I…"

"Will," says Stu, standing, "it's time to go now. Let's go." Stu grabs William by the arm, and he is too weak to shake free.

"Get him out of here," says Dana.

In the background, they are all staring at him. The guy with the dreadlocks is even laughing. The girl with the green-framed glasses looks worried. She looks around at everyone else in the room, then back to William and lowers her head. William must feel embarrassed. He must want to sink into the floor and disappear. He can never go back now. Eureka! is over for him.

"Stu, I … I didn't write it Stu. Ask Tom, Stu." William is being led down the hall by the arm. Stu puts him in the elevator. Will protests. Stu tells him not to come back. The elevator door closes. Under his breath Stu mutters something about one crazy motherfucker. In the elevator, our cameras register William's hysteria.

What will he do? He's outside now. He's become obsolete. He wants to go home and sit and be quiet. He wants to run. He wants to check his *Real* account to see if he did indeed write that letter. He's still capable. He won't come apart just now, not at this crucial moment. He has motivation and the will to see it through. He'll rush home and turn on his computer, log in to *Real* and see for himself.

He runs back to Harmony and goes straight to his room, to his desk, and logs in to *Real*. Without looking at anything else, he goes to his outbox where he sees, there at the top of the screen, sent at 8:30 a.m. that very morning, the "Letter of Resignation," the same one he read in the office. It cites his psychological problems and his problems with Dana as the reasons for his departure and asks that the resignation be effective immediately.

But he notices other things as well—another letter in his outbox. Before he can think further about the letter of resignation, he opens the mystery letter. It's addressed to his father. It's a long apology, also sent that morning. In it, William says that he wishes he had written earlier. He'd wanted to, but it was so hard. He hoped that his father would write back and that they could discuss whatever problems they had. William wants his father back. He wants to reconcile. And what else? His profile picture, yes, yes, he sees it. It's not quite him, not quite the recent him, the him of the moment. Let's be thankful it's not *that* him. No, it's a happy William, a William with a sparkle in his eyes, colour in his cheeks, and a smile on his face that says, "Nice to meet you, I'm a happy, normal guy. We should be friends."

But that isn't all. He sees that Ryan and Mike are back on his friends list—we're confident that his friendship with Ryan will improve. We're sure of it. It might take a little longer with Mike— William was pretty mean, after all—but Mike'll come around.

William can't change anything. I see that he's trying, but it's no use. His *Real* settings are locked. What's done is done. It's permanent. His *Real* is now our *Real*. His mail is our mail. His life is our life. He is who we say he is. And he's good. He's getting better. The treatment is starting to work.

He must be wondering, of course he must be wondering, if he changed those things himself, maybe in a waking dream. He's been so tired recently. I'm watching him as he's trying to work it all out. I see him now as he sees #Ten-Two-Twenty-Two, William Potenco on *Real* and wonders, how could he have done it? If he, the real William, didn't change those things, then it must have been him, #Ten-Two-Twenty-Two, the *Real* William Potenco. He must've done it. Who else could? But how, how could he have done that to himself? He trusted #Ten-Two-Twenty-Two, William Potenco, and now he has betrayed him. William must know that he is truly alone. He's become a stranger even to himself. And he's incomplete; he's not real like he is on *Real*. On *Real* he is as I know he's always wanted to be. On *Real*, from now own, there will be no more sadness—no more sad compositions or sad diary entries. No more diary entries at all, for that matter.

Don't get mad, William. I can see that he wants to smash the screen. I see it in his face. He would love to take a brick and smash in the skull of #Ten-Two-Twenty-Two, William Potenco, the man staring back at him from the screen. But it won't change a thing. He can't smash the Internet. He can't smash *Real*.

I watch him sit and stare at the screen. He rubs his eyes and chin and tugs at his eyebrow hair. He's confused, suffering, trying to figure out what to do next. I wish he didn't have to suffer so much, I do. I wish we could bring him in now. Soon, though—real soon. There is but one inevitable thing left for him to do.

He contacts Julia. He goes to www.thegirlnextdoor.com and she's available. He pays the fifty dollars and she's in front of him.

jewels: Willy! I hope you're feeling better. Are you?

Julia radiates happiness and warmth from her eyes and smile. She really likes him.

Will-i-am84: No, Julia. Can you put on the microphone? I, I need to hear your voice.

William speaks aloud what he is typing. Julia does as he asks.

"What is it, Will?"

Will-i-am84: Julia, I really wish I could talk to you in person, Julia.

"I'm sorry that's not possible, Will. What's wrong?"

Will-i-am84: Betrayal. Conspiracy. They're out to get me. I've betrayed myself, Julia.

"What the hell are you talking about, Will? C'mon, this has to stop," she pleads.

Will-i-am84: The computer is staring at me, Julia. Julia—the computer is staring at me.

"That's because you're looking at me, Will. You can see your reflection in the screen."

Will-i-am84: Don't you see that it's all a big lie? There is no privacy. They lied. They're watching me. I've changed. I'm no longer me anymore.

"Will, you're not making any sense. You're acting crazy."

Will-i-am84: Julia, they hacked in. Into my *Real* account. It's not me anymore. I'm not me.

"Just quit that, then. You don't need *Real*, William."

Will-i-am84: But you don't understand. He's betrayed me.

"Who's betrayed you?"

Will-i-am84: He has: #Ten-Two-Twenty-Two, William Potenco. He quit my job, he wrote to my bastard dad and he's smiling. Julia …

"Will, *you* are you. I care about you. Come—come to me. Leave that place. I'm in Montreal; just get on a bus and come. I've seen you. I know who you are. I saw you on *Real*. Come to me. Everything will be fine."

Will-i-am84: No, Julia. You saw him on *Real*, Julia. *Him*. Did you talk to him? What did he say? That animal. What did he tell you?

"Oh, Will." She lowers her eyes and shakes her head.

Will-i-am84: Don't be sad, Julia.

"Will, you're sick. Something's gone wrong with you. You need help."

Will-i-am84: It's my enemies, Julia. I have to find them, then I'll be fine, then I'll come. You'll see. You'll see, Julia. I'm right. You can't understand right now, but you will, Julia. It wasn't me Julia. It was the *Real* me. I didn't do it, I promise.

"Will, you don't even know what you're saying."

Will-i-am84: I do Julia. I know better than ever. I'll show you Julia. You'll see, you'll see, Julia…

"Will, I have to go. I'm sorry. I can't talk to you when you're like this. I have to go now. You get better and then call me again, okay?"

William starts to type, but she's already vanished.

"She'll see."

A look of unspeakable fear appears on William's face. He leans back in his chair, looking terrified. He begins to pace the room, back and forth and in circles, frantically. He's thinking. He's utterly alone. He has no one. He keeps repeating the words: logical, illogical, sound, unsound. He's thinking crazy thoughts. He's thinking of conspiracy, of little men in black, perhaps, of his recurring dream. It's had too strong an effect. A person can't sleep with a light on their head like that. Just put the damned curtains back up, William. There are no little men dressed in black, just honest, hard-working doctors looking out for the health of the citizens at large. It's all quite legit—quite legal, quite honest work we're doing. William will see, soon enough. When he wakes up tomorrow, all will become clear. He must try not to trouble himself about it. It's been hard, I can imagine how hard it's been on him, but he'll see, it will all get better. He's had a friend all along, and tomorrow he'll understand and realize it's all been worth it.

I would have liked to say that William took my advice and rested, but it seems that our techniques, our treatments, have had a too strong effect on his fragile mind. He did lie down, but only to get up again, to pace, to lie down, to splash his face with freezing water, to have a cold shower, to pace again—all the while mumbling long, rambling strings of unintelligible gibberish. It was almost painful to watch his mind unravelling.

II

It's 8:00 a.m. William's awake in bed when a loud knock sounds on the door – BANG! BANG! BANG! But he barely registers the noise, and turns his head only slightly to stare in the direction of the noise. *It's the little men dressed in black, William, and they're here to take you and throw you in a padded cell.* Haha! I'm joking—but honestly, he looks terrible.

He doesn't answer the door. That's fine, I had bet he probably wouldn't, so I told them to slide the letter under the door and leave. He sees the letter from his bed. William's a curious man. I had given him ten minutes, but he cracked in five and I lost. He gets up and goes to the door and opens the envelope.

The Public Health Bureau of Vancouver

File Number: 654419-8404-043513
Address: 6090 Northwest Marine Drive
Vancouver, BC V6T 1Z1
Officer: Degair
Room: -
Telephone: (604) 822-xxxx
E-Mail: elias.degair@phb.van.ca
Internet: www.phb.van.ca
Date: Tuesday, May xx, 201-

Mr. William Potenco
1 West Pender, Suite 8A
Vancouver, BC V6B 1R3

Subpoena as Accused

Dear Mr. Potenco,

You have been incriminated in the following investigation:

Accusation: concealed illness
Date: Friday, April 4, 201-
Place: 1 West Pender, Suite 8A

According to Article 23 of Special Decree 451, you are given the right to comment on this accusation. You are hereby asked to come to our offices to present evidence and apply for nullification of this accusation. Please come on the following date:

Date: Tuesday, May xx, 201-, 11:30 a.m.
Place: 6090 Northwest Marine Drive. Vancouver, BC. V6T 1Z1

Please bring Official Identification: (passport/birth certificate (full form)/drivers license)

In the event that you cannot appear on that date, you must notify us by telephone or written (electronic) communication. If you do not appear on the date specified, and present no sound reason, it is assumed that you do not wish to exercise your right to comment on the accusation. However, if you do waive this right, you will have no further right of comment and must therefore have to accept the presiding Doctor Officer's decision in this investigation.

Sincerely yours,

Degair, Doctor Officer

He reads the invitation and calmly places it on his desk. He walks into the bathroom and stares at his face in the mirror. He begins pulling faces and smoothing and tugging at his skin. He leans into the mirror to examine in detail the features of his face. He pulls the skin below his eye down to inspect his eyeball; he tilts his head back to look closely up his nose; he opens his eyes wide and shuts them tight; he turns this way and that; he tries to look into his ears.

What's he looking for? Physical traces of his illness? He can look all he wants; the signs are hardly physical. He should stop spending so much time thinking about it. He needs to get ready. He needs to have a shower, maybe a shave too. He should try to eat something. We're going to meet, he and I, and he needs his strength. It won't be easy. He has a little over two hours. It's time he steeled himself.

At 10:30 a.m. William exits Harmony. I had a couple of Syndics place a bloated dead albino rat at the entrance. William has had a strange association with dead animals recently. I wanted it to give him a little shock and see how he'd react. We need to keep him on the edge. What's surprising is that the rat doesn't startle him at all. He even smiles when he sees it. Or is that a grimace? He takes a bite of an apple in his hand while staring at the white rat, so I guess it doesn't affect his constitution much. It's curious. William's reactions are all out of place. He sees a dead crow and he cries, he sees a dead cockroach and he cares for it, and he sees a bloated, dead albino rat and he takes a bite of an apple. It seems we still haven't figured him out...

So eat the apple, then. His appetite means that he's not that nervous, or maybe he's that hungry. It's been a while since he's eaten. He munches the apple as he walks south down Carrall, west on Keefer, and then enters the SkyTrain station.

There are plenty of cameras in our SkyTrain stations. We've done a lot to make the stations as clean and healthy as possible, but they're still sites for contagion. It's hard balancing the good of the people with the demands of a modern, efficient infrastructure. Cars, of course, are infinitely better for the health of the people since they isolate the individual and keep him or her free from airborne disease, but they pollute more and they do cause congestion on our streets—such difficult questions. If William and all the rest only knew what we go through for them. We watch him enter the station, buy his ticket, take the escalator to the platform and board the train. The familiar whoosh of the doors closing behind him, and he's on his way.

He must be thinking about his crimes and wondering how to act when he gets here. He doesn't seem happy to have to come in and confess. I don't honestly think he was surprised to receive my letter. Some of my colleagues still think he's confused and hasn't worked things out yet. But I think he knows—he's worked it out now that he's been sick for some time.

William sits quietly on the train as it brings him to Main and Commercial where he transfers to the Millennium Line, which will bring him to me. He stares out the window as he so often did at work; he stares across the city as it passes by. He stares across the ocean toward the mountains. Maybe he's thinking of going to the mountains again. Maybe he wants to get away. He's always wanted to go for a long hike, get out in the wilderness, but he's been too afraid. Maybe we'll cure that too. It'll do him some good to get out in the fresh mountain air. He's stopped staring out the window and is looking down at his eyePhone. He's probably trying to log into *Real*, maybe thinking it was all a dream and that it didn't happen. He wants to be sure. But he's not dreaming and he'll never again be able to log into *Real*.

When he gets off the train he won't have much farther to go. University campus is big, he knows that, but does he know where we are? He'll need to look at the map. It's right where he gets off the train. There, I see him looking now; we're in the southwest, next to the Experimental Farms. Good, he sees. He still has fifteen minutes. At a good pace, it should take him only ten to get here.

I see you, William, I see you coming now, walking in my direction. Things are all ready for you here.

III

He's sitting in the lobby waiting. He's on the edge of his seat. He looks nervous as I approach.

"William, I'm glad you could come on such short notice. My name is Doctor Elias Degair. I've been in charge of your case. If you could follow me, please."

He stands without a greeting and follows me.

"What do you think of our building, William?" I ask as we walk. "It was designed by Morphosis, you know. Do you see how they use glass? The whole building—glass doors, hallways, floors, desks—glass everything. Do you know why everything is made of glass, William?"

"…"

"No? It's so everyone can see inside, William. It's so everyone—the public and all of us that work here—can see everyone else and see what we do. It's all about transparency, William. We've nothing to hide here, William, so don't be anxious. Okay?"

"…"

"We're almost there now. Just up these stairs—glass, of course—truly an amazing feat. A glass spiral staircase, William, impressive, no?"

"…"

"Not so talkative, are we? Well, that's okay. But look around you, William, look how very busy we are. Do you see how busy we are? The health of the whole city is in our hands."

He stops and looks around at all the people hard at work. Then we continue up the stairs and down a glass-walled hallway to my office.

"Very busy, indeed; sickness, disease and the health of the citizenry have no notion of time, you know. It's twenty-four hours, seven days a week, non-stop work … Here we are. This is my office. Nice, isn't it? I have an okay view. Not quite as nice as yours was at Eureka!, but I guess we can't all be so lucky … Oh, also, William, I should say, please forgive the temperature in here. I know it's very cold, but I'm going to have to ask you to remove your jacket. It will get warmer. It will get very warm, but for now it's cold. It's a standard interrogation technique to fluctuate the temperature. Cold to get us started and warm to ease you in. Do you understand? Do you see how I tell you this? All transparent, William. Do you understand?"

"No."

"Please, please, have a seat. Do you want a coffee? You like coffee, and you're very tired. I'm very tired too, William. I've been up with you for the past few days. We take our work very seriously here."

"No coffee, thanks."

"Okay, okay then, no problem … Are you comfortable? Are you ready William? You look confused."

He shrugs and looks from side to side. "I … I guess. I mean, I don't really know what's going on," he says.

"Well, William, the first thing you should know is that I've put the most sedulous care into your case. It's not on a whim that we've called you in. We've been following you and your illness for over a month now."

"What illness? You've been following me?"

"William, do you see this file in front of me? This is your file. It's big, and it has in it all the evidence we've gathered on you. Information about your habits, metadata—all sorts of things that we know from your daily life, your *Real* profile and your online activity. We know everything about you. For example, we know your IQ—upwards of 130, William, very impressive. We know, of course, your gender, sexual orientation, political leanings, religious beliefs. We know your favourite websites, search history, film preferences. We know …"

"You've been following me for a month? Why? What can you learn in a month?"

"William, this is not the olden days. We haven't been 'following' you, like in the movies on a stake out. Let me try to explain …"

"What am I doing here?"

"We'll get to that William. Don't be angry. First, I'd like to ask you something. This will help you understand. Do you know what the Chinese word for computer is?"

"No, of course not. Why would I know that?"

"Don't be insolent, William. I'm trying to help you. It's *dian nao*. To translate directly, it means electric brain. I find that fascinating. Don't you?"

"I … I don't know. Why are you telling me this? What's going on?"

"William, you've seen lots of movies; spy movies, movies about the police building cases against criminals. Do you know how long it used to take to track down all the information and build a case against someone who was a murderer or a thief or a traitor or a political enemy, for example?"

"…"

"Months and years, William, years. And even after they built the case, the police would have to bring in the suspect and question or torture them to get the confession. It was all very messy stuff—long, time-consuming, unpleasant stuff. But that was then. Today we're very fortunate to have our electric brains, our computers. They don't require much torture to open up and to give us your secrets. You turn on your computer, you're already connected to the Internet and it begins to record. It's marvellous. Everyone's thoughts are recorded; everything you do online is ordered, structured and saved in one long timeline, on platforms like *Real* and Eureka!, for us to read and reference. People like you who help build these things go unlauded—it's a shame. For us it's convenient that people use their electric brains rather than their real ones. It makes our job much easier. Do you see where I'm going with this, William?"

"No. I'm not a criminal, or a terrorist."

"Of course not, William. But you are sick. You're here because you're sick. The information I've mentioned, your IQ and so forth, that's all public, that's what our software got just from your electric brain, Smartphone, and *Real* account. That's what got us started. Our

239

software analyzed the metadata and saw the troubling signs. When combined with the rest of your information—your online search history, your *RealDiary* entries, evidence of your relationship with Julia—I diagnosed a very complicated illness, with symptoms of loneliness, depression, perversion ...”

“What are you talking about? I’m not sick.”

“Don’t cut me off, William. Of course you are. Does this sound familiar? On April 8, from 7:00 a.m. to 7:30 a.m. you visited www.porngurls.com and www.girlsxxxvids.com, you searched for the keywords: “asian,” “big tits” and “secretaries,” then you went to www.triplexxx.com where you searched for “red head” and “POV.” Are you starting to get it yet?”

“That’s not sick!”

“Maybe not in itself. In itself, it’s just perverted. But what about your diary, William? Do you remember this? ‘If future were a bucket, mine holds no hope and no dreams.’ Do you remember writing that? We have it all here. And what about this with your little camwhore, Julia? On April 17, you wrote to her on www.thegirnextdoor.com: ‘jewels, you make me so hard. I want you so bad. I wish I could be there with you.’ And then, of course, there was your little fête with Thomas Vickers and company. We have it all here, William, we ...”

“You better leave her alone. Please leave Julia alone.”

“Oh, William, don’t cry, we won’t bother your little girlfriend. Please try to relax. Here’s a tissue.” I hand him a whole packet. “Do you understand now, William, how sick you are? How socially unstable you are? Look at you. You’re a mess. We can’t let you infect others.”

“I’m not sick.”

“You are.”

“No I’m not! Your argument is wrong!”

“My argument was given to me by our software, William. I

diagnosed you. We're never wrong."

"I don't care. It's all wrong!"

"William. This is silly. I've just shown you. It's all right here."

"You can't do this."

"We can."

"But I'm not sick! That stuff is normal."

"William, you are far from normal. *I* am normal. You are sick. Not sick in the traditional meaning of the word, of course. No—your sickness is different, since you yourself, until now, didn't know it. That's what's so dangerous about it, William—but you are sick."

"…"

"I see you're confused. But let me reassure you that what's going on today is not punishment. What we're doing—what we've already begun—is part of your treatment, your cure. You're going to get better, starting today."

"What have you *already* been doing?"

"Here, look." I log into *Real* and turn my monitor so that he can see. "This is you."

"That's not me. That's him!"

"I'm sorry, William, I didn't mean to frighten you, but look please. Look at your *Real-ID*, look how happy you are. You're smiling; there are no more sad Canvas posts with that depressing Morrissey droning on in the background. You like Coldplay now, soon it will be U2, and so forth. It's a gradual process."

"That's not me!"

"How curious. William, calm down. Please. It *is* you. Last Friday we sent you a letter. It explained that your personal information had been lost. Had you read the second page, you would have seen that if you didn't reclaim this information, it too would be put into the public realm for all to see and use. That's what we've done. And so you see—

you, William Potenco, sitting here today, are no longer real. The *Real* William is more real than you are now. He has a social insurance number, a health insurance number and a credit history—you don't. He is going to have a good job, back working with his friends Ryan and Mike; he'll have a strong relationship with his father—his mother too, William, don't worry. But *he* is William Potenco now. Do you see?"

"…"

"Still confused, hey? You've gone a bit pale. Would you like some water?"

"No."

"Please, William, have some water. It's getting warm in here." I hand him a glass of water.

"Ryan hates me. He'll never take me back." He takes a sip.

"Ryan doesn't hate you, William. Ryan was trying to help you all along. We got to Ryan some time ago. The Ryan you think you knew, he doesn't really exist anymore, not in any way that you would recognize. He exists now as we want him to. He was trying to help you, William. He offered you a way out all those months ago when he told you he had a job for you in Winnipeg. He's consistently been on your side, but you kept turning your back on him. It's a pity."

"And Tom? Did you get to him to?"

"Thomas? Thomas Vickers is a non-entity, William. You should have listened to your friend Ryan."

"What did you do to him?"

"Thomas is gone, William, and we can't talk about that. We don't know where he is."

"You killed him?"

"No, William, of course not. This isn't one of your movies. We can't say where he is. It doesn't matter; it's beside the point. We're here to discuss you and what's wrong with you, not him."

"You can't take away my life."

"William, I can see that you're getting emotional. Don't cry. It's part of your affliction, that emotionalism of yours; you're going to have to learn to reign that in. We live in a world where emotion is best left to the professionals—actors and so forth. That will be part of your treatment: learning to be unemotional."

"My treatment? I want my life back. Let me go back on *Real*. I'll reintegrate. You can't do this!"

"We *can* do this, William. We can do all of this. It's for the good of everyone. We keep them safe."

"But you shouldn't do this!"

"No, William, we *should* do this. We can and we should. Understand? I think you understand. It's the world of big data, metadata. It's like you do at Eureka! It's like what the pioneer Sydney Rothsteen has done."

"Rothsteen?"

"Try and think of it like this: can we get oil out of sand? Yes. Do we care that it costs more to extract than it's actually worth? No. We need it and we can get it, so we do. Oil is black gold; big data is electronic gold. It's our new capital, a new currency for a new age. You know all this."

"What does that have to do with me?"

"William, the people need to be kept healthy. We need data to make that work. Just like we need oil for our society to function, we need data too."

"I … I can stop. I can stop doing the bad stuff. I can be good. I'm not sick. I'm healthy and I can reintegrate."

"You're fooling yourself, William, and we're very sorry, but what you're suggesting is not an option anymore. Part of your treatment is to stay away from the Internet. No more *Real*, no more Blabber—I know you're not on Blabber, but regardless—no more online porn, no Julia, none of that. In fact, you can give me your eyePhone right now, you can't have that either. We have to make room for the healthy new William Potenco, #Ten-Two-Twenty-Two, to grow. We can't have you interfere with him in anyway."

"…"

"Don't be alarmed, William. This is not a punishment. And you'll be excited about what comes next."

I take a small box from my desk and kneel next to William. I lean in and lower my voice to a whisper. "William, look at me. Do you know what I have for you here? I'm so excited to introduce this to you. This is a revolutionary product I have to show you today. It will make you happy. In this box is something amazing, something very few people in the world have even seen. In this box is one of the first sets—it's just a prototype, mind you—but one of the first sets of *Real*'s First Reality Lenses." I open the box and pause for effect.

"Yes, yes, designed and given to us by Sydney Rothsteen himself!" I'm too excited to whisper. "This is exciting, William! This tool is going to revolutionize medicine and the world, and you get to be a part of it! And just think: you'll get to help your hero, Sydney Rothsteen, after all!" I pause. "What do you think, William!? You don't look excited."

"…"

"Okay, I understand. You're too shocked for words, that's fine. But you know, William, within a few years, everyone will be wearing these, and you, William—you get to be one of the first to try them.

"Aren't you excited!? You look confused. Of course, your Lenses have been modified. They're not going to give you access to the Internet—they won't give you the augmented reality, or the night vision, or the gaming experience, or the holograms of celebrities that users of *Real*'s First Reality Lenses will get. No. What we've done is kind of reversed them. Here, look. They look like a normal pair of contact lenses, but actually, they're an impressive piece of technology. Did you know, William, that tears have much the same chemical makeup as blood? That means that contact lenses, equipped with the right technology, can show us what's going on inside your body without having to actually go inside your body.

"William, look—just look at these lenses, they're the latest in bio-nanotechnology. A receiver has been implanted in them to act as a display. The receiver uses cell phone towers so that we can see what you see. There are microscopic screens implanted in the lenses, each as small as fifty nanometers—that's the size of a single cell. And there are other biosensors, so we can feel what you feel: wind, heat, cold. We can feel if you tremble, if you're scared—it shows up on our screen. We can feel if you smile—that shows up too. We can measure your pulse and temperature, and we can conduct biochemical tests on your blood. It's amazing, William. 'Continuous non-invasive observation.' William, you don't even need to come in! Rothsteen is a genius! This technology is your cure. It makes you free. It's absolutely incredible!"

I get to my feet and look down at William. "Okay, William, it's time. Put them in. Go on. I'll take your eyePhone now too. And William, I should tell you, you can't take these out. They don't need to be cleaned. If we register a problem, someone will come to see you. If you do take them out, the Syndics will come. Have you got them in? Good."

I return to my desk. "Let me just see here. I have to activate you on my monitor. Okay, okay. Yes, yes! There you are. William, don't be anxious. I can feel your heart beating—or rather, I can see it beating fast. Amazing, right! Just relax, William."

"How…how long do I have to wear these?"

245

"Try not to cry, William. We don't want to overload the sensors. You have to wear them until our software tells us you're better; until you're strong again. Vancouver needs strong healthy citizens to make itself strong again. When you can contribute to that project, then we'll see."

"And you can hear me when I speak, too?"

"Of course we can. The lenses are equipped with microsensors that record and transmit everything back to us."

"What am I supposed to do now? How will I live?"

"That's up to you. You have all the freedom in the world. Just don't leave Vancouver, and don't touch a computer."

"But I have no job."

"You'll find one. I might suggest something in customer service. Get to know the people, William."

"…"

"Your heart rate is up again, William. Try and relax."

"Can I leave?"

"Of course. If you have no further questions, yes, you can leave. I suggest you go directly home and get some rest. You need it."

William stands and takes his coat. He's sweating. I'm sweating. I stand and accompany him down the glass spiral staircase to the lobby and the front door.

"Do you see, William? It's a beautiful day." I pat him gently on the back. "You'll get better, William, you'll see."

He walks away without saying goodbye, which I find a little rude. I thought he'd be more excited. I go back to my office to see how he is. His head is down and he's staring at his feet as he walks, when he should be looking around him. It's sunny and warm. I suppose it just hasn't hit him yet, how lucky he is.

"William," I say. "Look around you!"

"You can talk to me, too?"

"Of course. Now look around you at the beautiful day."

His pace quickens and he walks rather briskly back and boards the SkyTrain.

To see what another person sees, to notice what they notice—to experience what they experience—this is the way forward for us. It will create true empathy for us and for the people. Deep human monitoring is the wave of the future.

"William, listen to me. You're just the beginning. You know that? You sit on the train and you stare out of the window. You don't know it yet, but I can already sense that you're getting happier. I can see that your heart rate is back to normal. Your temperature is fine. Even though the sensors don't read it directly, I can feel that you're getting happier by the second. I think I even see a smile on your face. Is that a smile or a smirk I see reflected in the window? No, it's a happy smile. Well done, William."

He's thinking something over. He's planning. He's realized the obvious—everything *is* fine. That's it. He's smiling and thinking bright pleasant thoughts; planning his new future; turning his life around.

He gets off the train at Broadway and Burrard. So far from home—curious.

"William, why did you get off there?"

No answer. It must be that he wants to walk. Be outside with the people. He wants to live again, that's it. He's walking north. He notices the people, his head is up, he hears them. He feels the warmth of the sun on his face. He looks to the clear, blue sky and blinks his eyes. He looks around as he walks. He's at Vanier Park, next to the ocean. There are people in the park. He sees a family having a good time—citizens of Vancouver with their children and their dog, laughing and playing safely and healthily. William pauses, he takes a long, deep breath and smells the cool, clear ocean air. He hears the birds—it's almost as if they're singing for him.

"This is your happy ending and new beginning, William. No need to cry any more. That life is behind you."

He gets to the bridge, the beautiful art deco Burrard Bridge. An exemplar of our past technological and artistic achievements. To see it is to celebrate what humankind can accomplish. He walks onto the bridge, looks up to the golden pillars left and right where he sees the busts of two of Vancouver's historical luminaries: Captain George Vancouver and Sir Henry Burrard-Neale. He walks under the cold, grey, metal trusses to the centre of the bridge and stops to gaze over the railing. From joy, his heart rate increases. He takes a long deep breath, and looks out west over the sea.

"I can feel it, William, I feel the wind on your eyes and in the follicles of your hair. I see it all—the clear blue sky, the dark blue ocean below."

Appendix

www.en.pediapedia.org/ped/Real

Real

Real is an online social networking service. It was named by founder and owner Sydney Rothsteen (main article: Sydney Rothsteen), who wished to offer a "real" alternative to competitors. *Real* was founded under the name RealFriend as one of many "friend"-based social networks to emerge in the early 2000s. Unlike his competitors, Rothsteen's intention with RealFriend was to create a social network with more. It would incorporate the best online services into one platform. RealFriend's initial success was its ability to do that. On an interface that Rothsteen called the Canvas, ahead of its time both technologically and graphically, RealFriend combined real-time messaging with the capability of uploading and sharing photos, video clips, music and animation.

RealFriend also provided what it termed as its "room feature," a method of separating and sorting users' contacts into different rooms: the Family Room for family contacts, the Rec Room for recreational contacts, the Office for colleagues, the Cellar for second-rate contacts.

RealFriend set itself apart from its competitors through its marketing strategy, which targeted mature and sophisticated users. "The difference with us was that we didn't want college students, we wanted college grads," said Sydney Rothsteen. Membership in the fledgling RealFriend grew, surpassing 200 million only a few years after launch. The rapid growth of RealFriend was in part due to its features and in part due to its seemingly limitless funding. Unlike its main competitors, RealFriend did not have to secure investors or seek financial backing, which enabled the platform to operate on an aggressive business model that has come to be known as the "ten million member hurdle." Using this model, RealFriend, later *Real*, purchased or attempted to purchase all other social networks and wireless communication software that had achieved a membership base of ten million users (main article: *Real*'s Business Strategy).

RealFriend membership and profits grew at an exponential rate. Harold Brinks (main article: Harold Brinks), longtime Rothsteen collaborator and self-proclaimed "conceptual innovative genius," was appointed to lead RealFriend's creative department. With Brinks at the conceptual helm of RealFriend, users were introduced to the *RealFlea Market*, an online shopping service; *RealNews*, an online news service; and a number of other features. Famously, Brinks was behind the introduction of RealFriend's "intuitive advertising," which used intelligent software to allow advertisers to superimpose ads directly onto users' photos and videos (main article: *Real* Advertising).

In 2008, Brinks and Rothsteen launched *RealEconomy* (main article: *RealEconomy*). Initially conceived as a game and described by Sydney Rothsteen as "the world's most boring MMORPG," *RealEconomy* is today called the saviour of global capitalism and has become the third largest economy in the world, smaller only than those of China and the USA. Two years later, RealFriend broke into the lucrative China market. Shortly after, it dropped the "Friend" and became known as *Real* (italicized) (main article: *Real* vs. Coke).

Since then, *Real*'s growth in both members and data has been rapid. Currently, global membership is 2.5 billion users. *Real* collects 1000 exabytes of data per year and grows by two exabytes per day. Sydney Rothsteen is the richest man on the planet, earning $140 billion last year, twice the earnings of Carlos Slim.

The Canvas

"The Canvas is our bread and butter."—Sydney Rothsteen.

With the tagline, "Compose it on your Canvas," the Canvas allows *Real*'s users to drag and drop images, music and headlines onto an interface to create what on *Real* is called a "composition." The Canvas also includes a sketchpad that enables users to draw and animate their posts.

"On the Canvas," *Real* explains, "you can paste together, much as an artist would create a collage, links for videos, ebooks, music, news reports, pictures—in fact, anything. You can even draw and animate your own pictures. The finished product is a personal composition: a modern masterpiece." Sydney Rothsteen said about the Canvas: "This is not a sloppy wall that gets tagged, this is a canvas that gets composed."

The idea for the Canvas, Rothsteen said, came to him from two sources: "My good friend, artist Eric Fischl, said that 'collage is the most important innovation in art since perspective was discovered in the fourteenth century.' He's right." And Rothsteen also said: "Jack Kerouac wrote *On the Road* on a 120-foot roll of teletype paper. We want the Canvas to be like that, a never-ending roll of canvas on which each user can paint, post or compose whatever he or she would like. We view each of our users as an expressive individual with unique creative ideas."

On the Canvas, users have the option to be "affected" or "unaffected" by each other's compositions, and depending on the user's settings, can add, alter or change each other's posts.

The Identification Page: *Real-ID*

"Like a snakeskin jacket, the Real-ID *can be a symbol of each user's*

individuality and a representation of their own personal freedom."—Sydney Rothsteen.

When users join *Real,* they are given options through which they can tailor their profiles. These include standards like favourite musicians, favourite directors and films, favourite authors, culture, abilities, etc.

Moreover, a user can tailor his or her *Real-ID* in a sophisticated, detailed way. *Real* explains that "the individual is found in the details. Like each room in a person's house, each *Real-ID* can be made unique and personal through the largest database of fonts, images, styles and colours ever put together on the web."

Real-ID Numbers

One element of the individualization that occurs on a user's *Real-ID* page is his or her number. When a user signs on to *Real,* he or she is assigned a number, which then becomes a login name and hashtag. The numbers are written out, from "#zero," #zero-one," "#zero-two," up to "#zero-ten" and so forth. For example, 100 is #one-zero-zero, 1053 is #ten fifty-three, 30,678,967 is "#thirty-six-seventy-eight-nine-sixty-seven."

When a user logs in, below the profile picture are his or her name and number.

Today, account numbers can be bought, sold or traded on the *RealFlea Market.* Certain *Real-ID* numbers, such as those below ten thousand, or lucrative ones such as #zero-ninety-nine, are worth well over their number value in dollars.

Controversy: *Real* was attacked in the media by former competitors and rights groups for this feature, considered reminiscent of the numbering of human beings in prisons, Gulags, concentration camps and labour camps. Religious groups have claimed that the number represents a new mark of the beast.

RealVideo

RealVideo was part of RealFriend's original launch. The software enables users to post videos and music on *Real*, both on their Canvas, and on a separate database that can be accessed by other *Real* users. Later, *RealVideo* complemented its free channels with subscription channels. A *Real* user can now create personalized channels with original programming that other users can watch or listen to. For a small fee, users can sign on to each other's channels.

Real announced this change as part of an effort to reward users for their "personal creativity." All the major television, music and film networks reacted by setting up personalized channels as well, so that *Real* users can now access mainstream television programs, movies, music, concerts, and any other type of media on the platform.

RealNews

Initially an aggregate of global news headlines that operated as a ticker on the bottom of a users' screen, *RealNews* has since expanded into a global network that produces and airs both original features and user-based news programs, which it calls "Hands-on News."

Today, *RealNews* is the most viewed news source in the world, with as many viewers as there are *Real* members. It is aired in over 170 countries and claims to report "even from the North Pole."

RealSeminars

"They sound academic, because they are."—Sydney Rothsteen.

RealSeminars are online discussion forums within *Real* where people hold conversations in the form of posted messages on a range of topics. In a *RealSeminar,* users can discuss anonymously important ideas within a community of like-minded individuals.

What is created in a *RealSeminar* is called a "dialogue." Each dialogue competes with others for "voice." The top "voices," based on activity, number of users and theme, are posted, depending on preferences, on a users' *Real-ID* homepage.

RealDiary

RealDiary was one of the original features on RealFriend. Originally billed as a place to record private thoughts on a social network, *RealDiary* has since become a feature that automatically catalogues, in a safe and secure place, all of a user's activities on *Real*.

RealStory

After Harold Brinks took the creative helm, *Real*, in combination with *RealDiary*, launched *RealStory*. Under the slogan "We all have a story worth telling," *RealStory* is online publishing software that lets users, with one click of a button, generate and publish ebooks from the personal information that has been collected in their *RealDiary* and from what they've posted on *Real*. These ebooks are known on *Real* as "AutoBiographies," and can be downloaded or read on a user's *Real-ID* homepage.

RealFlea Market

Real's online shopping network, the *RealFlea Market*, allows members of *Real* to sell and browse through goods on the website. The *RealFlea Market* was introduced after *Real*'s one-millionth user signed on.

"It started small, but I figured that one million gave us a good base and made the flea market viable," said Sydney Rothsteen. Later, to facilitate use of the flea market by users of *Real*, *RealBanking* was introduced. It allowed users to transfer money in a closed service that eschewed hefty bank fees.

By the time *Real* surpassed two billion users, the *RealFlea Market* was generating more business than Amazon, Taobao, and E-Bay combined.

RealEconomy (main article: the *RealEconomy*)

RealEconomy began as an online MMORPG (massively multiplayer online role-playing game) for users of *Real*. In *RealEconomy,* which was created as a simplified version of our own economy with simplified sectors for extraction, production, assembly, marketing and sales, users were given the choice of what field they wanted to engage in (for example, technology, advertising, agriculture) and the means to expand in their chosen business or profession.

Shortly after launch, the currency in *RealEconomy*—known as *RealDollars*—began to be sold on the *RealFlea Market*. Just weeks later, in patch 1.3, *RealEconomy* launched its hybrid sector.

In the role-playing sector, all business is conducted in *RealDollars*. In the hybrid sector, actual goods and money mix with *RealDollars*. With the launch of the hybrid sector and as an incentive to get more people to use *RealEconomy*, Sydney Rothsteen announced that each new user of *Real* would be given one hundred *RealDollars* to invest or use in any way he or she thought fit. Early *Real* users were given more, on an escalating scale based on their *Real-ID Numbers*.

Sydney Rothsteen had fixed a low original exchange rate between *RealDollars* and global currencies, so that few observers thought it would go anywhere. However, with the global economy in a slump, many unemployed people saw *RealEconomy*'s hybrid sector as their only way to make money.

RealEconomy took off first in Portugal, Greece, Italy and Spain, where youth and elderly unemployment rates were high; and also in poor countries like China and India, where daily earnings in

RealEconomy, sitting in front of a computer, were better than the low wages offered in the local economy. Many in North America now see working in *RealEconomy* as a second income, although not as a steady job.

As of last year, *RealEconomy* is the third largest in the world. Viewed by many economists as the main reason for the Rebound and the "saviour of global capitalism," *RealEconomy* has forced a major readjustment of global currencies and is considered to be the "final nail in the coffin" of the U.S.-dollar based global economy.

First Reality Lenses [coming soon]

"Change reality with the flick of an eye."—Real marketing slogan.
Only recently announced, *Real*'s First Reality Lenses are revolutionary contact lenses, a wearable computer that will operate as an interface between the user, *Real* and the outside world. First Reality Lenses will enable users to stay connected all the time while on the go.

Details of the Lenses are still scant. However, some of the already announced features include gaming, photo and video, night vision, and hologram-augmented reality.

Quoted in *Tech* zine, Harold Brinks said, "Users will have literally all the information on the Internet in front of them and accessible at the flick of an eye. Imagine walking down a street and having your destination GPSed for you, so you'll never get lost. Imagine never having to reach into your pocket for your phone, or even touching a phone again. Imagine *Real* in front of you all the time."

Acknowledgements

I would like to acknowledge John Thorne for all his help in editing the original manuscript. I would like to thank Catherine Cunningham at Deux Voiliers Publishing for her help in turning that manuscript into a novel. I want to acknowledge Paul Zacharias and Perry Thompson for their contributions to the cover design. Katja deserves much more than a simple acknowledgement for putting up with my massive mood swings. Importantly, I would also like to thank Ian Shaw and Deux Voiliers Publishing for their confidence in me and their continued support in getting *Nothing to Hide* into print. And finally, Liz McKeen for her excellent copy-editing and Su Sokol for her meticulous proofreading.

About the Author

Nick Simon was born in Ontario, Canada in 1978. He resided for several years in both Winnipeg and Vancouver and has lived and travelled widely in China, Southeast Asia, and Europe. *Nothing to Hide* is his first novel. He currently resides in Berlin, Germany where he spends most of his time writing.

When he can't write he reads, and when he can't read or write he goes for walks. When he must he works. He's worked a variety of jobs: University instructor, English teacher, mail room stooge, launderer of stolen goods, dishwasher, cobbler, copy writer, data analyst, *et cetera*. He prefers sunrises to sunsets.

About Deux Voiliers Publishing

Organized as a writers-plus collective, Deux Voiliers Publishing is a new generation publisher. We focus on high quality works of fiction by emerging Canadian writers. The art of creating new works of fiction is our driving force.

We are proud to have published *Nothing to Hide* by Nick Simon.

Other Works of Fiction published by Deux Voiliers Publishing

Soldier, Lily, Peace and Pearls by Con Cú (Literary Fiction 2012)

Kirk's Landing by Mike Young (Crime/Adventure 2014)

Sumer Lovin' by Nicole Chardenet (Humour/Fantasy 2013)

Last of the Ninth by Stephen Lorne Bennett (Historical Fiction 2012)

Marching to Byzantium by Brendan Ray (Historical Fiction 2012)

Tales of Other Worlds by Chris Turner (Fantasy/Science Fiction 2012)

Romulus by Fernand Hibbert and translated by Matthew Robertshaw (Historical Fiction/English Translation 2014)

Bidong by Paul Duong (Literary Fiction 2012)

Zaidie and Ferdele by Carol Katz (Illustrated Children's Fiction 2012)

Palawan Story by Caroline Vu (Literary Fiction 2014)

Cycling to Asylum by Su J. Sokol (Speculative Fiction 2014)

Stage Business by Gerry Fostaty (Crime 2014)

Stark Nakid by Sean McGinnis (Crime/Humour 2014)

Twisted Reasons by Geza Tatrallyay (International Crime Thriller 2014)

Four Stones by Norman Hall (Canadian Spy Thriller 2015)

Please visit our website for ordering information
www.deuxvoilierspublishing.com

www.ingramcontent.com/pod-product-compliance
Lightning Source LLC
Chambersburg PA
CBHW020547020726
47494CB00006B/1961